THE TIME-TRAVELER'S DAUGHTER

EMMA STRIKE

D1526913

CONTENTS

ONE

CATHERINE CHRISTIE'S twenty-fifth birthday did not get off to a good start.

She rose at dawn as usual, dressed in her uniform of ankle-length skirt and white shirt, and was having breakfast in the kitchen when she heard footsteps on the front porch.

The door creaked open as Dolly, her tenant and oldest friend, opened it. 'Catherine, someone's here for you!'

She rushed over. It was rather early for visitors, and she didn't recognize the young man standing there.

'Miss Christie,' he said, white envelope in hand. 'I didn't think you'd be awake.'

'I almost wasn't.'

He quickly pulled his hat off. 'I'm Toby, from Mr. Milton's office.'

'Oh, of course,' she said, before her heart sank. Though Toby was a perfectly sweet office assistant, despite being rendered unrecognizable by a sudden crop of facial hair on his young face, his employer, Mr. Howard Milton, was her family lawyer, who was seldom the bearer of good news.

Toby handed her the envelope. 'It just so happens that I live not three blocks from here, so Mr. Milton asked me to bring this over for you.'

'Thank you,' she said.

'Oh, and happy birthday, Miss Christie,' he said with a shy smile, bounding toward his bicycle and riding away.

Catherine sighed, opening the letter.

'What's it this time?' asked Dolly.

'Another summons to Mr. Milton's office to take care of some urgent business.'

'Today, of all days? Should I come with you?'

'No, it's fine. I'll see you once I am done.'

THANKFULLY, THE DAY GOT better from there. Grade 5 got to know about her birthday, she suspected from the English teacher Stuart Townsend, and they surprised her with a card and a very boisterous musical interlude. Even Principal Vance's stern face peering through the glass pane in the door couldn't dampen her pleasure.

During recess, Stuart, buoyed by Dolly at his side, waylaid her. 'Dancing tonight?' he suggested hopefully.

She raised a hand to her mouth in faux horror. 'Dancing? If Principal Vance finds out, we're toast.' Speakeasies, dance halls, skirts more than two inches above the ankle — there were many ways to lose their jobs as teachers at Manhattan's finest public school.

'Come on,' said Stuart, 'he'll only get to know if he is there himself, and he could hardly call us out then, could he?'

The ever-eager Stuart hadn't been witness to Principal Vance's more ridiculous strictures, which were reserved for his women employees. But Catherine hoped he was right this one time. 'Maybe over the weekend?'

Dolly frowned but had to rush away to class. Stuart, whose schedule was empty, complained all the way as he walked with Catherine. 'It's your birthday, come on, let us spoil you a little. How about dinner?'

Catherine bit her lip. They'd had one lone date before, and she sensed Stuart had sped ahead of where she was in their relationship. Not to mention that the first hint of impropriety, romance or marriage were all enough to get her fired as well.

But it was her birthday, after all, and it might do her some good after whatever it was Mr. Milton had to say. 'Okay, Stuart, dinner it is.'

He beamed. 'I'll pick you up from your place at 6 p.m.'

After school, Catherine strolled to Mr. Milton's office with even less enthusiasm than she'd expected.

She paused in front of the glass- and wood-fronted building. All the worst days of her life were bookmarked with a stop to this office, or a visit from Mr. Milton. It wasn't his fault she hated him; he was a kindly man with porkchop sideburns and unkempt hair who was forever associated in Catherine's brain with death. He was also the administrator of her tiny but invaluable trust fund. It is what had kept her in school after her mother's death a decade prior, why she'd been able to hold on to the house.

She walked in; the door swinging shut behind her. The front office was busy, and she spotted Toby in the corner and waved out to him.

As Catherine entered Mr. Milton's office, he looked up from his pile of leather-bound legal books. He was grayer than she'd remembered, but otherwise unchanged. 'Catherine,' he said with a smile, 'how lovely to see you again.'

She couldn't lie to him. 'I hope you've been well?'

'Oh, can't complain,' he said. 'Happy birthday.'

'Thank you.' Though that they all knew it was her birthday was a bit of an ominous sign. 'I must admit it surprised me to get your letter.'

'Indeed,' he said, leaning back in his chair. 'I would imagine it is not the only surprise you will receive today.'

Catherine's heart hammered in her chest. Mr. Milton's surprises were seldom pleasant.

'No need to be anxious. Before your father died, he left me with a set of instructions for actions to be set into motion on your twenty-fifth birthday.'

She went still. 'My father?' What instructions could he possibly have left fifteen years ago?

'You might not remember this, but I was executor of his will as well.'

'I remember.'

She was ten when her father died, after a brief fight against an unknown disease that had ravaged his body. Mr. Milton came after the funeral. There wasn't much business to attend to. Or so Catherine had thought.

'He was a remarkably straightforward man, your father. The house and all his possessions were signed over to a trust, and your mother was guardian. She knew all this, of course. So there wasn't much for me to do, except wait till this day arrived.'

She clenched her fingers tight on her lap, a lump in her throat.

'His instructions are to sell the house you currently live in, liquidate all the investments held in trust, and hand them all over to you as gold.'

Catherine gasped. 'Sell the house! But why?'

He shook his head, as befuddled as she was. 'I said he was clear, not candid, and I am afraid I wasn't privy to his decision-making process. But you may find some answers yet,' he said, standing up and walking to the cabinet that occupied one entire wall of the office. He opened a safe, from which he took out a box. He placed it gently in front of Catherine.

She'd seen this box before.

'Your father left this for you.'

She couldn't bring herself to touch the shining black surface, its brilliance undiminished by age. 'What's inside it?'

'You must see for yourself.'

The red wax seal. She used to be enthralled by the way he'd melt it over a candle, pressing the red wax onto paper before stamping it with his signet ring. Catherine couldn't break it now with Mr. Milton watching; she'd wait till she got home.

'So what happens now?'

Mr. Milton contemplated her as though measuring how much she was ready to take. 'I've started the process of selling the house. Someone will bring a few interested parties over this week. The rest is easy enough.'

'So soon?'

'Is there a problem?' he asked gently.

'No, I just want to know. The... the gold. What will you do with it?'

'I am not a banker unfortunately, so once we liquidate all the assets, I will hand it over to you.'

She shook her head. 'Whatever am I to do with such a sizeable amount! The sale of the house will yield a significant sum!'

'Perhaps answers lie within,' he said, with a nod toward the box.

PHILIP CHRISTIE HAD BEEN a most remarkable man, filled with magic tricks and strange tales, but he didn't like other people much. They'd lived an isolated life. He'd apologize for it sometimes, but she'd hardly cared because he had packed a lifetime of wonder into a few short years.

He died a fortnight after her tenth birthday, and for the next five years, it was Catherine and her mother, Maggie. If her father was all the flashy things a young girl adored, Catherine soon realized it was Maggie who was the genuine hero in her household. A lifelong campaigner for women's suffrage, she died of the Spanish Flu in 1920 after seeing women finally get the right to vote across the country.

For the last few weeks, her mother knew she was going, and knew she'd leave Catherine alone. She'd left her detailed instructions, saying that when you raised a child on your own, you were in the habit of wondering every day what would happen if you were to die, so she'd had it all figured out when the time came.

As a result, Catherine was sorted, more or less. She had no relatives to help, and so after the funeral, she went off to the boarding school her mother had recommended, because of which she received an education far superior to most girls of the age. Maggie had also advised her not to listen to anyone who said she must marry to secure her future. That the world was filled with women who could do many things, and Catherine had the wits to be one of them.

And she said that being her mother was the thing she had been most proud of. That love doesn't need a lifetime to have meaning — the fifteen years she had with Philip and the fifteen years she had with Catherine were worth all the rest of it.

Catherine had wanted to ask her what she meant — the rest of what? She had also wanted to ask about her father, but she couldn't find the strength to conjure one dead parent when she was about to lose another.

❧

CATHERINE SAT AT THE small dining table in her small dining room. Dolly was out for the moment, and she was alone. She looked around, filled with disbelief that it wouldn't be hers for much longer — her last physical connection to her childhood and her parents would be lost for good.

The box sat there, as smooth as ivory and black as jet, a missive from the past. A little time machine.

The last time she'd seen this, her father was still alive. It was after they'd taken a trip together, a trip she had long since known was strange in every way. She was about eight years old and her father and she had gone to an amusement park, where they had jumped from a great height onto a giant trampoline.

Before she knew it, they were back home. Maggie had been extremely upset, and after they thought she'd gone to sleep, her parents had argued.

'How could you do this to me?' Maggie had whispered.

'I just had to know if she was able,' Philip replied.

'Why?'

'I don't know. I am sorry.'

'Do you know something I don't?'

'No.'

'Well, it worked. Are you happy now?'

The next morning she'd seen the box on the dresser in her parents' bedroom. She'd been tempted to take a peek, drawn in by the luminous surface, but when she went to find it later in the day when her parents were out, it had no longer been there.

She held her breath, flipping the lid open, breaking the wax seal.

Inside was a letter, several pages thick. With a shaking hand, she lifted it out.

Underneath was a red velvet pouch. She'd come back to that later.

She unfolded the letter, creaking with age. It was unmistakably her father's hand. She began to read.

My dearest Catherine,

Happy birthday, my darling daughter.

If you are reading this, it is because I am dead. I hope I have taught you better than to worry too much about such things. I had a wonderful life, of which you were my crowning glory.

I am not sure how long it has been since we last spoke, since I set this little box into motion when you were eight years old, hoping it would never come to use, but knowing that it would be smartest to hedge my bets.

There are some things that I should have explained to you during my lifetime. I chose not to, mainly because you wouldn't have believed me. But also because I had made a promise to your mother that your safety would always come first. Don't blame her, though: she was wise enough to know that I was trouble, and making me promise her this before you were born was one of the smarter things that she did in a life filled with incredibly smart things.

That is why I am writing this letter in a manner meant to imply rather than educate. I'm going to leave you a trail of breadcrumbs, which you will shortly discover are infuriatingly obtuse. You will have to work for the rest of the information, and only if you want to. I assure you there is a good reason for this, too.

If you decide you want to pursue the crazy journey that I have been on for most of my life, that must be your decision with eyes wide open, well aware that there will be <u>grave</u> danger before you.

I know you must think that your father has finally lost his marbles, that he's given into grave sentimentality and hyperbole and outright insanity, but I can assure you that I have not.

In this box is a medallion. Yes, as you can tell already, I lied to you when I said I had lost this all those years ago. Till shortly before I sent this box off to Mr. Milton, I wore it always around my neck. You will soon realize why I took it off.

This is no mere bauble, it is perhaps the most dangerous piece of jewelry ever created.

This medallion, dear Catherine, can take you back in time.

I believe it to be part of Tibeau's pirate treasure, the one item that our great, failed ancestor Thelonious Christie had off the scoundrel.

And this is where I will need to be cryptic. There are good reasons for this: it is the nature of time that things are constantly changing. The fates of people are not to be toyed with or taken lightly. So I can only lead you to the first clue, because that is the only piece of information I am certain you need to have to make possible what I already know to be certain. For in the end lies the beginning.

Here it is: This medallion has the power to take you to 1851, where you need to find the Duke of Westlake. He has a piece of this puzzle that you need in order to proceed any further.

How, you might wonder, are you supposed to do such a thing? Think back to the tale of that delinquent boy Ferdinand that I told you so many times. I didn't just love that story because you loved it; it was told to prepare you for just such an occasion as this. You used to know that story by heart, and I want you to remember every detail now.

If you pursue this path, please remember: be prepared for every eventuality. Take nothing for granted. But most importantly, you mustn't attempt to meddle with death. I am sorry I left you so soon, but there can be nothing more dangerous than attempting to change fate.

And if you decide you want nothing to do with it, that too is perfectly fine.

Please also know that the other instructions left for Mr. Milton regarding your house and assets are for your own good. Please don't resent him for it.

I am selfish enough to hope that you still think of me, often and fondly. I will think of you wherever I am. I know we talked little about things like the afterlife when I was alive, but for the record, no death can erase my memory of you. Of this I am sure.

With all my heart,

Philip

TWO

CATHERINE PUT THE LETTER down, standing abruptly and pacing the room.

Then she stopped in front of the box, afraid to touch the velvet pouch within.

She began pacing again, before coming to an abrupt halt and then reaching in, gingerly opening its slipknot.

Inside was the medallion she'd seen hanging from her father's neck for years, from its thick leather cord. And then one day, after their strange trampoline trip home, he had announced it had been lost, and that was it.

She held it up to the light. It was a curious piece of jewelry that resembled a bird in flight. Catherine had seen nothing else quite like it in her life. There was a set of wings at the apex of which was a space where the bird's body should be, but only a wire cage remained, as though some portion of it was missing. Catherine tried to remember if there had ever been more to it.

In the story of Ferdinand, they called the bird-shaped medallion the key that can unlock time.

It couldn't be.

She was about to slip it over her neck, but feeling overwhelmed, she put it away instead, along with the rest of the box's contents.

After pacing the room for another ten minutes, she returned to it, grabbing the medallion once more and pulling it over her head, clutching it in her hand.

At least this made some sort of sense to her. It was a piece of her past unlike the gibberish the letter contained. It was solid, and it was real.

And then she heard a key in the door. Dolly.

Catherine jumped, putting the box away in the kitchen cupboard, tucking the necklace into her dress.

Dolly stood there, and Catherine had a moment's confusion as she registered Stuart by her side. She'd clean forgotten about dinner.

'You're not ready!' said Dolly.

'Oh sorry, my appointment went longer than I expected. Give me five minutes.'

STUART TOOK THEM BOTH out to a lovely Italian restaurant. Catherine tried her best to enjoy herself, particularly when she saw the concern on Dolly's face. But the entire evening, she could feel the cold metal of the medallion against her skin, till it felt like the only real thing. Dolly and Stuart's words filtered down to her as if through a fog.

Finally, when Stuart went to the restroom, Dolly took her hand. 'Are you okay, Catherine?'

She took a tiny bite of her chocolate cake. 'Just a little tired, I think.'

'You seem distracted. What happened at Mr. Milton's?'

'I'll explain when we are home.' She'd have to tell her about the house — it was Dolly's house as much as it was hers. She'd lived there for the past couple of years, ever since they both took jobs at the school after attending college, where they met.`

'Stuart here is so keen on you, and I think you should give him a chance,' Dolly said, not for the first time.

'He only thinks he is keen on me because he doesn't know me. He's so exactly right for you and I don't know why neither of you can see it.'

Dolly scowled. 'Nonsense! You have had to be strong for so long, you've forgotten that it can feel quite nice to be vulnerable. Let him in, Catherine. What's the worst that could happen?'

FOR SEVERAL DAYS, CATHERINE felt as though she was moving through water. She'd told Dolly about their impending move, keeping the details of her father's will as vague as possible. Confused and concerned about how Catherine was taking it, she attributed her friend's off mood to this news and started the hunt for apartments they could share. 'It'll be nice to live a little closer to school, wouldn't it?' she said.

Catherine still didn't know what to make of the letter. She read it once, and then over and over again, concluding her father had some sort of break with reality before his death. But at the same time, there was so much that had never quite made sense about her life. Who was Philip, really? She did not know where he had come from. Who were his parents, he had told her about them but she had never met them, and why was that? Where were all their other relatives?

Then, she put away the medallion, put away the box, and told Mr. Milton that she was ready. She and Dolly packed up their belongings, and inside of two weeks, she had moved to a rented apartment in a nicer neighborhood closer to school and had kept all her savings in a safe in the closet.

And then she went about her life as though nothing had happened.

BY OCTOBER 1929, CATHERINE knew exactly why Philip had advised Mr. Milton to sell the house and all other investments. As the country was plunged into financial crisis, she watched as everyone around her lost everything. Then she lost her job and Dolly did too. With several younger siblings behind her, her family had enough on its hands. And so when Dolly learned of a position for a governess open in California, she gratefully took it.

Alone again, Catherine truly did not know what she'd do with herself. Thanks to the sale of the house and assets, she'd get by for some years without work, but what did her future hold?

One day, with nothing better to do, Catherine pulled the medallion out of the safe and put it on. It gave her a sense of comfort, bringing her closer to her father. For the next few days she kept it on. And that's when she noticed strange things happening.

It felt as if time would slip away from her. There were moments where she felt a strange tingle, like there was a cool breeze in the room. And then she would close her eyes and see the face of a man she had never seen before. A dark man, older and dressed in strange clothes from a different time.

It was frightening at first, but then it was almost as though she was seeing flashes of a moving picture in her head; she'd see him sitting in front of a fire with a book, talking with someone on business of some kind, riding on horseback through the countryside.

As the visions grew more frequent, Catherine took the medallion off. No matter what it had meant to her father, there was no good that could come of it. She put it back in the box for the next few days.

But then, one afternoon, she found herself standing in front of the New York Public Library. She entered and browsed the shelves with no actual idea of what she was looking for, till she chanced upon the *Who's Who of Victorian England*. The Duke of Westlake was easy to find; it was a title that had existed since the War of the Roses and was still in use. She went down the list of all the men who'd held that title and stopped at the year 1851. The XIIth Duke of Westlake inherited the position then, and later the same year, there was a XIIIth Duke of Westlake.

She found an encyclopedia which had a little more detail. Westlake was a title, Talbot was the name adopted by the family of Tibeau when they emigrated from Portugal to England.

Catherine let out a gasp that had fellow readers turn to her with disapproval. But she couldn't help it because as soon as she saw the name, she knew at once what her father was doing: he was leading her to the treasure.

The Tibeaus and Christies had been locked in a generations-long battle over pirate treasure. She had heard these names countless times as a young girl from her father, about how their ancestor Thelonious Christie and Joseph Tibeau had assembled and then lost the most spectacular treasure the world had ever seen. The star attraction: the Bell of Dhammazedi, a massive work of gold studded with precious stones.

On the voyage home, they were shipwrecked somewhere in the Indian Ocean, believed to have gone down near Mauritius, as this was where Tibeau and Christie had washed up. In the course of the ordeal, Tibeau perished and Christie returned to England, and died soon after. The treasure was never seen again.

Catherine had never really thought of it with any seriousness till that very moment. Pirate treasure, time-travelers — it all seemed like remarkable escapades invented for the amusement of a child. But now, she had to rethink it all.

Catherine turned the pages idly till she came upon a reproduction of a painting that made her heart leap. Dark brown hair curling at the temples, sharp lines in an imperious face. This was the Duke of Westlake, as of 1851.

It was also the man from Catherine's visions.

Catherine rushed out of the library, hand on her chest, out of breath. She returned home in a state. She opened the box and read the letter over.

There was nothing new to be gleaned from it. She had wrung it dry of meaning already. Did the Duke of Westlake have the dagger-like body that completed the medallion, or was her father speaking more metaphorically when he said the Duke possessed a piece of the puzzle?

Two pieces, meant to be one, a magnet through the ages...

It could only mean one thing. But how could she be sure?

She cautiously put the medallion around her neck again, this time pressing it directly against her skin.

If she had expected to feel anything from the contact, she was disappointed. If the visions were connected to it, she didn't know how to activate them. She wore it around the house for the next day and, finally, right when she was about to drop off to sleep, she saw him again.

The next day she returned to the library.

CATHERINE SLOWLY prepared. She didn't know what would happen when she tried to travel through time. It was wholly possible that she would arrive bare as the day she was born, and with no means to support herself, though she'd like to think her father had not planned for that to happen to her with no warning.

Her first stop was to visit a professor of English history at the New York University, a guest lecturer from her college days.

'I'm looking for information about the Duke of Westlake around the 1850s,' she said.

'Westlake?' he said. 'I am afraid there is a gap in my knowledge there.'

'Does a lost treasure ring any bells? The name Tibeau, perhaps?'

His eyes twinkled. 'Ah yes, the mysterious Bell of Dhammazedi! Don't tell me you are looking for it?' he said with a laugh.

She merely smiled in response.

'I can't tell you more, but you are free to explore my library,' he said.

Having done so, however, she found nothing.

'Often peers of the realm such as the Westlakes would have had private family histories written,' he suggested.

'Where might I find these?'

'If it is not in my collection, it isn't in the United States. An English library might send you a copy. But if you have an interest in the Tibeau treasure, look at this,' he said, heading over to his bookshelf and pulling out a hefty volume. He opened it to a map.

'This documents the sea routes used by the pirates of the time, from the East Indies to the Continent. Some believe Joseph Tibeau himself drew it.'

Catherine peered over it, heart racing. 'Can I have this book, please? I am happy to pay for it.'

'No, it is irreplaceable,' he said. 'But you can copy it, if you wish.'

Missing Dolly terribly, Catherine hired a university art student to make a copy of the map. Meanwhile, she began researching the garments of the time, taking a picture of a gown that her seamstress might recreate.

She looked into the money and banking systems in 1851 England and tracked down a collector of mostly useless curios who also had a stash of currency from Victorian England, enough to see her through a few months. Eccentric though he may be, he was shrewd about extracting every dollar from Catherine possible. With few discernible options, Catherine traded in her little pile of cash remaining.

She already had the gold she hoped to use once she arrived in England. Thus armed, Catherine booked her berth across the Atlantic. She didn't know enough about how the medallion worked to be sure it could transport her from New York to England, and she was better off making the journey in 1929 than eighty years prior.

She boarded the steamer with a remarkably small case. Inside it was a knapsack with two sets of clothing, a compass, a bag full of coins and notes, and of course, the medallion. It also held a reticule that could be hooked under her skirts. Through the days and nights on the open seas, she read what she could find about the year 1851 and the life in that era. She reread *Jane Eyre* and couldn't believe that soon she'd be stepping into such a world. If all went well.

Once she was in England, she wasted little time. She headed to Tower Bridge early the morning after arriving, and when there was no one watching, she hoisted her knapsack onto her back, grabbed the medallion hanging around her neck, closed her eyes and jumped.

THREE

IT WAS LIKE FLOATING. That might be the closest Catherine could get to explaining how it felt to fall through time. After rushing toward the ground in a terrifying freefall off Tower Bridge, it was as though she slipped through some invisible divide on some invisible carpet and knew that she would be fine.

She lay there on a thick bed of grass without quite feeling the moment of contact, with no idea where she was, or *when* she was.

But to think of that would bring on panic so extreme there would be no holding it at bay, and so Catherine willed herself to close her eyes and take a deep breath.

The first thing that struck her was the smell. That was a clue that it could be 1851 after all, with its streets covered in horse manure, and the lack of indoor plumbing.

Catherine opened her eyes and saw a darkness so extreme that it threatened to overwhelm her again. She needed to find something to focus on, something real and mundane. There was a dark house on the lot, either abandoned, empty or simply at rest.

She felt for her clothes — they were intact. Her bag was still rather uncomfortably on her back, and the reticule she had hooked onto the inside of her dress was reassuring in its heft.

'My name is Catherine,' she whispered, as though saying it aloud would prove to herself that she wasn't crazy, or dead.

But what if she was?

There was only one way to find out.

She stood up, testing out her legs. She was steady. Catherine took a few steps toward the house and then paused, waiting for the bark of a dog or the rustle of grass signaling someone's approach. There was no sign of life and so she continued creeping along. The home was grander than she at first thought, with windows quite high off the ground, and no way to get a look in. She circled it till she found a stone conveniently placed near a window, standing on it to peer in.

Through the sheer curtain, she could see a fire dancing in the hearth, and she felt a stab of recognition as though she'd been here before. There was a high-backed armchair before it, and a man's black boot.

As she looked for clues to where she might be, the man occupying the chair stood up, sending Catherine spinning away from the window. She pressed herself against the wall beside it, back and hands flat against the cold stone, holding her breath.

She imagined fingers pulling back the curtain, the face of the Duke framed by the window right beside her. The face from her visions. But was it really him?

A few moments later, she heard footsteps moving away. Terrified that the man would come outside to investigate, she jumped off the stone and crouched behind the bushes.

Catherine had no idea what time it was. She would have imagined that without electricity most homes would be in darkness soon after nightfall, and only the affluent would burn candles and fuel for long.

What kind of home was this? It was large, to be sure, but the grounds were rough and unkempt. Had she been correct in her interpretation of her father's words and the tale of Ferdinand, the amulet acted as a sort of homing device and she should be at the residence of the Duke of Westlake. And she'd be surprised if this was it.

After what seemed like an age with no one approaching, Catherine felt safe enough to gingerly approach the front gate. She scaled the short wall of the property, discovering that there was no road on the other side, only a path beaten by the hooves of horses. There were other houses around, signaling that she was in some kind of town or village. She'd have to go looking for an inn, but the last thing she wanted to do was draw attention to herself by appearing in the middle of the night all alone. Instead, as she walked through a meadow, she made the soft grass at the base of an oak tree her bed.

She wouldn't have expected to get much sleep on the ground like that. But within seconds of curling up with her knapsack as a pillow, she fell into a deep slumber.

CATHERINE AWOKE THE NEXT morning well past sunrise.

She sat up with a start, suddenly remembering where she was — or rather, where she *wasn't*.

The ground was cool and damp, and she stood up and stretched. She was indeed in a meadow, interrupted by the occasional tree.

There was smoke coming from a couple of nearby chimneys, including the house she had arrived at hours before. Looking around to ensure she was alone, she unhooked the satchel from the inside of her skirts, fumbling as she eagerly opened it. It was with great relief that she saw her belongings inside intact: her gold, bank notes and coins, and the letter from her father's chest. Taking out a few coins and stuffing them into the deep pockets she had specially requested be stitched into her dress, she put the reticule in its entirety into her knapsack.

There was little way of knowing how she looked, having no mirror. Feeling her face and hair, apart from a few strands of grass and some grit, it seemed as though she had passed eighty years into the past unscathed.

Catherine slipped her bag onto her back and took to the path again. It appeared she had been correct in her assessment: she had arrived in some kind of industrial town. There were smokestacks in the distance, and that was the direction in which she was headed. For where there were factories, there might be a place to stay.

Of course, finding one would take time. From the sun just peering over the horizon, she guessed it was about 8 a.m. It was well over half an hour before she at last came upon a street that seemed to be more in the center of things, where a bakery was just opening its doors, and Catherine suddenly realized how hungry she was. Hoping her appearance was not amiss, she entered the shop, heart in her mouth.

'Good morning to you, miss,' said the old shopkeeper, barely looking up at her as he wiped the counter with gusto. 'How can I help you today?'

'I would like some bread, please,' she said, surprised by the sound of her own voice.

He grabbed a dense-looking loaf from the pile on the counter, wrapping it in a piece of paper.

She reached into her pocket to take out her coins, holding her breath as she handed them over, hoping the man who had sold them to her for twice their face value had not fooled her. When the baker accepted them without comment, she knew that so far she was safe. 'You have a good day now,' he said.

Catherine was about to step out of the shop when she turned to him and asked, 'Would you know where I could find an inn of repute?'

'You'd have to be heading to South Street for that, miss.'

'Would you be so kind as to direct me there?'

He looked surprised that she didn't know her way about; this town must not get many visitors. 'Walk to the church. Just before it, you'll find a lane beside the haberdashery. The best inn you'll find in Twickenham is there.'

So that is where she was: Twickenham. It didn't ring a bell, but what she knew was that the Duke of Westlake did *not* live there. She thanked him and took to the street once more, breaking off small pieces of the delicious bread hungrily on the way.

The church stood reliably tall, and she could see it from a distance as she walked down the road, sidestepping mounds of yesterday's horse droppings. The center of town was gray and uninspired, and she grew more and more uncomfortable. It was bustling with men and women walking toward the factories, and one or two threw strange glances in her direction. Catherine finally glimpsed herself in a glass window at the haberdashery and noted with alarm the impact of the night spent asleep in the field. She pulled out a blade of grass that had wedged itself in her hair.

Luckily, she found the inn just where the baker said she would. If she had been hoping for luxury, this would not be it. The cramped front room was empty, but with no idea where to go, she waited for some time till a man appeared. She could tell at once that her early morning appearance was far from customary. She was acutely aware of the strangeness of a gentlewoman traveling alone in 1851.

So she came up with a story she hoped would work. 'Excuse me, sir, I need lodgings. I am waiting for my family to join me and they expect to arrive tomorrow, but for tonight I need only one room.'

'You are alone?' he asked.

'Only for the moment.'

He looked her up and down. 'We have a room.'

She crossed her arms across her chest. 'And how much would that be?'

He named his price, and she was about to produce it from her pocket, when he said tersely, 'We do not give it out for single women travelers. We are not that kind of establishment.'

'Oh! And I am not that kind of lady!' she cried with a blush. 'A family emergency caused me to set out alone, and tomorrow my father will be here.'

He shook his head.

'It would be a great kindness if you could accommodate me.'

Nothing.

She closed her eyes, trying to stay calm. 'I'll pay double.'

His eyes narrowed. 'In advance.'

She pulled out the money, and with a quick nod of the head, he turned around to search for the keys.

While his back was to her, she peered over the counter to look at the ledger that lay open on his desk.

April 16, 1851.

She was so relieved her legs almost gave way.

The man turned around and Catherine quickly took a step back. 'Follow me,' he said, leading her down a dingy hallway to an even more dingy room.

But she didn't care. She was in the right time, off the road and safe for now. And she'd hardly be there long, if everything went to plan. She sat on the bed and ate some more bread as she contemplated her next steps.

IT WAS AFTERNOON WHEN Catherine set out again. She had slept some more, had a hot meal, washed, and now there was only one matter of business left for her in Twickenham.

She secured a carriage, the cause for some speculation amongst the folks at the inn, which she happily ignored. Her knapsack slung over one shoulder, she boarded the coach. As she rolled up to the house from the night before, she realized it was far from the humble cottage she had assumed it was. It was a rather stately Tudor home, with a steeply pitched roof. But there was no way it was the Westlake Estate.

She got out of the carriage, trying to gather herself as she ambled up to the door and knocked. It creaked open a few moments later, a liveried servant of at least seventy years before her.

'I am here to meet the Duke of Westlake,' she announced briskly. 'I have just arrived from New York and I have urgent business with him.'

He appeared untroubled. 'I am sorry, miss, but the Duke of Westlake does not live here.'

Catherine frowned. 'I beg your pardon, is this not the residence of the Duke of Westlake?'

He pursed his lips. 'It is the home of Sebastian Talbot, not of the Duke of Westlake.'

The disappointment coursed through her. If Sebastian Talbot was not the Duke of Westlake, who was he and why was she here? She had hung everything on the belief that the two parts of the medallion attracted one another, assuming her father had directed her to the Duke of Westlake for this reason. She could only hope that whoever Sebastian Talbot was, he'd be able to help her. 'Forgive me, my information must be at fault. But it is quite urgent that I meet Mr. Sebastian Talbot.'

'He is currently away on business. But perhaps I can fetch someone with whom you may speak more freely,' he said. He showed her to a comfortable sitting room and ambled slowly down the corridor.

Catherine looked around. The house was simple, cozy, unlike her idea of a stately British home. Nor were there any personal items that might reveal more information about the man she sought. She sat down and waited.

In a moment the housekeeper, an elderly woman dressed in black, came in. 'Can I help you, miss?' she asked warmly.

Catherine stood up. 'Yes, please, I am looking for Mr. Sebastian Talbot.'

'You have just missed him, miss.'

'How very distressing,' she said, shoulders slumping. 'May I ask where he is?'

'Why, he has gone to London for the fair!'

'The fair?'

Despite her exceptional training, the woman couldn't help but look at her as though she was daft. 'The Great Exhibition, miss, the grand fair organized by Prince Albert! He will be showing his collection of Turkish rugs.'

Catherine nodded. Of course she remembered the event — it found mention in just about every history book as the crowning achievement of the year. 'But I was given to believe he was at home even last night?'

'Aye, miss you just missed him! He left for town only this morning, having received a message from town summoning him there.'

Catherine cursed her luck at such a near miss. 'May I ask a question that may seem impertinent?'

She looked at Catherine askance, but nodded her head.

'The butler told me that Mr. Sebastian Talbot is not the Duke of Westlake.'

'No, miss. If it is the Duke you seek, try the family estate.'

'I thank you,' said Catherine, standing up.

She walked toward the foyer. Directly before her was the door to a conservatory lined with curios and objets d'art. 'Is that a gallery over there?' she asked.

'Indeed. Does the young lady have an interest in antiquities?'

'Yes, of course! Who doesn't?'

She gave her a look as if to suggest that perhaps young women should have better ways to spend their time. 'You are welcome to look if you like.'

'You are very kind,' said Catherine, following the housekeeper into the room — and her mouth nearly dropped at the sight of some items.

Statues from Greece and figurines from Egypt, ivory work from India and carpets from Persia.

'These are remarkable! How did your master come about such a collection?'

'He travels the world looking for such treasures.'

'Does he keep them all for himself?'

'I am not much aware of his business affairs.'

'Is there someone who can share with me the history of these pieces? Do they belong to his family?'

'No, of that much I am sure.' She dropped her voice. 'He took nothing from his home when he left except the clothes on his back.'

'His home?'

'The Westlake residence.'

'So he *does* belong to that family?'

The housekeeper seemed confused. 'Why, of course!'

'But he isn't the Duke.'

'He isn't the Duke *at the moment*. Though by rights he should be. His uncle — I shouldn't be saying this — all but stole the title from him.'

Catherine pretended to admire a Roman bust. 'You seem to have been with him for a while?'

'Aye,' she said with a smile. 'I was his old nursemaid, you see, and when he left, he asked me to keep house for him.'

'And you were content to leave such a fine home?'

A shadow came over the housekeeper. 'I am content to be where Master Sebastian sees fit to take me.'

'The current Duke...?'

'Isn't a nice man, miss.' But then she remembered herself, and that was all Catherine could get out of her on the subject.

'Would you have a schedule of trains to London?' asked Catherine.

'I'll fetch one right away,' she said, hurrying away.

CATHERINE LEFT FOR THE train station, with nothing more to keep her in the town. London, she hoped, would provide more answers.

There was one giant question in her mind. If the medallion worked like she believed, it had brought her to the correct place. But as per her father's letter, it was in the possession of the Duke of Westlake in this time. If Sebastian Talbot was not the Duke of Westlake, she wasn't sure which part of the story was wrong — the fact that the medallion would do what she needed it to do, or that it was the Duke of Westlake she needed to find.

Making matters much more complicated was the fact that, judging by the collection Catherine had just seen, Sebastian Talbot might not be a duke, but he most definitely was a thief.

FOUR

'CATHERINE DEAR, WILL YOU please pass me the clotted cream?'

Catherine handed the white ceramic pot to the woman by her side, who was eagerly splitting a scone down the middle. Mrs. Mary Riley, wife to the head of the American delegation at the Great Exhibition. And for the past week, Catherine had been her de facto companion.

On the train from Twickenham, a direction had presented itself. She had picked up a newspaper to read on the journey, and it was in its pages she gathered her idea. London was teeming with international visitors who had come in for the Great Exhibition, many of whom were staying at the newly opened Ritz. On arriving, Catherine had gone directly there.

Checking into a cheaper establishment in the vicinity, she paid a visit to a restaurant in the hotel, whiling away a few hours in the lobby. She needed a plan and a cover story if she wanted to have any luck with Sebastian Talbot, and the hotel seemed just the place to find one.

An opportunity soon presented itself when she first saw Mrs. Riley making exhortations about the candied whole clementines the bakery had on display in honor of the French ambassador's arrival.

'We must have something just as splendid to represent the United States,' she was saying to the hapless woman behind the counter.

'There is nothing quite as American as apple pie,' Catherine had said conspiratorially. Mrs. Riley had spun around, eyes landing on her with glee. 'An American! My dear girl,' she had exclaimed. 'What a pleasure it is to be truly understood.'

And so Catherine got swept along for an emergency meeting with the concierge. In all the restaurants at the Ritz the following week they decided the dessert special would be apple pie à la mode ('But maybe just call it "with ice cream"? It might sound... more American,' suggested Catherine), and from that moment she had become indispensable to Mrs. Riley. On hearing that Catherine was alone in London ('What an extraordinary thing, traveling across the Atlantic all by yourself'), she had immediately invited Catherine to stay in the maid's room attached to her suite. An arrangement that suited her splendidly.

'The English certainly don't know how to eat, but the clotted cream is something,' observed Mrs. Riley, slathering great heaps of the stuff onto her second scone of the morning, adding a dollop of strawberry preserves. 'You really must eat something, dear,' she said as Catherine picked at her toast.

'It is all just so exciting,' she gushed. 'I find I have no appetite at all!' And for once, there was no deception involved. Two weeks into her extraordinary journey, she was no closer to finding Sebastian than when she was in New York. Hopefully that would change today.

'You had better get your fill now, because at the inauguration there will be quite the crush of bodies and no time for food.'

'Really?' she asked, eyes as wide as she could make them. 'Will there be quite so many people?'

'Oh yes, though we will be in a special enclosure, there will be thousands of people.'

AND Mrs. Riley was right. For the past few days, Catherine had been visiting the Crystal Palace, the extraordinary structure that had been created in Hyde Park for the event, watching as the giant glasshouse filled up with remarkable items from across the world. And yet she was still surprised to see how different it all looked on inauguration day, with thousands of people converging in order to view the ceremony, conducted under a regal purple canopy by Queen Victoria herself. Prince Albert was beaming with pride at the culmination of his efforts.

Catherine viewed it all from the front lines, thanks to her pride of place amid the American delegation. She took in the grand stage in hungry gulps. The domed archway, the towering crystal fountain, the royal presence — it was truly a sight to behold.

She scanned the elevated galleries too, where people lined up along the walkways on the first floor. From their attire, it was clear they were all from the upper echelons of British society. She couldn't wait to get up there as well, for a bird's-eye view of all the exhibits — the statues, the fountains, the steam power machinery.

And then Catherine froze.

A man gazed down at the proceedings from the balcony, dark-haired and chiseled, towering above the spectators beside him.

The man whose illustration she'd seen. The man who'd popped up in her visions. The man Catherine had believed to be the Duke of Westlake.

The man who must be Sebastian Talbot.

She glanced around her. Getting out of there in a rush would be impossible, with a strict protocol in place for the duration of the inauguration. She would try to keep an eye on him and then track him down as soon as she was able. But she knew it would be a monumental task, in this place, the largest structure in the world. Where would she even begin?

Once the launch was over and the crowd had dispersed, it didn't take long for the man to get lost. Catherine cursed her luck but had little choice but to plough on, for after the royal presentation had ended, it was the turn of the American delegation to hold their own inauguration.

IT WASN'T TILL AFTERNOON that Catherine could get away from Mrs. Riley, who was busy with visitors. She did not know where she might find the man from the gallery. It was possible she was entirely mistaken, and it wasn't Sebastian Talbot at all, because aside from his housekeeper's word that he would be here, she had nothing else to go on.

In all of her research about the Duke of Westlake, there had been no reference to carpets or exhibitions or antiquities of any kind. It was quite possible that she was on the trail of the wrong man altogether, but her instinct told her that her father would not have led her astray on so significant a point. If he said the two parts of the medallion were drawn to each other, he must be correct. If she didn't believe that, what was she even doing here?

Which raised the question: if the medallion was here, would she be able to feel it?

Catherine closed her eyes. She tried desperately to feel its draw, focusing all her attention on the metal sitting next to her skin under her dress.

Nothing.

If she was expecting some sort of magnetic attraction to guide her way, it wasn't about to happen.

She found an official-looking person walking around and stopped him. 'Excuse me, would you be able to direct me toward the display of Turkish carpets?'

'I don't know about carpets but Turkish, did you say? It is at the other end, miss.'

She walked in the direction he had showed, but was held up by the massive crowd where the Crown jewels were on display. She inched slowly toward the quieter end of the pavilion.

And there before her was the Turkish zone, with its brilliant canopy. Why would any of these belong to an English duke?

She entered and found a handsome turbaned man in traditional attire behind a crowd of visitors. She waited quietly till he had a moment.

'I was wondering if you knew where I might find Mr. Sebastian Talbot,' she asked.

The man was too distracted to pay her much attention. 'Sebastian? He was here not long ago, perhaps you might wait?'

She did her best to blend in, standing to the side. It wasn't long before the man from the gallery arrived in the pavilion, commanding the room. He was talking with some Turkish officials with his back to her, but she knew beyond a doubt that this was the man from her visions. It didn't matter anymore if he was the duke; it didn't matter even if his name was Sebastian. Her feet moved forward of their own volition. Whether it was the thrill of finding what she was after, or the draw of the medallion, she felt something she had never felt before.

And it was as though he felt it, too. He turned around, his lips parted, eyes searching the crowd till they landed on her.

Everyone else disappeared.

His eyes darkened as they met hers. He was older than she, in his mid-thirties, perhaps, his dark hair curling around his forehead, square jawed, imperious nosed and very, very handsome.

She dragged her eyes away, and he too turned back to the people with whom he'd been talking. Catherine continued her wait by a glass display case filled with stone-studded silver jewelry, visitor after visitor passing her by.

The man came to stand by her side. He towered above her with a presence so forceful she took a moment to compose herself before speaking. At last she turned to him with a brief smile. 'Turkey must be a land of many wonders,' she said.

'I have found it to be one of the most beautiful places I have ever beheld.'

'You are English?'

'And you are American.'

Her smile widened as she looked up at him through her lashes. 'Have you been to my part of the world?'

'I have not yet had the pleasure.'

She turned to him, holding out her hand for a handshake. 'I am Catherine Christie of New York.'

He took it and raised it to his lips. She cast her gaze down coyly at the floor, a slight thrill of pleasure at the brush of skin against skin.

'And I am Sebastian Talbot, of everywhere and nowhere,' he said as he released her hand.

She felt the loss of his contact and had to remind herself to giggle. This was the persona she had chosen for herself: the coquettish belle from across the pond. Hopefully, it would get her what she needed.

'These carpets are yours, I heard?'

'Indeed. They are from Turkey. Hand knotted, each one takes months to make, years even, depending on the size and intricacy. They are nothing new, of course. From the earliest days of the silk route, carpets have been coveted by all of Europe. What brings you to the Great Exhibition?'

'Do I need any other reason apart from such wonders as this?'

'You have traveled all the way from America to be here?'

'In a manner of speaking. I am with the American delegation, who are no doubt disappointed at the inadequacy of their display compared to the embarrassment of riches from the existing colonies.'

'Do I detect a note of regret that the United States is no longer a part of the Empire?'

She laughed long and hard at that, longer and harder than would please the ego of most men. But it didn't take her long to discover that Sebastian was not most men.

'I can assure you there are no regrets on that front, we are quite content with our lot. You notice that the treasures on display may originate from the colonies, but currently belong to the Crown.'

Sebastian smiled. 'I *had* noticed.' He paused, as though to say something else, but then appeared to think better of it. 'I hope you enjoy your stay here.'

'I am accompanying the American delegation chief's wife,' she said, and from the look on his face it had appeared that Sebastian had met Mrs. Riley and knew exactly how it must be going.

'No doubt you would like to see something of English life before you leave?'

'I would. The Ritz and the Exhibition are splendid, but it would be a dream come true to see how you all live over here.'

'Ah! Such dreams are the best kind — easy to fulfill. Follow me.'

He strode away to the next stall, Catherine in his wake. A pretty woman of about Sebastian's age stood there in a dress of muslin so fine Catherine itched to touch it. 'This is one of my oldest friends, Mrs. Jane Cheswick.'

Catherine introduced herself again.

The woman, almost a head taller than Catherine, looked at her with undisguised curiosity. 'What work are you doing with the delegation?' she asked.

'I am a companion to Mrs. Riley.'

'Oh how lovely, but you must be terribly bored.'

Catherine grinned. 'She has very kindly taken me under her wing.'

'Yes, yes,' said Jane, putting a hand on her arm. 'But there is so much more to do in London than spend your days here, whatever Sebastian might think.'

'Crowds aside, there are worse ways to spend a day,' he said.

'A day, but months?' she said with a shudder. 'We can do better than that for Miss Catherine. You know, Sebastian, it has been sometime since we have had an American in our circle.'

Sebastian nodded. 'Not since the ever diverting Scooter Thompson in 1849.'

Soon Jane proposed Catherine come with them to a garden party the following day.

Catherine looked pained. 'I don't know if Mrs. Riley will be able to spare me.'

'Oh, don't worry about Mrs. Riley,' said Jane, 'take me to her now and I'll sort out the rest. I think you may also fancy a shopping trip?'

She demurred at first, before admitting a deep love for British fabrics. 'But I would hate to inconvenience you.'

Sebastian dismissed this with a rude noise. 'Has shopping ever been an inconvenience to a woman?'

After airing their outrage, Jane and Catherine went to find Mrs. Riley. Catherine had not expected in her wildest dreams that meeting Sebastian and insinuating herself into his circle would be as effortless as this. So easy in fact that Catherine felt a twinge of guilt about what she had planned to do. But she had come too far and risked too much to back down now. Anyhow, this was simply the first step:

success was still far from guaranteed. If she were to fail, she would be
stuck here forever, an outcome too frightening to contemplate.

FIVE

THE GARDEN PARTY CAME and went, and the shopping expedition too. It seemed to Sebastian as though Miss Catherine Christie had always been a part of his little London circle. She was spending an inordinate amount of time with Jane, and by extension her brother William, who were both providing enthusiastic reports of their activities. Sebastian, busy with his various obligations at the exposition, was not in attendance at all times. But to compensate for it, he had taken to strolling down the transept of the Crystal Palace to the American zone to find Catherine when he had the time.

She was seldom alone. When Mrs. Riley could spare her, visitors surrounded her — gentlemen visitors. It was as though she were the most magnetic part of the displays from across the Atlantic, and Sebastian couldn't disagree.

After the first few weeks of the exhibition's run, the crowds thinned somewhat, and one lighter afternoon Sebastian found her free. 'Would you like to see some other exhibits?' he asked.

Catherine beamed up at him. 'I have got nowhere with the Indian display, it's been so crowded.'

She hooked her arm through his and led him straight to the area devoted to the East Indies. It was a Tuesday morning, and it was the least busy he had seen it.

'This is the place to start, isn't it?' she said. They examined the giant stuffed elephant at the center of the Indian exhibit, with intricate ivory howdah and golden cover.

'Imagine traveling on that thing.' She craned her head back to take in its size.

'I do not wish to be pedantic, but this is an African elephant. The Indian variety is smaller than this.'

Catherine shot him an incredulous glance. 'No, that's not pedantic at all.'

Bending over to get a better look at the Koh-I-Noor diamond, mounted on a frame designed to maximize the amount of light the majestic gem reflected, even Catherine was in awe. But Sebastian's own attention was divided between the stone itself and Catherine's rather dazzling emerald eyes.

Having completed her inspection, she straightened up. 'It is beautiful, but I don't see what all the fuss is about.'

This truly took him by surprise. 'It is fortunate then that it is not yours.'

Catherine laughed.

'Which of these many splendored things would you rather call your own?'

Catherine cocked her head, giving his question serious thought. 'The steam engine.'

Sebastian thought he must have misheard her, but Catherine charged straight off to the machine and tool end of the exhibition.

They stood before the mammoth pieces of equipment, the crowning achievements of England's industrial revolution. Impressive though they were, he wouldn't have considered them items for a young lady to covet. 'You can't seriously consider these giant machines more desirable than that magnificent jewel?'

'Don't get me wrong — I know which one I'd rather have on my finger, but it wouldn't be the best investment. Take your pick of these inventions and you will be rich enough in a hundred years to own all the Koh-I-Noors your heart could desire.'

Sebastian gave her a quizzical look.

She smiled. 'Why are you looking at me like that?'

'You are right, of course. A smarter man, and a richer man than I, would do just that and make a fortune in the railways alone.'

'You are surprised that I, a woman, would feel this way?'

'It is amply clear from your tone that such a position would be of particular offense to you. I think that surprises me the most.'

'Are your lovely English roses happy to be considered blinded by baubles?'

'In my experience, many women *would* prefer one of the world's largest diamonds over an engine. And more to the point, those who wouldn't take great pains to hide such a fact.'

'And why is that?'

'Because an interest in science and engineering has caught no one a rich husband.'

She raised a skeptical brow. 'I find it alarming that a desire for dangerously expensive pieces of jewelry would enchant British men of means.'

'I think they would prefer their woman to demonstrate a desire for neither.'

'Yes,' said Catherine, nodding sagely, 'they are quite right to do so. For there is nothing more dangerous than a woman unafraid to own her desire.'

Catherine turned on her heels and walked back down the length of the Crystal Palace. Sebastian, at her side, couldn't help but wonder if that tiny flash in her eye might be a desire for *him*.

'You know,' said Catherine, who seemed completely unaffected, 'it occurs to me you have no actual business at the Great Exhibition every day, do you?'

'Yes, you are quite right. I was here to support my friends from Turkey, who had underestimated the need for carpets to decorate the entirety of their exhibition space. So I helped them with some from my collection.'

'So why are you here still?' Catherine looked up at him with innocent eyes, but he had to wonder if she didn't know exactly what she was doing.

'I have a rather disreputable reason for hanging around.'

Catherine fluttered her eyelashes. 'And what might that be?'

'Perhaps it would be best to show you rather than tell you.'

IT TOOK SEBASTIAN A few minutes to convince Mrs. Riley to let Catherine leave the exhibition in his charge, on the assurance that he would see her back to the Ritz before sundown. And then Sebastian and Catherine were on their way in his carriage. It was only a short distance to their destination, and Sebastian was curious to see how Catherine would respond. So far, she had always said the thing he least expected.

They came to a halt before a shop, and he jumped out and held his hand out for her.

'What's this?' asked Catherine, taking his hand and stepping off the carriage.

'You asked me why I am still here. This is the answer. This is the shop I am running with the help of my friends from Turkey and a few other countries, who saw a business opportunity in the interest that visitors to the Great Exhibition show in the East.'

He held the glass door open, and Catherine's eyes widened. The store was an assault on the senses: spices redolent of a Turkish bazaar, resplendent silks adorning every wall, handmade jewelry atop velvet-lined busts.

'It's a little shop of wonders,' she said.

'And that's it?' he asked. 'No critique of my mercenary attempt to trade on people's fascination with the East? To prey on their provincial desires for the exotic? No disdain for my shopkeeping venture?'

'In America, there is no disdain for trade. As for the other stuff, you said your partners are Turkish, is it not? It's not exploitation if they are profiting too, surely?'

Sebastian stood back as the shopkeepers showed off splendid silk after silk for Catherine to see. They paraded their finest jewelry. They laid out their most aromatic spices. She admired them all, with praise both effusive and appropriate, but she showed not the slightest desire to own any of them.

Sebastian saw her fingering a scarf, feeling the soft fabric between the tips of her fingers. But at last, she smiled and turned away.

They left the store. Sebastian turned to her, and before he could change his mind, asked, 'Shall I take you back to the hotel, or is there time perhaps for a bit of a London tour?'

She looked delighted. 'Is there?'

He nodded. 'Jane has done an admirable job of showing you all that she loves about town. Perhaps you'd like to see some of our other contributions to civilization, apart from endless reels of muslin.'

SEBASTIAN HAD NEVER FANCIED himself much of a tourist. He had traveled to some of the world's most exciting locations and had enjoyed it all thoroughly, but mostly he stayed away from the attractions that drew visitors from foreign climes. And he had never bothered with the ones closer to home very much. But for some reason, it was of the utmost importance that Catherine see the best of London, so he took her to the Big Ben, Saint Paul's Cathedral and Tower Bridge in a whirlwind tour. She was uniformly delighted, full of questions about the history and current importance of each landmark. At last they ended up in the most quintessential of all British establishments: the pub. He chose one with a rich and storied history on the waterfront.

After a short primer on the cultural significance of a good pint of ale, they rushed back, for Mrs. Riley would surely be at the hotel by then, and Sebastian was mindful of his commitment. As they climbed back into the carriage, Sebastian couldn't remember a day spent in a woman's company that he had enjoyed so much.

'How did you get into the antiquities business?' she asked. 'If it is such a scandalous thing?'

'Once I lost my family title, I had to adapt. I had an inherent interest in history and archeology, and it is something I stumbled into.' It wasn't something Sebastian spoke of often, and it surprised him how easily the words rolled off his tongue.

She flashed him a grin full of mischief. 'Could it be the fact that it was scandalous that drew you to it?'

Sebastian smiled. 'Possibly. Though my family might find it has no leg to stand on if it judged me for my current mode of living.'

Catherine cocked her head again. 'Perhaps you'll tell me about it someday.'

'Perhaps. But I wouldn't want to spoil a splendid day with talk of that lot.'

'Splendid, you say?' She looked up at him, her eyes a dazzling green.

For a moment he fell silent. They were approaching her hotel, and Sebastian wished he did not have to part with her so soon.

'What's the big deal about closed carriages?' she asked abruptly.

'What do you mean?'

'You promised Mrs. Riley we would travel by open carriage, and that seemed to sway her decision to let me go with you unchaperoned.'

'Is it so very different in America?' asked a confused Sebastian.

She looked somewhat flustered by this. 'My family is what you might consider unusual. I wasn't raised in company very much, and my manners must be deficient.'

'There is the fear,' said Sebastian, 'that an unmarried woman's reputation will be spoiled by traveling in a closed carriage with a man.'

Catherine laughed and Sebastian felt wrong-footed, a sensation wholly unfamiliar to him. 'This amuses you?'

'Yes,' she said, 'and it should amuse you too.'

He found the ridiculous rules of propriety an annoyance to be worked around but not particularly amusing. 'And why is that?' he asked.

'Any truly scandalous behavior,' said Catherine, looking up at him, 'cannot possibly be so easily contained. If not having a cover over your carriage is all it takes to deter you, the crime can hardly be worth it.'

Sebastian's breath caught in his throat. Her eyes were dancing, lips parted, in an open and blatant invitation. One she knew he could not accept in the dying light of the afternoon, riding down the road. He was aroused, and she hadn't even touched him.

The coachman came to a stop before the entrance to her hotel. Before he could disembark to assist her, she had jumped off, leaving him staring down at her.

She was the very picture of innocence once again. 'Thank you for an absolutely delightful day.'

And with a tiny curtsy, she turned and walked through the gates of her hotel.

SIX

IT WAS A LOT more work seducing men in 1851 than it was in 1929. Not that Catherine had much experience of that kind of thing. But at least back home she'd have been able to get Sebastian alone without so much fuss, and then she'd have been able to make him want her.

Instead, she was trapped in this game that Catherine, so isolated all her life, felt ill-equipped to play. If she had come in the guise of a more scandalous woman, she might have had an easier time of all this flirtation. She'd had a taste of it in the carriage. How easily words of desire rolled off her tongue when this man was near!

How scandalous would it *really* be if she were to seduce Sebastian, or allow him to seduce her? He didn't look like he'd be overly shocked by such attempts.

It was with that in mind that Catherine entered a grand mansion on the arm of Jane, with William trailing behind them. She did her best to disguise her nerves at being in the home of the illustrious man of science, Stuart Johnson, one of the most influential inventors of the age. William and Jane seemed completely at home in such company, and she mimicked their matter-of-fact air.

Then she watched as Charles Darwin walked by, and she felt her mouth hang open. 'Is there a single famous person in England who isn't at the Great Exhibition?'

Jane smiled. 'Not one who is worth knowing. It is truly spectacular, is it not?'

'Will you all be here for the entire duration?'

'No, we are here for another month at least, but then we travel north.'

'All of you?'

Jane cast her a sidelong glance. 'I would like to think you are asking because you enjoy my company — and perhaps even William's — but I fear it is someone else's plans that concern you most.'

Catherine reddened and stammered out some manner of excuse.

Jane laughed softly, placing a tender hand on her arm. 'Oh dear, I apologize for teasing, it is only that I worry so about my friends and would like to see them all happy.'

But Catherine wasn't listening anymore — a woman had just walked in, dark haired and fine-featured, and she looked vaguely familiar from her research.

'But no... It couldn't be,' said Catherine.

Jane turned to see who it was. 'Oh, we must congratulate her on the success of *Jane Eyre*. Though I find it a trifle sentimental myself.'

'It is... Is that Charlotte Brontë?'

'Yes, dear.'

Catherine stood silently awestruck as Jane began a casual conversation with her favorite Brontë sister, who had no idea how far her fame would outstrip her death. She remained silent, as there was almost nothing she could say that wouldn't make her sound like a bumbling idiot at best, and a witch at worst.

There was a bit of a whisper that went up and all eyes were fixed on the entrance behind them. Catherine turned and saw that it was Sebastian.

Their eyes met across the room. Whenever he looked at her, she could feel it from the top of her head, right down to her toes. It was fear, apprehension, and something else she would rather not think about.

The whispering came to an abrupt stop as he entered, but the curious sidelong glances remained.

'What is happening?' asked Catherine.

'Oh, it's nothing to bother yourself with,' said Jane.

'There seems to be a buzz around Sebastian's arrival.'

'Yes, I don't know how these things are settled in America, but here one's past can be hard to leave behind.'

'It sounds like there is a scandal afoot.'

Jane smiled. 'Isn't there always? It is just about discovering whose.'

Sebastian approached them. 'Somewhat oppressive in here,' he said, gloved hand on his silk cravat. 'Let's go outside, shall we?'

Together they left the salon for the less stifling environment of the garden, but Catherine couldn't help wondering why the crowd here was so bothered by Sebastian when every other assembly they had attended didn't seem to care.

'How do you find this selection of British society?' Sebastian asked Catherine, a cynical smile on his face.

'Ms. Brontë rather bedazzled her,' said Jane with an indulgent grin.

'Not to mention Mr. Charles Darwin,' she said. There was nothing to be gained by being star-struck by the celebrities of the time; she came from the land of the Wright brothers and Hemingway, she told herself, and there was no room for distraction. 'It is all rather impressive,' she said, 'but I still want more than anything to see how common English people live.'

Jane seized upon this declaration with glee. 'We are not famous artists or inventors, or even adventurers like Sebastian here. We are likely as common as you will get. You should accompany us to our home in Mansfield. There is nowhere more British than where we come from and there you may finally get the chance to see how we live on our little island.'

Sebastian looked amused, but before he or Catherine could answer, Jane's face grew troubled. She touched Sebastian's arm.

'What's the matter?' asked Catherine.

'I fear our welcome here may draw to a close,' said Jane.

Sebastian turned around. His eyes traveled to a man who had just entered, young and fashionably dressed. 'If John doesn't want to see me, he shouldn't be here.'

'It is not John I am worried about, it is you.'

'I assure you there is no cause for concern.'

As Sebastian wandered off to speak to some acquaintances, Catherine turned to Jane.

'Could I ask what all this is about?'

'I fear if I tell you, I will frighten you away from us altogether.'

'Is it something to do with Mr. Talbot losing his peerage?'

She looked surprised. 'Why, yes. The man who has just entered, John Lewis, is the brother-in-law of the current Duke of Westlake, Sebastian's uncle James. The Duke's wife Ophelia and Sebastian have a somewhat complicated history.'

'Oh dear.'

Jane nodded, her color rising. 'She, there's just no discreet way to say it, sullied Sebastian's name in order to have the title pass to his uncle.'

'Sullied his name! How?'

Jane looked around. 'I suppose you will find out, anyway. You don't strike me as a silly sort,' she said. 'Ophelia seduced Sebastian and then accused him of plotting to kill James so he could marry Ophelia himself. It was all a most scandalous fiction, of course. Not the seduction part of it, unfortunately, but the rest of it.'

Catherine's head reeled. Could this be true? Could her father have put her in the path of such a man? 'Why, that is simply terrible! But why is that woman's brother involved in all this?'

'Sebastian had accused them all of conspiring against him.'

'Doesn't that make Sebastian the wronged party?'

'Given that everyone believes he is the one at fault, no, and John has made a bit of a nuisance of himself before by insisting on defending his precious sister's honor.'

That would explain why there were whispers on Sebastian's arrival. 'Can there be no recourse?'

'The current Duke is unfortunately very close to the ruling dispensation — not just the Crown, but several ministers.'

'But surely that man wouldn't drag that business up here?'

'That is what Sebastian is counting on, but I am not so sure. The last time we chanced upon John, the host asked Sebastian to leave before things got out of hand. He is seldom in society, simply to avoid such confrontations. He's made an exception of late, I suspect because of you.'

Catherine mumbled her objections to this half-heartedly. Soon after, she spotted John through a window, someone whispering in his ear and pointing in their direction. It didn't take him long to get worked up.

'What is that blackguard doing here!' demanded John, striding across the lawns.

Their host, a mild-mannered, bespectacled man who seemed to be the very image of a mad scientist, could barely summon the interest in their scuffle to provide an answer.

But Sebastian stepped forward. 'I have been invited, same as you.'

'You have some gall showing your face here!'

'No more than you,' he said, taking a sip of wine.

John sputtered his outrage. 'I challenge you to a duel!'

Sebastian raised a bored eyebrow. 'Not this again?'

'You may not cast aspersions upon my family, now or ever!'

'And surely those who were unaware of those aspersions are now learning all about them. You do your sister and brother-in-law a greater disservice by repeatedly making a scene.'

'I will have your answer!'

'I believe England has declared its last a duel fought and lost some years ago. What would Prince Albert say if he heard the Duchess of Westlake's brother had the temerity to ignore the law?'

John drew a dagger, a gasp going up around the garden.

Catherine took a step toward Sebastian, but Jane held her back.

Sebastian hardly blinked an eye. 'This has to be a joke, surely.'

'Do I look like I'm joking?' sputtered John. 'If you won't accept my challenge, you leave me with no choice to defend my family's honor in what way I can.'

'I can assure you, a less worthy beneficiary for your gallantry never existed.'

Another gasp. The man had nothing but scorn on his face.

'But do what you must,' said Sebastian.

Catherine grabbed Jane. 'But striking an unarmed man cannot possibly be tolerated!' she cried.

'None of this is permitted, including duels, but happen all too often, though not perhaps in such a place as this.'

Jane was not as droll as Sebastian about the affair, but William looked positively excited.

The men circled one another, Sebastian still unarmed. John struck out, missing once as Sebastian leaned away from his dagger's edge. As he swung again, Sebastian effortlessly grabbed him by the knife arm.

'Now I see why you needed to ride on the Duchess's coattails. You can't even take on an unarmed man on your own.'

With a roar, John freed his arm and swung wildly, slashing Sebastian through the middle.

At last, Stuart Johnson came rushing forward.

'Sir!' he said to John. 'This is utterly unacceptable! I must ask you to leave immediately or I will have no choice but to throw you out!'

John looked from him to Sebastian. 'This isn't over, Talbot.'

THEY ESCORTED SEBASTIAN TO a closed room, and Catherine and Jane stood anxiously outside it. Johnson had rushed his injured guest away so fast they didn't have a chance to check on their friend. William was inside and had promised them an update.

A few moments later, a servant approached the door holding some dirty cloths from the kitchen and a basin of water.

Catherine stepped forward. 'No, stop!'

The servant paid no heed, entering the room and closing the door behind her.

Such was her opportunity, and Catherine would have to take it.

'What are you doing?' asked Jane.

'They can't use those cloths on him! His wound will get infected!'

Catherine flung the door open and every set of eyes in the room turned to her, including Sebastian's, who looked only mildly surprised.

'Stop!' she said. 'We need clean cloth to dress the wound!'

Stuart Johnson looked at her as though she was speaking in tongues.

'A dirty cloth like that can cause illness, even death.'

'This is definitely the first I am hearing about such a thing,' said Johnson.

'I have worked as a nurse in America,' she said, thinking on her feet. She crossed over to Sebastian as though she belonged there.

'Bring me a basin of water and soap, and another of boiling water, but before that some clean cloth and your strongest alcohol.'

Sebastian looked at her with hooded eyes, his expression inscrutable. 'It's okay, Johnson, Miss Christie can be trusted.'

Johnson stepped back. Sebastian continued to watch her most curiously as she examined the wound. John's knife had sliced through his vest and shirt and through an extensive amount of skin, thus producing a lot of blood, but it had not cut deep.

A footman was dispatched to fetch the items she'd requested, and another returned with a length of white muslin and a decanter of whisky.

She glanced up at Sebastian with a whisper of a smile. 'I need to clean this properly. I must ask you to remove your shirt.'

He raised an eyebrow, and then quietly complied.

'Give them some space, please,' said Johnson. The room emptied of all but the two of them and a footman.

She helped him out of his ruined clothes, by which time the boiling water had also arrived. And there it was: a small dagger-shaped piece of metal, unmistakably forged from the same curious stuff as her own medallion, which even now was hidden under her dress. She stole a couple of glances at it as she cleaned the wound. 'With some rest and the proper care, this will heal without stitches,' she said, her voice shaky.

'Stitches?' asked Sebastian.

'Sutures, a surgeon could sew the skin together if it was too deep.'

'Little Catherine,' he whispered. 'So full of surprises.'

Even through the fear and excitement of finding the missing piece of her medallion, she couldn't ignore the wide expanse of his chest, hard and chiseled, wondering how it would feel under the tips of her fingers. Skin prickling at the thought, she did her best to keep her eyes on his wound, raising them to his face with what she hoped was a fitting amount of embarrassment.

'Where did you learn to do this?' he asked.

It had been her mother who taught her first aid. She'd learnt, apparently, from Catherine's father, who had a habit of showing up with nasty injuries.

Not altogether a surprise if he made a habit of traveling through time.

She couldn't tell Sebastian any of this, of course. 'I care for the needy, back home, at-at our church, and there is a pastor that has taught me all he knows.'

As she spoke, she caught another glimpse of the pendant, now certain it was identical in its sheen to her own and would fit into its cavity. Two parts meant to be one.

Catherine tied the bandage around his shoulder to apply some pressure to the wound. 'Quite impressive,' said Sebastian, as the footman helped him back into his ruined shirt and jacket.

Catherine nodded. 'Hopefully it will feel better by the morning.'

'Thank you. I feel better already.'

Catherine pursed her lips. 'You should lie down.'

'Yes, but I must leave here and not cause our host any more unease.'

'Will I see you at the exhibition?'

He thought for a moment. 'I have some business to wrap up, so I will be back. But in a day or two, I must leave London. If my presence reaches the ears of the Prince, my Turkish friends may suffer the consequences of my ill repute.'

She took his hands in hers. 'Promise you'll come to see me before you leave.'

He looked down at her, searching her face. 'I promise,' he said.

He left amongst murmurs, and shortly so did Jane and William, dropping Catherine off to the hotel on their way.

Catherine's mind was full and her heart reluctant to take the next steps she knew she must. She would cause Sebastian more pain than he'd already endured. But there was nothing to be done for it: she hadn't planned on getting close to this man, it had happened of its own accord, and now she had no choice but to go ahead.

With Sebastian set to leave London, Catherine knew she had no time to waste. It had taken a knife fight and the threat of gangrene for her to get his shirt off once. What would it take to get it off again?

He had the missing piece of her medallion. She knew that now. All she had to do was get her hands on it.

SEVEN

THROUGH THE GRAND ARCHED ceiling of the glasshouse that was the Crystal Palace, a beam of light found its splendid target: a slight girl in conspicuously unfashionable dress, her bronze curls cascading down her back. All around her buzzed a million men and women, all visitors at the Great Exhibition of 1851.

And yet all Sebastian could see was the curve of her neck as she looked up at his friend William, who was attempting to explain how the giant telescope in front of them worked.

'I know it all sounds terribly confusing,' he said. 'Surely a place such as this has wonders more befitting a woman such as yourself. There are the splendid silks from Lyon or from India, the Koh-I-Noor, the largest diamond in the world.'

Catherine's brow furrowed. 'But surely the Koh-I-Noor isn't the largest diamond? I recall hearing there is one larger displayed in this very hall. They call it the Daria-I-Noor.'

William shook his head, so certain in his knowledge and his ability to impress her. Sebastian took a step forward to stand by her side.

'The lady is quite right, you know, though the Koh-I-Noor is very much the gem *du jour*, a sign of our Empire's might. As for this grand telescope, from what I have seen, Miss Catherine understands more about how this blasted contraption works than you do.'

Catherine looked up at him, a sparkle in her eye and a smile playing at the corner of her mouth. 'I was wondering when the collector would make his appearance. We had quite given up on you.'

He fought a wholly inappropriate urge to tuck a curl behind her ear.

'How is your wound?' she asked.

'Better. Thanks to your timely ministrations.'

A look passed between them, containing the memory of intimacy past. It was quite lost on William, who cleared his throat and pointed at the Turkish pavilion. 'You see those rugs over there?'

Catherine followed the line of his pointing finger. She nodded.

'Those are Sebastian's latest obsession.'

She looked up at him through her thick curtain of her eyelashes. 'How fascinating.'

Sebastian doubted William had picked up on her sarcasm. He'd already shown her the Turkish display that had several pieces from his own collection, and she'd been suitably impressed. But in the few short weeks he'd known Catherine, he had realized that carpets and diamonds were not the baubles to hold her attention.

She was... He couldn't put his finger on it.

'Miss Catherine, will you be attending the reception tomorrow night for the French minister?' asked William.

Catherine sighed. 'I will have to miss it, I'm afraid.'

His expression was almost pitiable.

Catherine continued, 'My hostess detests balls and will not come, so neither can I, even though I would so love to see this place all decorated.'

Sebastian looked around. 'How much more ostentatious could it get?'

'Exactly!' she said with a smile.

William rallied upon hearing this, because for this at least he might offer a solution. 'If you would do us the honor, my sister and I would be glad to escort you.'

Catherine looked from William to Sebastian, eyes wide.

Sebastian smiled. 'Sadly, I have no sister and cannot offer you her services as a chaperone. But if you accept William's invitation, I will see you there, and hope to have the honor of a dance, Miss Catherine. As a final parting of sorts; I leave town the next day.'

She frowned. 'I don't know if you should raise your arm that much.'

'A trifling flesh wound won't stand between me and such pleasure.'

Catherine nodded. 'Though one hopes your enjoyment will not be cut short by another duel.'

'Not here, they wouldn't dare.'

'Then I look forward to it.'

And then Sebastian did something he had never done in his life. From the inside pocket of his jacket, he pulled out a small slender box. He held it out to Catherine. 'For you,' he mumbled, unaccountably embarrassed.

Catherine looked at it with delight.

'What is it?' she asked, her eyes dancing.

'A little token. A trifle.' And then he rushed away.

Sebastian entered the Crystal Palace at the appointed hour. It would be like finding a grain of rice in a Turkish bazaar, trying to find Catherine in the madness that was a public ball. And she was, he hated to admit, the only reason he was here, despite the threat of

John's renewed aggression. For a moment he considered leaving without further delay.

But then, a familiar voice called out his name. Sebastian turned to see Jane approaching. 'There you are,' she said.

Sebastian scanned the room. 'I was just about to turn tail and run out of here. It is worse than I expected.'

'No need to transform yourself into a complete hermit, Sebastian. There are still those in your acquaintance who will not shy away from your presence.'

'I feel the weight of your compliment,' said Sebastian, raising her hand to his lips. 'One must wonder why I'd prefer to stay away from such an adoring audience.'

'Oh, Sebastian, you seem to have a newfound penchant for sulking. You may be persona non grata now, but it wasn't long ago that London was your playground.'

'So think how my current state must compound my misery. To have fallen so far.'

'I can think of one young lady whose enthusiasm seems sincere. Catherine is quite taken by you.'

The vein of excitement running through him at the very mention of her name was hardly typical for Sebastian. Jane was right: he'd had his choice of eligible females, and some not so eligible during his heyday. But it had been some time since a woman in polite company would dare to seek him out.

Perhaps that was why Catherine's attentions felt so good. It had just been too long since a beautiful woman had looked at him with anything like flirtation in her eyes, much less fussed over him.

But he wouldn't give Jane, his oldest friend, the satisfaction of knowing his interest. 'I think your imagination is running away with you again. She hardly seems so impressionable as you imply.'

Jane nodded thoughtfully. 'She has an air of independence, it is true, but sometimes she seems a little lost.'

He frowned. 'I cannot say I have seen anything of the lost child about her. She is in possession of her wits more than most young ladies of her age.'

Once again, he searched the room. The cacophony was almost deafening, between the conversation and laughter and the music from the ballroom, echoing around the soaring ceiling and bare, stone floors.

'That sounds rather like admiration to me,' said Jane. 'What would you suppose her age to be?'

He took his friend's arm and led her through the melee, hoping to secure them both a drink. 'I would answer that question if I didn't know it to be a trick to test just how far I have fallen. I am not fool enough to speculate about the age of unmarried young ladies.'

'Would you think she is over one and twenty? She is quite an unusual beauty, is she not?'

'And why would it matter what I think?'

'Merely trying to figure out a puzzle.'

'What puzzle is that?'

'Why you deny your admiration for her, while you have seldom been shy about your dalliances before.'

'And why, pray, does it matter?'

'No reason,' she said with a delicate shrug. 'Or perhaps it is because my brother seems to have fallen quite hard for the girl, and I want to know where you stand before I clear the way or advise him to stand down.'

Irritation settled over him at the thought of William and Catherine together, but he tamped it down and changed the subject. 'Where is that bore of a husband of yours, by the way? He wouldn't be happy to see you standing up with me in so public a place.'

Jane smiled. 'At this ball you could be the most abhorred man in England and it would hardly matter. Now, let's go find that girl of yours.'

It was no mean feat finding Catherine and William amongst the teeming masses that thronged the area cordoned off for dancing. When they at last did spot them, William was twirling Catherine around, and she was laughing up at him. Jane snuck a look at Sebastian, and he did his best to maintain his air of nonchalance.

'You might have no choice but to make a declaration to her if you care about her reputation, after you and she were holed up alone in Johnson's study.'

'She will be gone from London in a few months and no one will know what happened in that room.'

'And what happened, precisely?'

'She has some nursing experience. She tended to my wound.'

Sebastian noted she did look rather well, and rather happy, by William's side. And there was no doubt of his feelings for her.

'Am I correct in suspecting that you'd rather not see William with her?' he asked.

Jane bit her lip. 'I sense her heart isn't in it. And that also, perhaps, there is a bit too much mystery about her for my simple brother to handle. You, on the other hand, would do well to intervene. If only for a season, you could try to remember how it feels to be happy.'

'As though dancing with a woman solves my problems.'

'Not any woman: Catherine Christie. Destined to return to the New World unless you say otherwise.'

'Once again, you have sped to your destination without me by your side. Pray explain.'

Jane waved her hand as though it must be obvious. 'She will return to New York, if you choose to let her, at the end of the exhibition. If you'd rather she didn't, it is in your control to change that.'

'Are you suggesting that I amuse myself with her as though she were a plaything and dispense with her as I see fit? How very cynical of you, Jane.'

'I only suggest that you allow yourself some happiness.'

'I have long stopped considering a woman's hand as a route to happiness.'

'That is because you choose the wrong women,' said a dashing older man, sliding his arm around Jane's waist. It was her husband, who had made it clear that he wanted Jane to have nothing to do with her old friend on many an occasion, a diktat Jane had happily ignored.

'Nice to see you have lost none of your ability to interrupt at the most inopportune moment, Cheswick,' said Sebastian.

'I have never known any moment with you to be anything but inopportune,' he said, holding his palm out to his wife. She slid her gloved hand in his and with a small smile at Sebastian spun out onto the dance floor with her beloved husband.

SEBASTIAN GRABBED A hard-earned drink as he waited for Catherine to finish dancing.

He couldn't help but watch her. It was in the moments when she was quiet, when William got his mouth away from her ear, that he noticed what Jane had been talking about. She took on a more serious look, but he didn't think her lost: it seemed almost as if she was afraid.

Their eyes met as though she had felt the intensity of his gaze. There was a moment between recognition and smile. As the music stopped, she whispered in William's ear, her eyes still on Sebastian, and they came towards him. She was wearing the scarf he had given her around her neck. He had never seen one worn in such a manner. It was beautiful and strangely erotic to see his gift disappear into the blue silk of her gown's bodice.

'We were beginning to think you'd stayed home,' said William.

'And miss such delights?' he said, eyes lingering on Catherine's face a second longer than necessary.

'Would you be so kind as to get me a drink?' Catherine said to William, hand on his arm. 'I am beat!'

They watched William leave. 'If I didn't know any better, I'd think you were trying to get rid of him.'

She laughed. 'Isn't a woman allowed to be thirsty?'

'Some of us welcome it,' he said.

She fluttered her eyelashes, but did not seem offended by his words, though she could have hardly mistaken his meaning. 'I thought you and William were friends.'

'We are.'

It suddenly struck him it might have been William that she was afraid of. He had seen the mildest of men act like beasts given the right provocation, even one as seemingly benign as William. And independent or not, Catherine was an unaccompanied woman.

'A lady is also allowed to rid herself of unwanted attention.'

She shot him a surprised look. 'You believe his attentions to be unwelcome?'

He bent down and whispered in her ear. 'Tell me, Catherine, am I wrong?'

She trembled ever so slightly, a hand on her stomach. 'I had heard Victorian England was a place of repressed desires. I have been much mistaken.'

'In what way?'

'Your manners may be more formal, but the desires are as close to the surface as they are back home.'

'Dance with me,' he said, holding his hand out, glad for the skirts between them as he put a hand on her waist. There was danger in getting too close to Catherine Christie.

'It is hard to hide what the heart wants, as greater men than William have discovered before him,' he said.

'And women too.'

Sebastian paused. 'You do not strike me as a woman to be overcome by matters of the heart,' he said finally.

'It is only that women have been taught better than men to conceal, not that they feel any less.'

'Some women, perhaps.'

'Are you accusing me of being unfeeling, Your Grace?'

Hearing her address him so was almost too much to bear. 'Not a duke anymore, Catherine, as I've told you before. Just Sebastian, please.'

'You didn't answer my question.'

'You, unfeeling? I'd say no, but that would be presumptuous of me on so short an acquaintance.'

Her eyes fastened on his chest. 'It was a rather interesting amulet you were wearing the other day.'

'It is a family heirloom.'

'Why do you hide it away? I can see you still have it on. I don't believe I have ever seen anything like that before. It must have a fascinating history.'

'It is possibly part of the treasure of a Portuguese pirate.'

'A Portuguese pirate!' Her eyes glittered. 'May I ask how it came to be in your family?'

'Would it surprise you to hear that I have pirate blood in me?'

She flashed him a rather wicked smile. 'I don't believe it would. There must be a matching treasure chest to go along with it.'

'Alas, no.' He looked down at her face, so strikingly different from the English women around him. Her hair was aglow, her skin dewy and pale, her eyes emerald green, her full mouth alive with amusement. She looked away, and he followed her gaze to William on the sidelines, wineglasses in hand, scanning the crowd for them.

'Oh dear,' she said.

'He is rather an eager pup, isn't he? Come now, Miss Catherine,' he said, leading her toward the exit, 'perhaps a bit of air would do us both some good.'

Even outdoors, there were far too many revelers to enjoy an inch of space in the shadow of the Crystal Palace.

'Perhaps a walk through Hyde Park is in order.'

'It is rather dark, is it not? It would be a bit of a scandal to be with you, alone, out there.'

He searched her face for even a stitch of hesitation and found none. 'It would.'

Before they could weave their way through the crowds on the carriageway in front of the Palace, John Lewis appeared with a contingent of guards he had mustered up from somewhere.

Sebastian swore, and Catherine grabbed his hand. 'Come quickly,' she said.

They were rushing toward the garden when he heard footsteps behind them. Sebastian turned to find William standing there.

'He's arrived with Westlake men! What is he trying to do?'

'I don't know and there is no time to figure it out,' said Sebastian. 'I'd best leave.'

'I'll send you your coach.'

'How, where?'

'Send it to the bridge over Serpentine River,' said Catherine.

Sebastian turned to Catherine. She should go back with William, he thought. But she stared back up at him defiantly.

'They won't think to look there,' she said.

No, they wouldn't. They'd check the main road, not the lanes within the park.

'Go back with William,' he said.

She shook her head. 'You'll be less conspicuous with me, and also less likely to come to harm.' She seemed to know exactly what she was suggesting: together, they'd be one of the many couples looking for a moment alone in the park.

William, color heightening, hurried away.

'It will take William an age to locate my coach,' he said as they set off toward the river.

'Hopefully it will take a while for the guards to work out our whereabouts as well.'

As they headed into the gardens, they were far from alone — a few shadows in the distance that were best undisturbed.

'You'll be leaving London soon?' she asked.

'Tomorrow.'

'Thank you, Sebastian, for making my visit so very memorable.'

'I am sorry it had to end this way.'

'What happened?' she asked.

He knew she was asking about John and the title and perhaps she deserved an explanation, but he couldn't bring himself to rake it up. 'It is a long and complicated story that would be best left for another time.'

'I am sorry then that we shall not have that time.'

Sebastian looked at her. 'In your society, there is no peerage. Modern, and perhaps better.'

'I don't know — there are plenty of men still born to wealth, which they guard as jealously as the nobles of England guard their lands. For women, the situation is as dire in America as it is everywhere else. We seem to have the right to nothing, nowhere.'

They came to stand on the arched stone bridge, as if they were looking out at the water, though they both had their eye on the path, watching for Sebastian's carriage or John and his men.

'I am sorry for involving you in such a scheme.'

She sighed. 'It makes little difference. My situation is hardly less grim than yours.'

'How so?'

'Once I return home, I have two fates before me: becoming a dreaded governess,' she said with a shudder, 'or entering a loveless marriage with a man who is poorer than even me.'

He frowned. 'Surely there is someone who can help you? The Americans you travel with? Some childless yet conveniently wealthy relative?'

'If only we all had such relatives! But you know what hurts my heart even more?'

'What?'

She looked up at him, her eyes dark pools in the moonlight. 'That I will never know love.'

He smiled grimly. 'If you feel so strongly, I can vouch for the strength of young William's ardor.'

She raised a skeptical brow. 'Is that what you really want?'

His eyes went to her mouth and then to the hand she held to her stomach, and finally they traveled up to her bodice, and the scarf that disappeared into her gown.

Catherine turned toward the water. 'Just two weeks ago, I was told William was professing his love to the younger Miss Crenshaw. I believe he was heartbroken when his father refused to bless the match.'

He smiled. 'It is hard to deny a certain fickleness in his attentions.'

'What about you? Is it easy to break your heart, Sebastian?'

He looked at her quizzically. 'I keep away from all such dramatics.'

'That is not what I hear.'

She sat on the railing of the bridge, and he leaned against it as well, stretching out a protective arm behind her back, careful not to touch her. He looked impatiently for his carriage; there was still no sign of it. But he noticed another couple in an advanced embrace by the bank of the river, who luckily were not bothered by the two of them.

Catherine followed his gaze, and they exchanged a look. She was smiling and far from scandalized. 'I hear that you have quite a reputation with the ladies,' she whispered.

He could smell the lavender in her hair. She tilted her head back, the light of the moon illuminating the pale column of her neck, and he could imagine bending over to taste it.

'You must have me confused with another Sebastian, lapsed Duke of Westlake.'

'I was told you had your heart broken and have never been the same since.'

He rolled his eyes. 'Jane!'

'Don't be angry with her. I made her tell me.'

'You and she are both mistaken. I know this because I have no heart.'

'Oh, that can't be true.'

His breath caught. What would this strange and bewitching creature do if he kissed her right now? That rosebud mouth was all but begging for it. She was watching his lips, as though she was wondering the same thing.

He lowered his mouth to hers slowly, giving her all the time in the world to pull away. As his lips made contact with hers, a shock went through him. Surely a kiss couldn't feel this good?

Far from pushing him away, she grabbed his shirt and pulled him close, wrapping her arms around his neck. He groaned as she deepened the embrace, melting into him, as though her body was meant for his.

'Catherine,' he muttered, trying to put some distance between them. He turned to the path and could now see men running toward them from the Crystal Palace. The guards. Where was his damn carriage?

'It's not too late to run,' she said, panting for breath.

But he knew it was. He pulled Catherine back to him. If kissing her was the last thing he did before being imprisoned, or worse, so be it.

Her arms snaked around him again as his lips slipped down to plant a trail of kisses down to her shoulder. He felt her fingers on the base of his neck as he opened his mouth to taste her.

'Sebastian,' she whispered. 'They are coming.' And then she pulled away.

'Catherine, I had no right,' he began.

But she wasn't listening. He looked down just in time to see her grab his amulet.

'Catherine, what in heaven's name are you doing!'

The guards were only sixty seconds away when he saw Catherine's other hand disappear into her bodice and grasp another piece of metal.

'I must ask your forgiveness, Sebastian,' she said.

Just as the guards closed in, Catherine swung her legs around so she dangled above the water.

'No!' he yelled, but it was too late. Even as he reached out to grab her, she somersaulted off the bridge.

He expected to feel the thick silver chain attached to his amulet jerk against his neck, but it never came. She had got it off him somehow.

John was at his heels now.

He lunged forward to get a hold of her dress, a foot, anything. As she tumbled headlong toward the water below them, with no time to think, he was leaning too far over the railing to ground himself. His fingers made contact with skin and cloth, but instead of stopping her fall, she was taking him down with her.

EIGHT

SHE SHOULD HAVE KNOWN that seducing a man, no matter the era, wouldn't be *all* that difficult. What she hadn't known was how much she would enjoy it. When Sebastian's lips touched hers, she thought she'd be able to hold back. But it was hopeless. The rush of sensation was overwhelming, unlike anything she had felt before.

Was it the man or was it the medallion, drawing her to him with such ferocious need? She struggled to dam the flood of feelings, but it was only on seeing the guards approach that she finally commanded herself to follow through with the plan as intended, wrapping her arms around his neck, pulling him down to her and slipping her fingers into his shirt.

He seemed oblivious to her actions, and she got it off with no trouble at all. She regretted for a moment what she was about to do. Having to push him away was hard enough, even without the dramatic flourish that would follow.

As she pulled away from him, his chagrin at his behavior turned to confusion, his anger to rage and finally a flash of fear as she pushed off the bridge. As she fell, time all but stood still — she could see and feel every fleeting second as she tumbled through the air, her back to the ground, arms flailing. She saw the moment he extended his hand, with the men at his back, when it touched her foot. She felt a crushing disappointment, expecting her body to jerk up like a yo-yo on a string, and then shock when instead his weight joined hers as the surrounding air turned to honey and they fell toward the shallow pool.

This time the landing was rushed. Catherine crashed onto the ground, feeling the weight of Sebastian's body as it hit the hard, cold earth beside her.

She was too winded to speak. Suddenly Sebastian straddled her.

'What in the devil just happened! Who are you! Where are we?' he demanded, shaking her shoulders.

She was trembling, and as soon as he realized what he was doing, he stopped, but his eyes were still fiery and as they landed on her breast for a brief flicker, she felt herself go cold.

What if she was entirely mistaken about the kind of person Sebastian was?

But his eyes were on the medallion, both parts of it still around her neck. He yanked the dagger, its metal chain still intact, and sprang to his feet. He stared down at her as though she was some dangerous wild animal.

It took a minute for Catherine to regain her ability to breathe as usual. She looked around, hoping to get her bearings, but it didn't take her long to realize she did not know where they were. It was not Hyde Park, that much was clear. It was dark, and there was no sign of habitation.

Catherine had done her best to concentrate her intention as she had begun her descent, but the unexpected arrival of Sebastian for the journey had done nothing to help. And of course, she had no actual idea how all this worked.

Sebastian was pacing. 'Of all the mad, infuriating creatures I have met in my life and, believe me, there have been many, you must be the very worst of the lot.'

She reluctantly rose to her feet. 'It is a shame you feel that way, I really thought we were beginning to understand one another.'

'I think that is the source of the problem.'

Catherine, hands on her waist, turned to him. 'That's rather rich! It is I who should be angry at you and not the other way around!'

He crossed his arms. 'Is that so? Pray, illuminate me why!'

'What in heaven's name prompted you to grab me? I wasn't about to drown in the Serpentine Lake!'

His nostrils flared. 'I was trying to help you!'

Catherine rolled her eyes. 'I didn't need your help! You only have yourself to thank for the fact that you are here.'

'Did you expect me to let you steal the medallion so easily?'

For a moment she was mum. Then finally realization dawned. 'You don't know what it is, do you?'

He was silent and perfectly still, but Catherine caught the confusion in his eye. 'You do not know what is going on.'

He looked both aggravated and embarrassed. 'So enlighten me!'

She took a deep breath. It gave her no pleasure to do this. 'We have traveled through time.'

His eyes widened, and he collapsed onto a boulder beside him.

'I am sorry, but you must believe I never intended for you to be here!'

'It's true?' he said.

'What's true?'

He shook his head. 'The stories... the legends... It is all true!'

So perhaps he knew *something* of the medallion's significance. 'Look, you don't want to be here, and I don't want you here. I'll take you back to your time right away. You can pretend this never happened.'

He stood up again and looked at the medallion around her neck. 'Give me that and I'll take myself.'

'I can't do that.'

'Why not?'

They both had their hands on their hips like feuding children. 'Because then I will be stuck here!'

He let out a ragged breath. 'Where are we? *When* are we?'

'I-I don't know, I think it is 1831.'

'What do you mean, you don't know?'

'I am not sure if I focused properly.'

He threw his hands up. 'Who are you, really?'

Her arms hung limply by her sides. 'You know that already.'

'Why are you here?'

She shook her head.

Sebastian grabbed her by the arm and started walking into the darkness.

'Let go of me! Where are you going?' She was almost running to keep up.

He turned to her without stopping. 'As you can see, we are in the middle of nowhere, and neither of us have any idea where we are. It is probably a good idea to find out.'

She wrenched her arm away, bringing him to a halt, but he kept his eyes on the dark horizon, as though expecting some sudden illumination.

'If the medallion works like it is supposed to,' she said, 'we should be in England.'

He swung around, his eyes wide. 'That is a broad statement. There is some doubt about even the country we are in?'

She wasn't sure why she blurted out the lie, but in that moment it felt like the only way. 'I can't be certain. I haven't done this before. The pieces don't work on their own.'

And then he nodded, and she wondered: how much did he actually know? The legend of Tibeau's treasure had mentioned nothing in particular about time travel. But despite his initial disbelief, he didn't seem as shocked as she'd been when she'd discovered what the medallion could do.

For the moment, however, they both put aside their questions and turned their attention to their current predicament. If Catherine had to guess, she would say they were near the coast, which was about where she had wanted to be. She could smell the salt in the air, she could imagine the crashing of the waves. She licked the tip of her finger up to feel the direction of the breeze.

'I think we should go that way,' she said, pointing in the opposite direction to where they had been heading.

'And why is that?'

'I think the beach is there, it will be easier to navigate.'

He ran a hand through his hair, letting out an exasperated sigh. 'You clearly have some idea of where you need to be. Does this look like it?'

'I don't know.'

'Where?'

'I would like very much for us to be in Bath.'

Sebastian looked around. 'I doubt very much this is that, though we may be close enough. We might as well settle in for the night.'

'I don't think—'

'Enough!' he said. 'How long do you think it would take me to overpower you, force those wings from you and leave you stranded here?'

'You wouldn't dare!'

'Don't try my patience!'

She shook her head. 'I don't understand why you just won't let me take you back!'

He sat down, took off his boots, stretched out on the grass and closed his eyes.

'This discussion will have to wait till morning.'

CATHERINE AWOKE AT DAWN to find Sebastian still asleep. They were in a fallow field, barren apart from a carelessly strewn boulder here or there. Yellow wildflowers waved good morning as she rubbed her face.

His face was more peaceful than she'd seen it. He'd lost some of his intensity at rest, though the dark slashes of his brows were as imperious as ever. Her eyes slipped down to his mouth, full, soft and surprising. She remembered how they had felt slipping down the column of her neck.

Would she be able to slip the necklace off his neck once again without detection now that he was asleep? Not only did she doubt it, but she also suspected that if he caught her in the act, she may find she had reached the limits of his forbearance.

Catherine got up, brushing what debris she could off her clothes. She wished she was in a less fussy dress, but at least the skirts had been generous enough to hide the reticule she had attached before the ball, bearing all her money and maps. The sudden nature of their departure had meant only the essentials made the journey; there had been no way to bring her knapsack of clothes.

She took a few steps in what she believed was the direction of the water and saw at once they were closer to a beach than she had thought the previous night. She reached the edge of a cliff, surveying the area below, and saw a few houses in the distance. When she turned to call Sebastian, he was already striding toward her.

She felt a moment's panic again at his angry glare. If only she could get her hands on the dagger, she could jump off this very cliff and then, with him safely deposited back in his own time, she'd be able to return alone. But he was stronger than her, and the risks were too great. She didn't know enough about him to gamble her own safety, and she didn't know enough about how the medallion worked to know what was even within the realms of the possible.

Instead, she arranged her face into what she hoped was a welcoming smile. 'Look there,' she said, pointing into the distance. 'There are houses; a town.'

'But that's not Bath,' he said.

'We should head in that direction though.'

'Yes,' he said, pinning her down with his glare. 'But first we talk. Who are you?'

'That part you know.'

'So you keep saying.'

'I haven't lied to you about that.' Only that she was from 1929. Should she tell him now? But that would mean admitting the medallion worked in isolation, and something told her this information was best not shared for the moment. Specially since she didn't know how it all worked.

'Why are we here?' he asked.

'I am here because I have something to do. You are here because you grabbed me.'

'What do you have to do?'

'It is a private matter.'

The stormy look came back. If she thought he'd cool down overnight, she was wrong. His anger seemed even closer to the surface. She could hardly blame him, but she would be damned if she'd let him see that.

'I am under no obligation to share that with you. I will gladly take you back home and come back here myself.'

'But for that I will need to part with my medallion?'

'Yes.'

'Why would I do that?'

'Because I promise to bring it back to you when I can.'

His jaw clenched. 'And I don't believe you. So begin talking. How did you come to have the other part of the medallion?'

'It belonged to my father. How did you come by yours?'

'Same. It is from Tibeau's treasure?'

'I believe so.'

'What is it you want to do here now?'

Catherine thought fast. 'I am looking for an heirloom that belongs to my father's family, which has gotten lost over the years. It is a precious gem.'

His eyes narrowed. 'I thought you preferred steam hammers to diamonds?'

'If my family had owned a steam hammer, that is what I would come for.'

'You are too good a liar for comfort.'

'It's the truth!'

He gave her a calculating look. 'I believe you are hunting for something — or someone. For now, let's leave it at that. How did you know I had the rest of the medallion?'

She thought back to the hours she'd spent in the library. The sketch she'd seen of him in the encyclopedia must have originated somewhere. 'I saw a picture of you in the newspaper.'

'Then you know about my past — what they have accused me of?'

'Yes! I don't care about that. Far more significant than some family battle for power is the fact that you steal antiquities!'

His brow furrowed.

'I visited your house in search of you before coming to London. Your housekeeper showed me your collection. I know what kind of man you are.'

He cracked a smile at last. 'In that case, you know I am precisely the kind of man for this situation.'

NINE

SEBASTIAN HAD ENDED THE previous evening in a rage. He'd welcomed the sleep that came over him like a blanket, but it had done little to cool him down. And the questions spiraled.

It wasn't from his family that he'd heard of Tibeau's treasure containing artifacts that possessed miraculous, time-bending properties. He had heard whispers on his own archeological digs, amidst profiteers and historians who had deeper knowledge.

The rumor went that the old men Christie and Talbot had fought over something more valuable than gold.

But that had been all Sebastian had known. He thought he'd done well to hide the depth of his shock from Catherine. He needed her to believe him in control. She'd betrayed him, made a fool of him, and he'd be damned if he'd let her know how badly it stung.

But he wasn't about to go anywhere either. Sebastian was nothing if not practical, and it made sense to stick with this woman for several reasons.

'I can help you find what you are looking for,' he said.

She frowned. 'And how is it supposed to help me to ally with a common thief?'

'A common thief!' he said. 'What you saw at my home was my very own personal collection; there was no theft involved. I pay dearly for what I find and there is nothing common about collecting antiquities from some of the oldest civilizations in history.'

'And what about the people from whom you are taking these objects?'

'Ah! Well, that is a different discussion. I can assure you there is none in England who considers what I do theft. And I seem to remember you making a pretty speech outside my shop about it not being objectionable if the owners profited. The matter at hand is not about my ethics but about yours, which seem to be variable depending on what you need in the moment. What are you after, Catherine?'

She shrugged, turning away from him, skirts spinning around her. 'I told you already.'

'And this heirloom, is it in England or America?'

'Eng-England.'

'What is your actual name?'

'Catherine Christie, as you know.'

When they first met, he had not considered the name of Christie more than a coincidence, but now he knew better. 'Since I believe you are hunting for what is anything but a trifle, you will need someone with experience finding things, for which I am ideally suited. Not to mention, you will need a man.'

Catherine rolled her eyes. 'A man like you? I would rather travel alone and take my chances.'

He stepped closer to her, and she took a step backward, finding herself up against a tree trunk.

She stared him down as he traced a finger down her cheek. 'Precisely what kind of man did you take me for when you kissed me so ardently on the bridge?' He may have meant to be menacing, but his voice sounded wistful instead.

She side-stepped him, and he leaned against the tree with a sardonic smile.

'The kind of man who could be easily distracted by a kiss.'

He grinned. 'I confess, that is true. And quite the kiss it was. I wonder if you would have kissed poor William in quite the same way?'

'If he had the dagger around his neck, I can assure you, yes.'

She was lying, but he'd let it go. The less time spent dwelling on that kiss, the better. It was not an event he'd be revisiting, no matter how attractive the inducement. 'So now you have admitted to that, tell me what you are really after here.'

'I've already told you.'

'And I already said I don't believe you.'

She shook her head and put some more distance between the two of them.

'But I suppose it doesn't really matter, for I know what you are looking for.'

'And what is that?' she asked.

'The Bell of Dhammazedi.'

She looked at him with horror. 'You have got to be kidding me. What would possess me to look for such a thing as that?'

'You and I both know Tibeau's treasure connects both our families. They've been looking for it for centuries.'

'So? My family is distantly related to George Washington, but I am not rushing off to claim the Presidency.'

He ignored her quip, focusing again on the necklace. 'That you went as far as to use that little medallion around your neck is proof enough it is the treasure you are after. And that you have come to find me, of all people, given our family history.'

From her face, he could tell that there was genuine confusion there.

'What do you know of my family?'

'That there are only two tribes of people who have ever risked everything for that treasure, and they are the Talbots and the Christies. And here we stand today, in the greedy snare of history.'

Her expression darkened.

'How have you not heard of this?' he asked. 'In my family they seldom speak of anything else,' he added wryly.

'I was unaware that my family had been actively searching for the treasure in recent times. Tell me what you know.'

'I will, but first I need to find a quiet place to take a piss.'

CATHERINE AND SEBASTIAN CLIMBED down the cliff face to the beach. It would make for an easy walk to the town, but there was no cover to be had, so Sebastian found something of a nook behind a rock in which he could achieve a measure of privacy.

Just as soon as he'd turned his back to her, Catherine continued without him. He let out a string of expletives, finished his business and jogged back to where she should have been.

There was no sign of her.

He had a moment of blind panic. His hand went to his chest, sure that she must have stolen his medallion and left him there. But it was in place around his neck and under his clothes.

He walked to the water's edge and craned his neck back to see if she had gone up the cliff for some godforsaken reason, but it would have taken her longer to climb up all that way than it had taken him to empty his bladder. So he jogged ahead in the only direction that made sense: toward town.

He heard the screaming first.

'Help! Help!'

He ran as fast as the loose sand allowed him, and only when he rounded the bluff that had been obstructing his view of part of the beach, did he see her: Catherine, surrounded by three men, clawing wildly as the tallest one hoisted his very unwilling cargo upon his back.

'Stop!' he shouted, speeding up.

Catherine raised her head, arms flailing, but the men didn't even bother to turn back. Sebastian overtook them at last, circling them with his hands up to bring them to an annoyed halt.

'What is going on here?' he demanded.

Catherine kicked and screamed atop the shoulder of her captor, but it was the smallest man, a head shorter than Sebastian, who seemed to be the leader.

'What's it to you?' he said.

'How dare you accost my companion in this manner?'

The man looked Sebastian up and down. 'Companion, you say? This wench?'

'My wife, to be precise,' said Sebastian. Catherine went still for a second.

The man took Sebastian's measure and sensed something of an opportunity. He stole a look at the third man, who might be his brother. 'And who may you be?' he asked.

'David Talbot, son of the Duke of Westlake.'

This seemed to interest them.

'Let me go!' shouted Catherine again.

Sebastian glanced at the knives hanging from their belts, cursing how very unprepared he was. 'Please, sirs, I implore you to unhand my wife and my family shall reward you handsomely.'

The two shorter men exchanged another look, and the tall one set Catherine down on a signal from them.

'If you be his wife, why didn't you say so in the first place, woman?' the leader asked Catherine.

She huffed indignantly. 'I don't recall you giving me much of a chance to explain myself — grabbing me like that!'

'You are dressed like a whore, and so we took you for one.'

Sebastian took a step toward him. 'Continue just as you are if you wish to have a cavalry of the King's men on your tail. Let us pass without further incident and you have much to gain!'

The short man sized up Sebastian and then drew a knife. 'We already have our reward, don't we lads?'

The other men laughed.

Sebastian dared not look at Catherine. 'You would be put to death for a moment's fun?'

'More than a moment, I reckon.'

Sebastian pulled a ring off his finger. 'Take this — the signet ring of the Westlake family. It is worth a fortune.'

The leader inspected it. 'This little gold isn't enough to get you your woman back.'

'That's just the deposit. It might not be worth much in itself, but if you take it to the Talbots, it will be precious. Come with this to the castle and claim your gold. You have my word.'

The men looked at one another. 'How do we know it is not a trap?' asked the leader.

'I have already given you my assurance. I will be home in a week; come then. But if you do not, you will soon learn what a mistake it is to make a duke your mortal enemy.'

The leader glared at Sebastian before waving at his man to release Catherine, who ran to Sebastian's side. He took her by the hand and wasted no time hurrying along.

'We come in a week!' the man yelled after them. 'And we'll have more than your woman if you don't keep your word!'

SEBASTIAN AND CATHERINE WERE quiet for the rest of their walk to the town. As they neared, he saw it was larger than he had at first thought. 'This is good,' said Sebastian, 'in a town this size, we may find proper lodgings.'

Catherine only nodded. He took in her ashen face and stopped. 'Did they hurt you?' he asked, voice dangerously sharp.

'No,' she said with a shudder.

After some inquiries, they were sent toward the main street where there was an inn.

'We will pose as husband and wife,' said Sebastian.

'Why?' asked Catherine, aghast.

Sebastian stopped and turned to her. 'You saw what happened back there. There is no telling what happens to single women travelers in such times as these.'

They arrived at the inn. Sebastian made the arrangements and returned to Catherine. 'Anyhow, there is only one available room,' he said. 'And it is the only inn in town.'

She stared at him, open-mouthed.

He looked at her with an eyebrow raised. 'Your outrage would have been more becoming had you not thrown yourself into my arms not twelve hours ago.'

'That was... that was different!'

'Was it?' he said, bending down so they wouldn't be heard. 'You may have wrapped your alluring body around me for reasons less carnal than I would have liked, but there was no hesitation nor, I suspect, regret.'

Catherine seemed to have several things she'd like to say, but the innkeeper cleared his throat.

'The room will be empty at 2 p.m. and no sooner I am afraid,' he said.

'We shall return,' said Sebastian as they exited.

Once on the street, Catherine walked ahead of him.

'Come now, no need to be angry. I have good news, too.'

She stopped in her tracks and glared at him.

'I have found out that it is 1831 and we are in Portishead, near Bath.'

She let out a sigh of relief. 'I missed the mark on the location, but we aren't far, and it is *when* we should be.' She looked up and down the street. 'Where shall we go now?'

'As the one who allegedly had all the plans, why don't you tell me?'

Catherine smothered what looked like a fiery desire to wring his neck. It gave Sebastian the most acute pleasure.

'I think I saw a public house down the street. Perhaps we can go there for breakfast and to wait?'

'Of course,' he said cheerfully. 'I hope you have money. For I have none.'

'Yes,' she said through gritted teeth, 'I do.'

He looked her up and down, wondering where this money might be hidden. Several salacious ideas crossed his mind, and from the glare she gave him, she seemed to have guessed the direction of his thoughts.

They found the dank pub open and ordered what food was to be had at the simple establishment, along with tankards of beer. As she tucked into a plate of eggs and bread, she seemed somewhat revived.

'I didn't thank you for saving me,' she said at last, setting down her drink.

He looked away, almost embarrassed.

'I am sorry too that you had to give up your ring.'

'Are you? I am not.'

'What will happen when they arrive at the Westlake house next week?'

The ring had belonged to his father in the year 1831, and he never took it off his finger. Sebastian had received it on his death, one of the few pieces of his inheritance he still had claim over. 'The family will assume it is a fake, I would imagine.'

'What will they do?'

'My father is the current duke, and not a man you'd like to mess with. I can only imagine the matter will be dealt with severely.'

Her brow furrowed.

He frowned. 'Are you sorry for them? They meant to violate you.'

'Meaning to do something and doing it are not the same thing.'

'It would not have been their first offense, I can assure you. They'll get what's coming to them.'

She let out a sigh. 'You are right.'

He shook his head.

'What?' she asked.

'I was just thinking about the other Catherine I met, the one who batted her eyelashes, smiled just so and tried to seduce me.'

A smile touched her lips. 'Sounds a fascinating creature.'

'A fictional one too, by the look of it.'

'Tell me about the treasure,' she said.

Sebastian drained his glass and signaled to the barkeep for another. 'Which part of it? You clearly know the important bits.'

'The rivalry.'

'Your grandfather's grandfather's grandfather, or something like that, and my forefather were involved in what was the biggest haul in pirate history. And that is saying something given they thrived in the era of pirates. The Bell of Dhammazedi was the crowning glory, said to be the biggest bell ever cast, forged from precious metals and studded with gems, but there was also an entire chest of gold and other riches.'

'They worked together?'

'They started as friends, co-pirates if you will. Then my ancestor fell in love with a local woman and spent several years in the Burmese countryside and suffered something of a transformation. But when his lover and child were killed by a local landowner, he contacted Christie, and together they looted those he held responsible, and set sail for Portugal.

'They were traveling from Chittagong to Portugal when disaster befell their ship. They washed up on the island of Mauritius, and that was the last the treasure was seen. Tibeau died while they were there, and Christie returned empty-handed, only to die soon after. That is the end of my knowledge. But you clearly know more than you are letting on.'

Catherine shook her head. 'You overestimate me. The only thing I can add is that Christie must have got his hand on at least this medallion, because it is now in my possession. And Tibeau must have sent your pendant on to your family, because you have that.'

Sebastian nodded. 'Fair enough. They salvaged a few belongings of his and this must have been amongst them.'

Catherine paused.

'What is it?'

'As you know, the story ends with the Crown getting its hands on the treasure. An industrious bounty hunter is believed to have found it at last and brought it to England, but then the entire lot was seized.'

'I have heard they uncovered a treasure, but it was never certain that it was Tibeau's treasure, as they never recovered the bell.'

'It was Tibeau's treasure, bell notwithstanding.'

'And when did that happen?'

Catherine smiled. 'In 1831.'

TEN

SEBASTIAN'S EYES WIDENED. 'DON'T tell me you plan to set sail to retrieve it?'

She didn't answer right away, pulling a piece of paper out of the satchel she had unhooked from the inside of her skirt earlier.

'What is this?'

'A map.'

Sebastian grabbed it from her and held it up to the light. 'No, I mean the paper. I have seen nothing like this.'

Catherine snatched it back. 'A factory in America has made great strides in producing paper,' she said. 'Can you focus on what matters?'

'Where did you find this?'

'That doesn't matter. Look at this. What if Christie and Talbot only *thought* they had landed in Mauritius, but where they actually landed was here.' She pointed at a landmass he didn't recognize. 'This is Kallan Island.'

He looked at the map, jaw clenched. 'Even if you are right, how does it help? What is it you plan to do? Are you going to take us there?'

Catherine took a sip of beer. She had to lay her cards on the table if she wanted him to help. In the rude course of the morning, she'd had to admit that the risks of trying to go it alone seemed to outweigh the benefits to be gained from being rid of his aggravating company. Short of trying to abduct him back into his own timeline, there was nothing she could do anyhow. If she was to be stuck with him, she might as well make the most of it.

'I do not intend to go to the island at all,' she said. 'I plan to get to the treasure when it arrives in England, before the Crown can take control of it.'

He leaned back in his seat, arms crossed across his chest. 'And when do you expect this feat will occur?'

'Two weeks from now, because that is when the Crown, ever meticulous in its record keeping, logged the treasure.'

He went still. 'Where? And how does it matter if it came from Kallan or Mauritius?'

'Because around the same time, there was news of a ship that had been shipwrecked returning from Kallan. Quite the coincidence, isn't it? However, where it came into port was not mentioned.'

'And how do you propose to figure such a thing out?'

'I have an idea or two,' she said.

'How do we commandeer it?'

'We'll come up with something.'

Sebastian nearly spat out his beer. 'That is a bit of a tall order.'

She shrugged. 'There is almost no information about what happened, but we know the Crown seized the treasure, which implies that something transpired to cause it to change hands. What happens if they don't take control of the chest, what happens if we take control of it instead?'

'Not exactly a minor task.'

'As crazy as it sounds, we can at least try to set things straight.'

Sebastian raised a brow. 'Just now you were talking about how obtaining antiquities from ancient civilizations was akin to theft, and suddenly you want to steal pirate treasure that was unambiguously stolen from the East Indies?'

'I never said what I intended to do with it.'

'Do you fancy yourself some kind of modern-day Robin Hood?'

The truth was, she didn't know what she'd do with the treasure. She had arrived on this mission simply knowing it must be done. 'That is no concern of yours. We already know you have no ethical objections to pillaging, so why the compunctions now?'

'I don't have any compunctions. I am simply worried about yours. Because I am not sure you are telling the truth still.'

'You can doubt me all you like, but the question is, are you in or are you out?'

'Oh, I'm in. As long as we agree that whatever we get at the end of this is split down the middle. I will not be part of your saintly schemes. And if you aren't okay with that, it is up to you to say so now or forever hold your peace.'

'Okay,' she said, 'seeing as I have little choice in the matter, I am prepared to work with you.'

'Is it the bell you are after?'

She shook her head. 'I don't know. The bell was not recorded as part of the raid, so if it arrived on these shores, it went missing soon after. But the rest of the treasure is substantial enough to make it worth our while.'

'Okay,' he said.

'Okay.' She extended her hand. He took it, giving it a firm shake.

'So now that we've established that, how do you propose we track it down and intercept it?'

She pursed her lips, reluctant to part with the information he was demanding from her. 'There is mention of a man in the stories from my family. A man from Bath.'

'Name?'

'Stanley.'

'And he lives here, now?'

'I believe so.'

'And it is to find him we are here?'

'Yes. I believe he has a role to play in whatever fate befalls the treasure. If we find him, we may find another clue.' Breadcrumbs, as her father had called them. She was merely following the trail.

Sebastian shook his head. 'That isn't much to go on.'

'It is only little if we don't succeed.'

'Fair enough,' he said, raising his glass. 'Tomorrow to Bath.'

EVENTUALLY, CATHERINE PUT HER head down on the table and dozed off. The stress of the morning and the long walk had finally got to her, along with the pleasant buzz from the beer.

It was sometime later that Catherine awoke with a start when a pewter tankard hit the ground. She found Sebastian watching her with a smile on his face.

'What?' she said, running her hands over her hair. 'Was I snoring?'

'Are you always able to fall asleep in the middle of a busy room?'

'Time travel seems to be a tiring business,' she said, dropping her voice.

His eyes narrowed. 'That makes it sound like you have had some experience of it. Have you done it before?'

Catherine paused just a beat. She could tell him. She *should* tell him. But something held her back. She shook her head. 'How could I have? You need both parts of the medallion, don't you?'

Sebastian let this pass without further examination. 'The innkeeper will expect us in an hour,' he said. 'I'll go now and plan for tomorrow's travel to Bath.'

As Sebastian left, Catherine decided that she too wanted to stretch her legs, after so many hours spent seated on a hard wooden bench. She stepped out of the pub and was amazed at how similar to 1851 this town looked, while her own world of 1929 and 1851 were like night and day.

She and Sebastian would need a change of clothes. The blue gown she was wearing was barely acceptable in 1851, let alone 1831. She'd chosen it for the ball because of its flattering line and fetching low bodice, which she had covered at the last moment with Sebastian's scarf. She'd taken the scarf off the night before and tucked it away in her bag, which then led to her being mistaken for a prostitute on the beach that morning. But it wasn't just a desire for modesty that spurred Catherine's quest: her skirts were spattered by mud from the morning's exertions and heavy with sand, and Sebastian's were hardly more presentable. They could have them washed when they arrived in Bath, but for now, they needed an alternative.

She went from one establishment to the other — local bakery, greengrocers, milliners — till she finally found a woman who could provide her with well-worn garments in approximately both their sizes, in exchange for a small sum from Catherine's precious reserves.

When she found her way back to the inn, Sebastian stood before it, exasperated once more. 'Have this morning's misadventures taught you nothing? I asked you to wait at the public house for me.'

'I didn't go far.'

He shook his head.

She smiled. 'Were you worried about me?'

He looked annoyed. 'Come now, our lodgings are ready.'

They walked up the creaky wooden stairs and entered a small room. It was hardly large enough for one. Sebastian closed the door behind him.

'I have arranged for us to leave at first light. Once in Bath, there will be more choice of place to stay and I hope to be more comfortable there.'

Catherine's eyes went to the narrow bed.

'There really is no more room,' said Sebastian. 'Even if we pay for it. But have no fear,' he said, looking down. 'I will sleep on the floor.'

The clothes had been dropped off as promised, and the innkeeper had placed them on the wooden table. Sebastian took in the pile of humble garments, somewhat confused.

'I thought we needed to blend in a little better. Not to mention we are filthy right now,' she said.

He looked at her with surprise, picking them up. 'They look like they will fit. Thank you.'

By the time they had finished supper, it was dark out. They sat at the table in the parlor, and Sebastian had acquired a local newspaper from somewhere and read snippets to her, making her laugh with reports of a pig that had run away from a local farm, only to be found herding sheep along with a dog that had befriended it. But the warmer she felt toward him, the harder it was to ignore his closeness.

When they could delay it no longer, she returned to the room first and got ready for bed. It relieved her to see, as she pulled back the bedcover, the sheets were clean. In due course, Sebastian knocked on the door and she opened it, standing awkwardly to the side so he could step in.

'There is only one blanket,' she said.

'Don't worry on my account. I shall be quite comfortable.'

She picked up one of the two pillows and handed it to Sebastian. 'Thank you,' he said.

As he took it from her, their hands brushed.

He was so close, she could feel the warmth of his breath. She remembered his mouth on hers, the feel of his hands on her waist.

She moved to the small table in the corner and busied herself pouring a glass of water, but it did nothing to dispel the tension with his eyes on her as she drank and wiped her mouth with the back of her hand.

'Goodnight, Catherine,' he said, his voice a seductive murmur.

She turned away and climbed into bed, her back to him as she pulled the covers up around her.

He put out the candle, and her eyes sprang open. She was quite rested after her nap that afternoon at the pub, and sleep proved elusive.

The bed, with its thin mattress, was hardly more comfortable than the wooden floor upon which Sebastian rested. She was aware of his every breath; he seemed as close to her as he had been on the bridge. It had just been the evening before, but it seemed an age ago.

It was a strange way to spend a night together. If this was her time, would she have invited him into her bed?

Eleven

THEIR CARRIAGE ARRIVED THE following morning. Two horses and a large, black and rather grand-looking vehicle were at the inn's doorstep. Sebastian hopped on to the driver's seat and took the reins.

Catherine eyed him suspiciously. 'Where did you get this?'

'I have my ways,' he said, getting comfortable. 'Get in.'

She didn't budge. 'I hope you don't expect me to pay for it.'

He grinned. 'I said I have no money. Not that I have no resources.'

'Is this another bill your family is going to be stuck with mysteriously?'

His smile grew wider. 'Let's just say the Westlakes will have some mysterious creditors to placate this summer.'

Catherine climbed in. Sebastian was in quiet control of the animals and the road, and she contented herself with watching the scenery pass by at a relaxing pace. There was no scope for further conversation till their first stop to rest the horses.

'Are you much of a horsewoman?' he asked.

'Oh no, the pleasure of driving us will be all yours.'

'I'd have expected a woman like you to be adept on horseback.'

'And why is that?'

'Those who court trouble should always have a means to get away.'

She thought wistfully of the cars and trains she'd left behind, and how much easier this entire expedition would be without the daily troubles of simply existing in these simpler times.

It was not long to Bath, and hardly onerous on relatively good road, and they arrived by afternoon. Sebastian took them to lodgings he seemed to be familiar with.

'Do you know Bath well?' asked Catherine when they disembarked at a small inn on the outskirts of the city.

'Enough to know that there are cheaper and perfectly acceptable rooms farther away from the spas.'

Catherine entered the room with a rush of relief: it was a suite of sorts, with a bedroom and attached sitting room. 'We can take turns sleeping on the settee,' she said.

Sebastian's brow shot down. 'There is no need to be churlish, now. The bed is large enough for the two of us.'

She went into the bedroom and slammed the door to the sound of his laughter.

THE NEXT MORNING, SEBASTIAN and Catherine set out to hunt for Stanley, with only the vague description Catherine had of his house being near the Abbey. It was, Sebastian had warned her over breakfast, the heart of Bath.

'Does it get very crowded?'

'Yes. You will find some bustle you are accustomed to in New York, I'd imagine.'

Catherine stifled a smile as she looked around. Though New York of 1831 would have differed from her version of the city, it would be nothing like the charming Bath.

'Remind me to tell you about New York someday.'

On the way there, ensconced in the comfort of the carriage, a driver they had retained from the hotel at the reins, Sebastian pointed out some of Bath's landmarks. Catherine looked on in awe at the beautiful Georgian architecture, the historic Royal Crescent forming a truly majestic sight.

Soon she had to admit Sebastian hadn't been wrong in his cautioning her about crowds. When they approached the thoroughfare close to the Abbey, it was bustling in a way that Catherine had not yet experienced in England. These were not the orderly hoards that descended daily upon the Great Exhibition. There appeared to be some sort of Church fete that had taken over the street, and the jostle of bodies and the smell of horse manure, the heat of the cobblestones trapped between the stores and stalls and scores of visitors was overwhelming.

Leaving the driver instructions to wait, they then took stock of their options. With only a vague idea of where the man lived and a first name, they quickly concluded that despite Sebastian's reservations, they would have to split up if they were to have any chance of finding him at all.

Sebastian, they agreed, would take one side of the road, and Catherine the other as they went door to door asking after Stanley. 'See the Abbey there,' said Sebastian. 'In thirty minutes we meet at the entrance, whether or not we have anything.'

Catherine went on her way, and it was some effort even getting the shopkeepers to listen to her above their festive bustle. She was distracted by a boy of about five years standing in the middle of the street, shouting for his mother. She was about to give up and head to the Abbey when, at the very end of the line of shops, she had some luck.

'Sir, I am looking for a man named Stanley, who lives close to the Abbey.'

'Old Stanly Parker?' asked the man behind the counter at the store selling handmade shoes.

'I believe so, yes,' she said.

'He lives just up the way in the grand old house.'

'Which grand old house?'

'Once you get there, you can't miss it. It is painted green, with gold trim.'

Catherine thanked him for his help and headed toward the Abbey with a new optimism. It had started to drizzle, and the boy was still standing in the middle of the street. A man in a hat was bending over to help him, presumably, but the child was having none of it. Catherine was headed toward them when she felt a hand on her arm dragging her away.

'We don't have time for any of that,' Sebastian hissed.

She turned to him in anger. 'You scared me! And why not? What's the rush? That boy is clearly lost!'

He glowered down at her. 'Will you listen to me for once? How do you propose to help him, not knowing a single soul here?'

He had a point, and it registered that he looked more put out than usual. 'Did something happen?' she asked.

He looked around. 'I don't know, but there was a man in naval uniform. I can't be sure, but I think he was following me.'

'Why would he do that?'

'I don't know, but when I asked for Stanley, it seemed to catch his ear. What have you learned?'

'There is an old Stanley Parker who apparently lives down the road in some sort of green house.'

'A green house?' he repeated with a frown.

'Yes. Why is that strange?'

He shrugged, and they proceeded in the direction the shoemaker had indicated. Sebastian kept throwing glances over his shoulder.

'Is he still there?' she asked.

'I don't see him.'

They continued down the street, which was less crowded the farther from the Abbey they went. They made a few unnecessary stops hoping to spot someone following, but could not see the man in naval uniform.

When they finally reached the house, it was just as the shoemaker said: there was no missing it. Both Catherine and Sebastian craned their necks up to take in the shamrock structure that was eccentric to say the least, sandwiched between two perfectly staid homes.

'This has got to be the place,' said Catherine.

The house looked as though it had been built in several eras by several craftsmen, the Tudor roof and Georgian columns at complete odds with one another. And the shade of green was wholly alien in its brightness.

Catherine walked up the three steps to the doorway and knocked. But no one opened it, even after a full five minutes. The drizzle was turning to rain, and they were about to abandon hope when they heard footsteps approaching.

'What do you want with Stanley?' came a man's voice.

Catherine swung around and saw a man in a blue naval frock coat and tricorne hat standing at the foot of the steps, flanked by two other men in civilian attire. She glanced quickly at Sebastian.

'Do I know you?' asked Sebastian, standing taller and looking down at him with a hauteur befitting a duke.

But the man was not so easily put off.

'No, but you will know my sword if you don't answer the question,' he said, his hand at his waistband.

'There is no need for all that,' said Sebastian. 'He's simply an old friend. My wife and I are on holiday in Bath and we were just looking him up.'

The man looked Catherine up and down. 'An old friend, you say? An old pirate friend, perhaps?'

'No,' he said, 'just an old friend of the family.'

The two men took a step toward them, their eyes on Catherine. Sebastian took her hand.

'It's strange,' said the captain, 'that just a day after Stanley is rumored to have returned to Bath you too should appear, looking rather out of place.'

So he was here! 'Last I checked it wasn't a crime to go looking for someone,' Catherine said, pulse racing.

The captain looked at Catherine menacingly and Sebastian shielded her with his body. 'Stay away from my wife.'

The captain sneered. 'I don't know what you are implying, sir, but we are officers who serve at the pleasure of the Crown.'

'Now, now, dear,' said Catherine, stepping forward. 'We seem to all have got off on the wrong foot. Let's just finish here and then I am sure we can all go on our way.'

'An American?' said the captain, tipping his hat back to inspect her. 'Who are you?'

'The name's Talbot,' said Sebastian before she could reply.

'Your first name?'

'David.'

'Talbot of the Westlake family?' he said, eyes narrowed. 'I am intimately acquainted with the family, and I have never in my life heard of a David.'

Catherine went cold, but Sebastian didn't miss a beat. 'I am the second son of Jeremiah Talbot. And you have not heard of me because I have been in the former colonies for some years now.'

'Whereabout?'

'New York,' said Catherine. 'David and I met in New York and have made a home there.'

'And you are?'

'Catherine Talbot.' It was raining harder now, and she shielded her face with her hand.

'And how do you know Stanley, exactly?'

'We met him when he was in New York a couple of years ago.'

The captain looked at his men. Catherine held her breath, not sure if the lie would land.

'Go on.'

'He was there on some business. I didn't ask him what it was, in case you are wondering, and he didn't tell me. But he is a great character, and we became friends through a common acquaintance. And that, sirs, is truly the extent of it. We were in his part of the world, and we thought we would look up an old friend, as one does.'

The captain looked from Catherine to Sebastian. They stood there, getting soaked to the skin, water dripping from their faces. It looked to Catherine as though the captain was finally tiring of this fruitless line of questioning.

'Bently,' said the tall man behind the captain. 'Let them go.'

Catherine filed his name away for later. 'May I ask why the very act of looking for Stanley is a problem? What has he done?'

'That does not concern you. But I *can* share that he is wanted by the law. And for your future safety, I would suggest that you stop your pursuit of him. If you hear from him, report it to the authorities.'

Twelve

CATHERINE WAS QUIET ON the way home, shivering in the cold, soaked down to her petticoats. She could not wait to get back to the inn. But once there, she had Sebastian's stormy countenance to contend with.

'That was too close,' he said, tossing his drenched hat on the back of a chair.

'Yes.'

He stripped off his shirt, and Catherine turned to face the wall in a hurry.

'I think it's time to tell me who exactly Stanley is and what you know about him.'

'I know little more than I've told you.'

'Which is nothing!' said Sebastian, pacing the room. He walked to the armoire and threw it open. 'Where are our other clothes?'

'They are still out for cleaning,' said Catherine, turning around, as Sebastian pulled his wet shirt back on.

'Damn this infernal place!' exclaimed Sebastian. 'Tell me what you know.'

She felt herself flush. 'It is part of a story my father told me when I was a little girl.'

Sebastian's face was inscrutable. 'You brought us here because of a fairytale?'

'It is the same fairytale that taught me how to use this!' she said, holding up her medallion. 'It is how I found you, how I knew how to get here!'

He shook his head in disbelief. 'Perhaps it is time to ask yourself if your father knew what he was doing.'

'We are here, aren't we!'

Sebastian glared at her, looking as though a hundred retorts were on the tip of his tongue, but then thought better of it. He stormed out of the room and an exasperated Catherine shut herself into the bedroom.

She stripped her dress off, grabbing the bed clothes and wrapping herself in them as tightly as she could, wondering where an equally drenched Sebastian had disappeared to.

It was over an hour later she heard him enter again. He came to the door of the inner chamber and knocked.

Catherine pulled the blankets tighter around her as she got off the bed, opening the latch and pulling the door back a few inches.

'Take these,' he said, thrusting something out toward her.

Catherine put out her hand and felt the brush of velvet against her skin. She beheld with wonder the pile of clean, dry clothes he was holding out. She took them from him, closed the door and quickly rid herself of the blankets. There were petticoats, a shift of the softest muslin, and a gown of green velvet with a ruffled collar. She gratefully donned the layers, which were a little large, and she'd show more bare skin than perhaps was acceptable, but it was beautiful.

Catherine opened the door and stepped into the sitting room. Sebastian was in dry clothes too, a jacket of equally luxurious black material with tails, and a waistcoat of the same green velvet as her dress. His eyes raked over her, but then he averted his gaze.

'Bring me your soiled garments please,' he said gruffly. He left the room once again, returning empty-handed. 'They will be cleaned and returned to us in a day or two.'

'Thank you,' said Catherine.

It was only then that she realized on the small table at the side of the room was a plate of bread, cheese, and fruit and a carafe of wine.

Sebastian looked vaguely embarrassed. 'We haven't eaten since morning.'

She was so ravenous she didn't mind the silence that hung between them. The food and drink soothed her nerves, and by the end of the meal she was content once more.

Sebastian's glare too had softened. 'Tell me this fairytale then,' he said gruffly.

She shook her head. 'You will laugh at me. Or worse.'

'Believe me, it is too soon for me to find the humor in any of this.'

She poured them both more wine.

'Okay,' she said, taking her glass and standing up, pacing the small room. Her voice was soft, but as the story picked up pace, so did she.

'There was once a boy by the name of Ferdinand. When he was fourteen years old, he found an old dusty medallion at the bottom of his grandfather's trunk. Now, many boys might say that a necklace was not an exciting discovery. But Ferdinand's grandfather was a strange sort of person, with many curiosities in his room that no one was allowed to touch. And he had tales of adventures so grand a young boy simply had to wonder.

'Notable among such tales were the adventures he'd had with a man named Stanley from Bath. After each of their trips, wherever they were in the world, they would end with a healing dip in the waters of Bath's spas. So miraculous were these waters they made all their pain and injuries disappear. Whether a Portuguese pirate or the arrowhead of an Andamanese pygmy had inflicted them.

'So, when Ferdinand got his hands on what was, by all accounts, a most curious piece of metal, it fascinated him. Why, it almost looked like an angel with wings! It had been forged from what appeared to be pewter and gold, but he couldn't rule out some strange alchemy. Ferdinand put on the necklace, tucking it away under his clothes, so no one would discover that he had it.

'And that was it for several years till Ferdinand was a man himself. He wore the medallion out of habit more than anything, for it certainly had been most useless in bringing him closer to adventure. Then one day, after he had a terrible fight with his father, after his hunchbacked boss at the drafting office where he worked fired him, he walked toward Tower Bridge on a deserted night. He climbed atop the railing, clutching onto that medallion, and told himself that if only he had been born hundred years before and had gone off for those adventures with Stanley instead of his grandfather, he would have been the happiest man on earth. His life would have been different. His future would have been worth something.

'When he jumped, Ferdinand expected to drown like a kitten in a pond, for he didn't know how to swim. But instead of meeting a wet and ignominious end, he floated onto a field of heather, in 1831, in the town of Bath, just meters away from where Stanley lived.

'And that's when his life truly began.'

SEBASTIAN HAD GONE COMPLETELY still, and Catherine couldn't take his silence anymore.

'You think it is ridiculous?'

He shook his head, his face aglow with unspoken emotion. Catherine could hardly expect him to trust her, given all they had been through, what she had done to him. 'How did you even know it would work? It is a child's fairytale, for heaven's sake,' he said at last.

She let out a deep breath. 'My father left me a letter which I inherited on my twenty-fifth birthday. He hadn't given me any sign during his lifetime that any of this might be real. He died when I was ten. So I was as much in the dark as you had been till then.'

'What made you go through with this? I hate to cause you pain on this front, but it doesn't sound as though your father was the most reliable of men.'

'He was... a magical man,' she said, wiping away a tear that had escaped. 'But I can't say I disagree. I went through months of denial, disbelief even, but then I started doing the research.'

'How does one research something like this?'

'He told me to look for you.'

'For me?' he asked, eyes wide.

'Well, the Duke of Westlake. He said the duke had the missing piece of the puzzle, which I took to mean the other piece of the medallion.'

His brow furrowed. 'How strange.'

'Yes, and the medallion did the rest. But before I left, I read as much as I could about the lost treasure and how it came to be in the possession of the Crown. And from there, I fell down a rabbit hole which led me to a picture of you in the newspaper, since your family scandal was a matter of public interest.'

He scowled at the mention of this. 'But how could you be sure? That picture did not reveal my locket. As you well know, I never wear it so it can be seen.'

She closed her eyes. The truth was her best bet here. 'I didn't need to see it. When I put the medallion around my neck, I started having visions. And they were clearly of you.'

Sebastian swung around. 'Visions?'

But he didn't look as skeptical as she had expected him to. 'Yes. Have you been having them too?'

He shook his head. 'Not visions. But a feeling. A feeling that seemed to make much more sense the moment I saw you at the exhibition.'

She warmed at the memory of that moment.

'Maybe we should take the necklaces off,' he said huskily.

'If you think it would help.'

Sebastian shook his head abruptly. 'No, that won't work. The risk of being separated from them if we had to leave this place in a hurry outweigh the potential benefits.'

She had to agree.

Sebastian gave her another searching look and sat down at the table again. 'This story tells me how you found me, how you got us here. It doesn't, however, explain why you embarked on this insane scheme.'

'Why do you go off to Egypt and Persia in search of valuables?'

'That is an entirely different proposition. There is a simple way in and a way out that doesn't involve falling through time. And there is an established means of doing business: money. Even if we can get within spitting distance of the treasure, we still have no way of getting our hands on it.'

She sighed. 'All I know is that my father wanted this. After a lifetime of keeping me away from whatever crazy reality he was part of, he gave me this when he thought I would be old enough to make use of it. And I trust him.'

He looked at her darkly. 'Do you trust him, or are you in search of him?'

She frowned. 'What would make you say a thing like that? How would I even do such a thing?'

He leaned back, his hands behind his head, his expression unreadable. 'I don't know, Catherine. But what I do know is that there are many ways of making a fortune, and this might be the most ludicrous one I've ever heard of. The only way I can make sense of it is if you are actually after something else entirely.'

Catherine felt the blood pound through her veins. His words angered her unaccountably. 'No. You are wrong.'

And without waiting for a response, she turned on her heel and went to the bedroom once more, shutting the door behind her, ensuring the lock was firmly in place.

Thirteen

'ARE YOU GOING TO sulk all evening?'

Sebastian glowered out of the window. He cut a dangerously handsome figure in his emerald-blue frock coat and black top hat. She had tried to ignore just how dashing he looked, particularly as he had made it clear in the past few days that he would like to keep her at arm's length.

Since Catherine had told him the story of Ferdinand and Stanley, they had not once mentioned her father. They had not mentioned much, in fact, giving each other as wide a berth as possible while still living in the same quarters. Sebastian had been out of their room for days on end, on business he was annoyingly cagey about.

On Catherine's part, she had been trying her best to make some local contacts. So far, she'd met no one who'd been able to shed light on Stanley or the strange green house by the Abbey. Thus, she was determined to make inroads into Bath society, to finally get some answers for herself.

'You know how I feel about this harebrained idea of yours,' he said.

'The only reason you think it's harebrained is because you didn't come up with it yourself.'

He cracked a smile at last.

'And you dislike people as a rule,' she continued, 'but in this situation, you can hardly deny that we need to reach out to *someone* if we intend to make any headway at all.'

'I am not sure what is to be gained by reaching out to the Bath social circuit,' said Sebastian.

'For the past few days, I've been patient as you tried your best with local authorities to discover more about the mysterious captain or the man he claims is wanted by the law. They remain a complete and total mystery.'

Sebastian was back to his glaring, but Catherine wouldn't be put out. 'So, if we are to assume the captain was telling us the truth, which is not a certainty, someone at the ball tonight might have an idea why he is a wanted man. If we find out that Bently was lying, we can let go of this angle and try some other way of reaching Stanley. The ball today is to be heavily attended by local and outside guests. It is quite a prestigious affair, organized every year by the Society for the Arts. We might meet someone who can help us.'

'So you keep insisting. But this is all the more reason we should not show up uninvited.'

Catherine waved his concerns away. 'Who will even notice that we are uninvited when we arrive dressed in all our finery in this beautiful, only somewhat stolen, carriage?' She was wearing the dress of green velvet that Sebastian had got for her, having since taken it in an inch or two around the bodice, adjusting the ruffles to a less modest, but more flattering line.

'You forget, Catherine, you may be a stranger to this place, but I am not. We are only twenty years before my time. The possibility of detection is ever present, given that it is too late to change our names and try to pass off as other people.'

'I don't see why not. The only person who knows you as David Talbot is the captain.'

'And he might well be there tonight.'

'If he sees us, so what?'

'We have already established this identity,' said Sebastian. 'He can hardly accost us for attending a ball but were he to discover we are also masquerading under some other name, I doubt he will let us go again.'

They arrived at the grand orchestra house, transformed into a public ballroom for the occasion, a glittering star shining against the dark city sky. Carriage after fine carriage stood in line, waiting to release their well-heeled occupants onto the pavement. Catherine peered out the window, taking in the beautiful men and women in their finest.

'Come now, Sebastian. It can't be all bad. How lovely they all are.'

'Oh yes, but there will not be a drink to be had all evening... and don't get me started on the food. There will be no space to stand, let alone breathe.'

'That's the spirit,' smirked Catherine.

He shot her a dark look that made the hair on her neck stand up.

As he stepped out of the carriage, she regained her composure. He came around and opened her door. He held out a hand, assisting her down the step. As her fingers touched his, she all but shivered.

It had been a lonely week. And the weight of expectation on this evening left her feeling vulnerable.

Or so she told herself. It was why she could smell the soap on his skin. Almost feel the stubble on his cheek. She'd tried to forget its rasp in the days that had gone by since their tumble off the bridge, but the memory of their kiss was seldom far when he was close.

He stood before her, making no effort to put distance between them as she'd come to expect. He smiled down without even a trace of cynicism.

'Shall we, my lady?'

THE EVENT WAS EVERY bit as crowded as Sebastian had said it would be. But at least the drinks were flowing. They both were handed glasses of claret by circulating waiters as soon as they entered.

Catherine tried to get the lay of the land. The event was indeed one for the who's who of Bath, and she could hardly walk up to anyone she wished and start a conversation.

Catherine and Sebastian parted ways to maximize their chances of learning something useful. 'I will meet you at the entrance in an hour,' said Sebastian. 'If we have something by then, fair enough. Else we leave.'

Catherine meandered around the dance hall. She listened to the splendid orchestra and watched as the couples floated across the dance floor.

A few times, she approached women with an inane question about the time or the direction of the exit, but they all answered and then hurried on.

She was a hair away from despair when at last she caught the eye of a young lady, part of a group of revelers, including another young woman and two young men, one of whom was in a redcoat.

She approached the group, standing by the woman whose attention she had caught. 'Excuse me,' she said.

Four faces turned to her.

'Yes?' said one lady, hardly over twenty years old.

Catherine never enjoyed talking to strangers. She hadn't been in society much, so her distress was genuine. 'I was wondering if any of you may have seen Miss Lydia Kingsley? She was supposed to meet me here by this balcony. Silly me, I can't seem to find her anywhere.'

The blonde turned to her friends. 'Lydia Kinsley? The name is familiar,' said the man in uniform who, with his golden hair and sparkling light blue eyes, was undoubtedly the other girl's brother.

And indeed, it should have been, for Catherine had read about her in the paper. She was a famous opera singer who lived in Bath and was in likelihood in attendance.

The woman and her companions all looked equally lost. 'I'm sorry but none of us are acquainted with her, so would not know even if we had seen her.'

Catherine wrung her hands. 'Oh, it really is quite a bother, with the crush of tourists, no one seems to know one another and I was sure you must be of Bath —'

'And we are,' said the woman.

'I apologize for intruding,' said Catherine, looking up at the men in the party coyly, a skill she had not used since she'd left 1851.

The redcoat stepped forward. 'Perhaps I can assist you in your search. I have several colleagues here and we could spread out and quickly cover the ballroom.'

Catherine was wide eyed. 'That is so very kind of you. But I wouldn't like for you to go to so much trouble when it is probably just a silly misunderstanding, and she has already left.'

They could not dispute this. But the other man in the group, a darker-haired gentleman with a hand on the other woman's elbow, had another suggestion. 'Perhaps we can be of help, if it is a ride home you need.'

'Oh yes,' said the other woman. 'We wouldn't stand to have you stranded here on your own.'

'Oh no, not on my own at all. It is just that, oh it is no matter. Don't worry about this, I'm so sorry to have disturbed you.'

She was about to walk away, taking a little longer than perhaps necessary, when the fair-haired woman intervened. 'Please, join us.

You look terribly alone, and it is such a fun evening.'

'How very kind of you, Miss...'

'Miss Eliza Franklin,' she said with a curtsy. 'And this is my brother, Thomas, and our friends Miss Judith Whitcombe, and her betrothed, Mr. Michael Martelle.'

With a little curtsy of her own, she introduced herself.

'I thought I detected an American accent,' said Thomas.

'Have you met many Americans?' asked Catherine with a smile.

'A few, in the line of duty.'

'Oh how lovely,' she said, almost cringing at her own inanity. She suddenly longed for Sebastian by her side, who, for all his grumpiness, was never at a loss for words.

'What is it like there?' asked Eliza. 'I have always longed to travel but have only gotten as far as Paris one year when an aunt of mine took me.'

Catherine smiled, her heart sore at the idea of home. Even in the state of turmoil she had left it, she'd have done anything to be back right then. Except the home she craved was no longer hers to return to. 'America is so very lovely,' she said wistfully. 'But if you ask me to tell you about it, I will probably go on for the entire evening!'

Judith took her by the arm. 'Oh, please do. We are tired of our own company.'

Catherine smiled gratefully at her new friends. Thomas appeared as if by magic with a fresh glass of wine, and she answered all their many questions as honestly as possible. She had to be careful not to let slip any information that was out of place almost hundred years before her own time.

'America is so very vast, but where I am from, New York, there is a kind of magic that I can't explain. London is splendid in its own way, with its storied history, and I felt very much at home there. But New York has a certain gritty underbelly, which may not be everyone's idea of wonderful, but it is mine. With so many people coming there from around the world, there are always some new delights to be found. New pockets of culture, new discoveries of food, new garments being spun and new fashions that result from them.'

'It sounds perfectly magical!' said Eliza, hands clasped, eyes aglow. 'If only I could visit, I would be quite content.'

Judith and Thomas smiled indulgently: this was not the first they were hearing of Eliza's yen for travel.

And if there was something that Catherine had discovered about herself in the past months, she had a talent that should by rights alarm her if it wasn't so very useful: she could sense a need in the people around her and use it to her advantage. Whether it was Mrs. Riley's desire for an American friend so far away from home, or William's desire to feel strong and clever. What Sebastian truly wanted still eluded her, but Eliza proved easier to understand.

'Oh, you truly must,' said Catherine, leaning forward. 'It really is a wonderful thing to travel.'

'And you crossed the Atlantic on a steamer?' asked Thomas.

'A vast one with enough space for this entire ballroom to fit in several times over.'

'You did not feel very sick?' asked Judith.

'I'm fortunate that I did not.'

Thomas looked truly impressed. 'I know sailors in the Royal Navy who can't say the same!'

She giggled.

'And it was quite safe? Were you traveling alone?' asked Judith.

'I traveled alone. And it was quite safe.'

'Oh, my family would never allow that,' said Eliza.

'Yes, I'm sure they wouldn't,' said Catherine quietly. 'But I have no family.'

The surrounding faces cycled between horror, pity and kindness. 'Oh, you poor, poor dear,' said Eliza. 'And so young, too! Are you here in England for long?'

'That I'm afraid is something I can't quite answer at the moment.'

'What brings you here?' asked Judith's fiancé, Michael.

'I was in search of some family of my father's, but so far I've had little luck.'

'Are any of your relations here in Bath?' asked Thomas.

Catherine's mind raced — to call a criminal a family member would mark her as poor company in anyone's eyes. Perhaps for now, Stanley should remain a secret. 'I had thought I had, but none of the family I came to visit are left.'

'So you *are* alone!' exclaimed Thomas.

'Not quite,' said Sebastian, appearing at her elbow, wrapping his arm around her waist.

Catherine craned her neck up at him, laughing into his face, hoping her new friends wouldn't notice her heightened color. 'I should say that I *arrived* alone, intending to find some relations. But I found a family of another kind altogether. This is my husband, David Talbot.'

Eliza clapped her hands, all pity forgotten. 'How delightful! A holiday romance!'

Now she could only hope they would not come into contact with the mysterious captain who had heard a very different version of their love story.

'How perfectly charming,' Eliza continued. 'I must hear how the two of you met. What a dashing couple you make!'

'Another story that could take all day to tell,' she said.

'That is the perfect kind of story, isn't it?' sighed Judith.

'I am afraid we need to get going tonight,' said Sebastian.

'Oh no,' said Catherine, leaning into him. He felt dangerously pliable beside her, and dangerously good too. 'I've only just met these lovely people, having completely missed Lydia altogether.'

A benign smile replaced a split second's confusion. 'Perhaps a few more minutes, dear.'

Eliza's face lit up. 'I have just the idea. Thomas's regiment is having a ball this weekend. The two of you must attend. I insist.'

'Splendid idea,' said Thomas.

After Catherine looked at him imploringly, Sebastian bowed. 'We would be delighted.'

Catherine and Eliza spent the next ten minutes sorting out the details of when they'd meet next. The ball wasn't soon enough, of course, and Catherine happily assented to her new friend's invitation to meet 'Bath's finest tailor'.

'He is awfully clever with bonnets and bodices and I've given him enough business over the years that he should happily make you something in a day or two if I press him,' promised Eliza.

'That would be grand,' said Catherine. 'I had no idea I would attend so many formal events in Bath, and I am woefully under-prepared.'

Sebastian at last caught her eye, the bored glaze making it clear that she had stretched his tolerance to the extreme. Catherine said her goodbyes and promised to meet Eliza and Judith the following day at Eliza's home.

Sebastian steered Catherine through the packed room. 'You seem to have made quite the impact.'

'Aren't they lovely?'

'Yes, but I thought there was a purpose to our being here.'

'Of course. And that purpose will be advanced, I hope, at the military ball where we might finally learn the true identity of Stanley and the captain, if not sooner.'

But then Sebastian stopped in his tracks.

'What's happened?' she asked.

But he wasn't listening. He was transfixed by a woman before them, hardly more than a girl, but one of stunning beauty, with a head full of golden ringlets, eyes almost violet. She was on the arm of a man who looked like he could have been Sebastian's brother.

The man did not notice them, but the lady's eyes fell on Sebastian's face and she started almost violently, some of the blush fading from the perfect curve of those cheeks.

'Sebastian,' whispered Catherine, 'we need to leave now.'

They rushed out, Catherine leading and Sebastian behind her. He pulled his hat down low over his brow as they waited for their coach outside the theater. It wasn't till they were seated in the carriage that Catherine worked up the courage to speak.

'Who was that?'

But Sebastian raised a hand, silencing her. They didn't say a word then, or as they settled in for another night at the inn. But Catherine already had her answer, because there was only one real possibility: they had just crossed paths with Sebastian's uncle James and the beauty on his arm was Ophelia, the woman who had broken Sebastian's heart.

FOURTEEN

THE NEXT MORNING, CATHERINE ate breakfast alone. Sebastian was gone again before she even awoke.

As she got ready for her appointment with Eliza, her mind wandered. Had she misjudged Sebastian? Their brief encounter with Ophelia the night before made it clear that he was far from at peace with what had happened with her. It didn't matter, Catherine told herself, except that it raised a giant question mark over Sebastian's motivation for wanting to stay with Catherine. She had like a fool been telling herself that they were on this quest together now, but she realized she might have been wrong.

From what she had heard from Jane, this would have been about the time Sebastian's uncle and Ophelia got married, and though Catherine was unaware of the details, it was quite possible that her relationship with Sebastian started around the same time. Could Sebastian be trying to change his own future? Could he be doing exactly what he had accused Catherine of attempting to do with her father? Could he be hoping for a different outcome to his own relationship?

A shadow hung over her as she proceeded for her meeting with Eliza, but it lifted immeasurably when the coach pulled in front of the terraced houses of the Royal Crescent. She soaked in the golden buildings, standing in a majestic semi-circle around an expansive green.

'Catherine!' cried Eliza, greeting her at the entrance as though they were long-lost friends, with Judith quick at her heels. A few moments in their presence was enough to lift her spirits the rest of the way. It had been months since she had any time to just enjoy herself. And with Eliza and Judith a morning of levity was possible, even with everything else that was going on.

After a cup of tea, they set off for Eliza's tailor. 'Jonathan is the canniest businessman,' said Eliza. 'Bath is overrun with tourists, many of whom are here for too short a time to buy his divine creations, which often take weeks or even months to put together. So he's hired a team to make gowns that are almost ready, that can easily be adjusted for different body shapes and sizes. And I think they will be quite the thing for you.'

It was truly a delight to go through Jonathan's beautiful designs, less of a delight when Catherine saw how much they cost. She should have known that Eliza — high born and well bred — would not even imagine that money could be an object for Catherine, and she had done nothing to disabuse her of the notion. But it was too late now, and Catherine felt it was worth the cost to build a relationship with Eliza. After some consideration, she found a charming, pale yellow confection in muslin and had herself fitted for it.

'How long will it take, Jonathan, for this to be ready?' asked Eliza, not waiting for him to reply. 'It is so very important that you give it to us by tomorrow.'

Jonathan, a sharply dressed man of about fifty, looked at her with horror. 'By tomorrow, Miss Eliza, it will not be possible. The best I can do is the following afternoon.'

Satisfied with this reply, Eliza steered Catherine toward the gentleman's coats and Catherine chose one. But when Jonathan insisted she bring her husband along for a proper fitting, she had the perfect excuse to get out of the purchase.

Their next stop was the Pump Room for afternoon tea.

'Oh, I almost forgot,' said Judith, 'just after you left last evening some of David's relatives arrived! One James Talbot and his bride-to-be Ophelia.'

Catherine feigned surprise as her pulse raced. 'Is that so? I confess to being so new to the family that I have not met many of his relatives. James and Ophelia, you say? The names ring a bell — I believe they are cousins. Did you have occasion to speak with them?'

'No,' said Eliza. 'But one of our acquaintances knows them and said they are soon to be wed at the family estate. He'll be attending. She is quite a beauty, don't you think, Judith? Uncommonly pretty. Of course, so are you in such a different way, Catherine,' she added, extending a hand, 'she is golden, you are dark. She is quiet and watchful, and you must be the soul of every party you attend!'

Catherine should have felt more pleasure than she did at these words. But all she could think was that if Ophelia was the sort of person Sebastian was drawn to, he could hardly find her attractive as well.

'I must ask David all about them,' she said. 'Though he has been away for so long that he probably doesn't have a clue either. He's been so bothered with helping me find my family that I fear he has practically forgotten about his own.'

Eliza made sympathetic noises. 'Is there no hope of finding your relations in Bath? You know I have lived here all my life and perhaps I can be of some help.'

She smiled. 'It is so hard to match my memories of people I've been told about with people I am hearing of here. We went in search of one person and then we were told, quite rudely I may add, that he was wanted by the law!'

Her eyes were round with horror and Eliza and Judith's mouths hung open as they absorbed news of this scandalous relation. 'Why, what has he done?' asked Judith in hushed tones.

'That's just it! I don't know. I don't even know if I want to know! But there was a person — a captain by the name of Bently — who told us this piece of news. So now I have given up on Cousin Stanley.'

Eliza's brow shot up. 'Stanley, you say?'

She nodded. 'There is a green house near the Abbey. Do you know it?'

Judith and Eliza exchanged a horrified look. 'Oh yes, everyone knows that house! If that man is your relative, you would do well not to seek him out!'

'Why ever not?'

Eliza leaned forward. 'There are all kinds of stories about the goings on in that house. Of disappearing people — kidnappings, murder even! If your relative lives there, Catherine, I think it is best left alone.'

BY THE TIME CATHERINE got back to the hotel, it was evening. She, Eliza, and Judith had walked around the center of Bath. The history of the place, most notably a house opposite the Sydney Hotel, where Jane Austen once lived, had fascinated Catherine.

When she entered their room, it startled her to find Sebastian there. But he seemed to be back to his usual self.

He folded the newspaper and put it upon the small round table without looking up at her. 'How was your expedition with Eliza?'

'It was productive. I have acquired an appropriate gown for Saturday evening.'

'And you are still determined to go?'

'Even more so, given what Eliza told me this evening,' she said, taking the chair opposite his. 'The occupants of the green house by the Abbey are well known in these parts for all sorts of suspicious behavior, rumored to go as far as murder.'

He raised an eyebrow. 'Her sources?'

'Idle gossip, I would imagine. But that doesn't mean it isn't true. What is more interesting is that she mentioned the disappearance of several people from the green house.'

Sebastian leaned against the table, a lock of brown hair falling over his forehead. Catherine tried to ignore the image of Ophelia and him together. He would have been barely more than a child, of course, and Ophelia just eighteen herself. Painfully young, painfully beautiful. How long were they involved? How did it end so badly?

'And you no doubt think these are time travelers,' he said.

She nodded, trying to return to the moment. 'Wouldn't that make sense?'

'I can assure you it would not.'

She shook her head with a smile. 'You think I believed any of this before a couple of weeks ago?'

'I haven't yet formed any opinion on what you may believe.'

Catherine ignored this. 'Seeing as you yourself have traveled through time, you can't still cling to the idea that it is impossible, can you? It would be too much of a coincidence that my father would concoct an elaborate tale to lead us to exactly where we are right now and we should find a dubious, yet unrelated, mystery.'

'I don't like assumptions. Particularly where you are concerned,' he said, crossing over to the sideboard. Filling two glasses of wine, he handed one to her. 'But if I were to assume for the moment that you are right, how does going to another ball help advance our knowledge?'

'We need to find Stanley. And we need to know what the captain is up to.'

'And dancing solves this somehow?' Suddenly, his face hardened.

'What is it?'

His jaw clenched. 'I forget that that is precisely how you insinuated yourself into my life.'

She flushed. 'It is a military ball, and we might meet people who can shed some light. If you see another way, feel free to propose it!'

'If we attend, how do you suggest we escape detection, with my uncle prowling about?'

'There is no reason to assume he will be there. Given their wedding date is fast approaching, they will return home soon. But I am sure you know that.'

'What on earth do you mean?'

'You were, what, fifteen years old in 1831?'

'Sixteen.'

'You must remember when your uncle returned home and brought his bride with him.'

He looked at her with angry eyes. 'Not down to the day, no.'

'There is always the option of you skipping the ball. I can go with Eliza.'

He nodded. 'Before that, there is somewhere else we need to be. There is a professor, a historian who is an expert on the families of Talbot and Christie and their obsession with the treasure. I thought you might like to come.'

'Of course,' said Catherine. 'Where will we find him?'

'He is just outside of Bristol. It shouldn't take more than a day to reach there. We can leave tomorrow, stay the night, meet him in the morning and get back here in the evening.'

'But my dress. I am scheduled to pick it up day after tomorrow!'

'We can send the man from the hotel.'

'That won't do. What if it doesn't fit properly?'

'I'm sure you can make it work.'

And with that, Sebastian left once again.

THEY SET OUT ALMOST before dawn the next day. Sebastian was driving himself, probably to avoid her company, thought Catherine. She told herself she didn't care; that she was happy to have the time to herself.

It was a long and bumpy trip with several breaks to tend to the horses. When they stopped for lunch, Sebastian finally sat down with her.

'Where did you learn of this professor?' asked Catherine.

'He has written — or rather will write — several books about the subject of the treasure over the next two decades,' he said, draining his glass of ale.

'Have you read them?'

He shook his head. 'Unfortunately not. I always thought the business tedious, and the treasure most likely exaggerated, so I didn't bother. Till you abducted me,' he said, tearing a piece of bread. 'I had no desire to get anywhere near the professor or pirates. But I am surprised you haven't at least heard of him in your research.'

Catherine kicked herself mentally. She was sure she would have found the books in 1929 had they still be in print, but they had not been available in New York at least.

'I am surprised too. How wonderfully convenient it would have been if I had found them before setting out.'

'Alas, there seem to be some inexplicably large holes in this plan of yours,' he said dryly.

'So you tracked him down? Is that what you've been doing for the past few days?'

'It was one thing I've been doing.'

'And you wouldn't like to share the rest?'

'No, I don't believe I would.'

'Could I ask if you have been trying to track down Ophelia?'

His frown was swift. 'And why would I do that?'

Catherine gathered her courage as she took a sip of beer. 'You clearly have feelings for her.'

The corner of his mouth shot down. 'Yes, I have feelings indeed.' And with that, he left the table.

THE NEXT TIME THEY spoke, it was when they arrived in Bristol. Their innkeeper in Bath had recommended the establishment as a fine one. And they weren't disappointed. They were keeping up the pretense of being married, so once again they found themselves in a room with only one bed, though it was bigger this time.

'Before we turn in,' said Catherine, 'I'd like to know more about tomorrow's meeting.'

Sebastian sat down, rubbing his face. It had been a long day's journey. 'There is no one I know of in this year who knows more about the treasure than Professor Whitmore. If we are looking for information, I can think of no better place to start.'

'Fair enough. Does he have anything to gain or lose from this situation, this meeting? Do we have to be worried about him?'

'If you are asking if Whitmore is looking for the treasure himself, I suppose it's possible, as it seems anything is possible. But I do not believe that to be the case. He is a respected scholar, and the author of several books. Which I would imagine would be quite difficult to do if he had been busy raiding pirate ships.'

'Will we be revealing our identities?'

'I suggest you stick to the truth, as far as possible. As far as my identity goes, we'll keep my name secret.'

She nodded. 'We are looking for my relations. And in so doing, hope to learn what he knows of the treasure.'

'Exactly. What we are after is any kind of clue to lead us to our next port of call. And it could be anything.'

'And if we fail?'

'Then it is back to Bath and the hunt for Stanley.'

Catherine had to agree. Without some information, they had few options.

'It really is a shame about this bed. It looks quite comfortable,' said Sebastian.

Catherine walked around it, measuring it with her eyes. 'I think we could put up a wall of blankets between us. And you could take one side of the bed and I could take the other.'

Sebastian turned to her. 'Are you inviting me into your bed, Catherine?' he said, his voice dangerously silken.

Her shoulders went back. 'Simply to ensure that you are comfortable after an entire day driving us here.'

Sebastian smirked. 'Thank you, that is very gracious of you. But I don't think it would be a good idea.'

'Of all the silly notions —' she began before swallowing the rest of her words. She was supposed to be from his time, share his values. America of 1851 may be different, but not *that* different. 'Surely we are in possession of our senses enough to control ourselves?'

Sebastian looked away. 'Be that as it may, I would not like to be accused of impropriety.'

She felt herself withdraw. 'I wouldn't do that,' she said coldly.

He took off his jacket and hung it on the back of a chair. 'You might find you surprise yourself one day. I'll take the couch, thank you.'

Fifteen

PROFESSOR CHARLES WHITMORE LIVED on the beautiful campus of a university, a cluster of old buildings on the outskirts of the city. His cottage was a quaint stone structure with a smoking chimney and a slightly crooked wooden door, overlooking a sprawling green. And she could only hope that what waited for them within was just as charming.

Sebastian rapped the door firmly three times. Catherine's heart beat so loudly that she was surprised Sebastian couldn't hear it. She was unaccountably perturbed about this meeting — it was their first real chance of learning anything meaningful, and it was also their first chance of failure.

After what felt like an age, the door opened with a creak and there stood a man very unlike the garden gnome Catherine had been imagining from the setting. He was tall, silver haired, sharp featured and elegant.

'Professor Whitmore?' said Sebastian.

He examined them both with bright eyes. 'Yes?'

'We have come to meet you on a matter of interest to you,' said Sebastian. 'As the leading authority on the lost treasure of Tibeau.'

Professor Whitmore raised a quizzical eyebrow. 'And who are you, may I ask?'

'My name is Sebastian Jones, and this is my wife, Catherine. We are interested in the treasure's history and we have been told that you are an expert on the subject.'

'You hardly look like the usual bounty hunters to me.'

Catherine looked from Sebastian to the professor and flashed him a smile. 'That is probably the case — we are looking for an unusual bounty: lost family. My maiden name is Christie.'

He gave a brief nod, stepping aside and ushering them in. 'In that case, please do come in.'

The inside of the professor's cottage was cozy, with every available surface covered in books and papers. They made space for themselves in a small seating area. It was clear that Professor Whitmore still had questions as to their antecedents.

'So you are of the tenacious family Christie?'

Catherine grinned, and so did Sebastian. She was nothing if not tenacious herself. 'I've grown up hearing all these stories about the family, but we were all the way in New York and I met none of them. With my father's passing, I decided it was time to come and find my roots.'

'I'm sorry for your loss,' said the professor. 'How are you related?'

At least on this front Catherine could be truthful. 'It is all a little vague. I do not have any relatives I am close to, anyone who can give me any information about the family. You see, my father was a bit of an adventurer, and he ended up in New York about thirty years ago and never came back home.'

'It sounds very much like he was a true Christie, and if you have traveled here all the way from America for this, so are you.'

'Yes, and to meet my husband's family,' she said, throwing Sebastian what she hoped was an adoring look. 'I didn't want to make the same mistake as my father of not nurturing connections before it was too late.'

'Was he a direct descendant?'

'Unfortunately, there's almost nothing that I can share with you about the details.'

'No cause for concern, we'll piece it together,' Whitmore said kindly.

'From what I gathered, there was a family in both England and Portugal, and it is from the English branch that my father descended.'

The Professor nodded. 'The local Christie clan was very invested in recovering the treasure. But as far as I know, the line died with Jaime Christie, in the year 1795. But there may well have been children by some less prominent members who have been lost to history. For instance, I did not know that a descendant of Christie lived in New York for all these years, and yet here you are. What was your father's name?'

'Philip. And his father was Louis.'

'Do you know when they left for America?'

She thought for a moment. 'As far as I know, Louis went over there when he was a young man.'

Whitmore walked over to a stack of books piled precariously high on his dining table. He miraculously pulled out one from the middle without unsettling the lot. He thumbed through it and then brought it over to Catherine. It was a notebook, and on it was a family tree.

'Look at this,' he said. 'See if anything rings a bell.'

Catherine scanned the page, starting with Thelonious and ending with Jaime. 'No, I can't say it does.'

'Is it possible that your father is descended from one of the women in the family and later adopted the Christie name for himself?'

She felt overwhelmed, and more than a little annoyed. Why hadn't her parents ever told her any of this? What were they trying to hide from her? She shook her head. 'It is possible.'

'If I may ask,' said Sebastian as Catherine continued to read, 'how did you become interested in Tibeau's treasure?'

'Ah. Well, that is a bit of long story. To get into that, I must get a pot of tea on first.'

The professor disappeared into the tiny kitchen and put on a kettle. Then he popped back in and waved them over to where he stood in the dining area.

'You see that there?' He was pointing to a sepia-tinted hand-drawn map of the world. It was a work of art, and on it were little markings.

'Those lines you see are the trade routes followed by the Portuguese, and the colonists who came after them. My primary area of study is the rise and fall of the Portuguese empire in India, and this emerged as one of its byproducts.'

Catherine followed the lines crisscrossing from various ports in the Far East and India to Europe. 'The difference in Tibeau's route in 1677 and what you see here was his point of origin. After some time in India, he ended up in Chittagong and then Burma.

'He pillaged the region with impunity. There were objects that had been collected by zamindars — landowners — who allied with Tibeau, over the years, in exchange for trade opportunities with Europe.'

Catherine had, of course, learned as much as she could about the history of the treasure before embarking on this insane adventure. But her search had been limited to the books available in her time, and Professor Whitmore was, to the best of her knowledge, no longer in print in 1929.

'What has never been known,' the professor said, 'was how Tibeau and company were shipwrecked. There was a map of the treasure, but over the next 200 years, it has led generations of adventurers astray. The island of Mauritius has been raked over the years, and it is unlikely that they were ever there.'

'Either that,' said Catherine, 'or the locals made the most of the situation.'

'It is possible, of course, but with some of the relics involved, unlikely. The treasure trove was so very vast that it would have been hard to hide it all. Some individual relics were also physically massive.'

'They could have used them for their own worship.'

'Miss Christie, I don't think you understand the nature of the Bell of Dhammazedi.'

The details, it was true, had been very vague in the books Catherine had read. She had imagined it to be of considerable size, perhaps from a family altar of some sort.

'How large is it?' asked Sebastian.

'While images do not exist, in the literature I have reviewed, they describe it as being taller than the tallest man, as wide as an elephant. But believe it or not, the bell is not the most valuable part of that treasure. It is up to you if you want to trust what I'm about to say is true, but there was a man in Yangon who is believed to have been an alchemist of sorts.'

Sebastian froze. 'An alchemist?'

The professor nodded. 'I can see you are inclined toward disbelief. Before I proceed I will ask you this: why do you think Tibeau and Christie had a falling out after such a successful career together?'

'You think it is something to do with the alchemist?' asked Catherine.

'It is a great mystery for most scholars only because they choose to disbelieve the version of the story that makes the most sense.'

'Please do not assume we are *both* skeptical,' said Catherine. 'I, for one, am not in the least.'

'Well then. The alchemist was famed in the East Indies for his skill with metals, creating alloys stronger than anything seen before. And there was much ado about his attempts to make one that had great mystical powers. It happened in secret, because had the Crown or even the local rajas learned of such efforts, they would have either tried to claim his work for their own purposes or shut him down for practising witchcraft. So little is actually known about his methods, but legend goes that he created a pewter-like substance that had the power to turn back time.'

Catherine and Sebastian exchanged a quick glance. She arranged her face into an astonished look.

'I apologize, but that sounds patently ridiculous,' said Sebastian.

'Shhh,' said Catherine.

'I don't blame you for such a reaction. It had been my first as well. But, for the sake of discussion — and your wife — humor me. Legend goes that this man had attempted to create such a substance and had successfully crafted several objects from it.'

'Several objects?' Catherine said, with genuine surprise this time.

'Yes, and that Tibeau had entered a deal with him to buy some more rare raw materials that the alchemist needed and, in return, would receive a token for his own use.'

'And Christie?' asked Sebastian.

'He wasn't a part of this arrangement. It was during Tibeau's time immersed in the local life. He was married to a native, you see. He had access to people in a way that Christie never had.'

'What finally happened?' asked Catherine.

Professor Whitmore raised a hand and sprang up, rushing to the kitchen, apparently just remembering the tea.

'What do you think?' she whispered to Sebastian.

He looked thoughtful. 'It fits what we know, that much is true.'

Whitmore returned with a tray bearing teapot and cups, continuing the conversation as though there had been no interruption.

'Nothing is really known beyond a point. It is believed, however, that on that voyage home with the bell, Tibeau had in his possession some sort of talisman or amulet that allowed him to bend, manipulate or move through time.'

'How'd he end up dead with such a thing in his possession?' asked Sebastian.

'Good question. Christie, it seems, found out about it, and realizing that it was the true treasure, fought Tibeau for it. And that it was this object that led to Christie running Tibeau through with his sword.'

'Christie killed Tibeau?' gasped Catherine, genuinely astonished. 'My family always told me that Tibeau had died of some sort of disease!'

Whitmore shook his head. 'I'm afraid your ancestor caused his death.'

'And did Christie get the medallion from him?'

'I don't know. Is it even real?' wondered the Professor, pouring their tea at last. 'Amongst believers in the lore of the Alchemist of Yangon, there is much speculation. We believe the alchemist died shortly after Tibeau's acquisition of the medallion and he took his secrets with him to the grave.'

'How can you know that?' asked Sebastian. 'If he had the power to turn time, perhaps he's just in another era?' His sardonic expression gave the appearance of cynicism. And Catherine wasn't wholly sure that, even having used the medallion himself, Sebastian truly took any of this seriously.

'That would be one theory,' said Professor Whitmore.

'Is anything known of how the device works?' said Catherine, taking a sip of the bitter brew.

'I am afraid I cannot help you there. The legend is tangential to my work, which is more historical than it is metaphysical.'

Catherine nodded.

'But coming back to your family, after Christie returned from the fatal voyage, he was a changed man.'

'Which would make sense if he found himself in possession of a time-traveling medallion.'

'And yet he was unsuccessful in retrieving the rest of the treasure,' pointed out Sebastian.

'Yes,' said the professor. 'Many say he went mad on that voyage. And that is pretty much that, till the next generation of Tibeaus — who changed their name to Talbot at some point — and Christies tried to retrieve it.'

'What happened to this object after Christie's death?' she asked.

'It is not known.'

Sebastian interjected. 'Do you have any theories where the shipwreck took place?'

Whitmore looked at the map on the wall again. 'Unfortunately, no.'

Catherine stole a glance at Sebastian. She didn't know whether he'd approve of what she was about to do. But from her reticule, she retrieved her map.

Whitmore smiled as she unrolled it and placed it before him. 'Ah, yes. The famous map. So you have something from the family, after all. You know it has led several people astray? All the surrounding islands have at some point been searched by either pirate or naval officer from the Portuguese or British crowns. And they found nothing there.'

'Including Kallan Island?' she asked.

'Oh, yes. In fact, I'm fairly certain the French took a stab at that one too.'

'And nothing?' asked Catherine, deflated.

'Either that, or there was an elaborate cover-up to hide the discovery of the treasure.'

'You believe they were on the wrong track? That the map is a fake?'

'Not a fake, exactly. It is my belief the map was a decoy, meant to be read with a key of some sort. And without that key, it was designed to lead the searcher astray.'

'And it wasn't drawn by Christie at all?'

'I believe Tibeau created this before his death.'

Catherine gasped. 'And Christie stole it! Another instance of my ancestor's infamy.'

Whitmore smiled. 'I wouldn't worry overmuch. Tibeau was hardly of exceptional moral fiber himself.'

'What kind of key would you think would belong to such a map?' asked Sebastian.

'It is impossible to tell. It could be a scrap of poetry. A painting somewhere. It could really be anything. It depends on the ingenuity of the mapmaker.'

'Could the answer lie with a gentleman by the name of Stanley?' asked Catherine.

Professor Whitmore waved his elegant fingers in the air, dismissing the suggestion abruptly. 'Oh, stuff and nonsense. There is absolutely no evidence that this Stanley character even exists.'

'Oh,' said Catherine, 'how unusual. May I ask why you say that?'

He looked annoyed. At last, the genial historian was gone. 'You are not the first people who have come looking for Stanley.'

'We haven't come looking for Stanley, it is just that his name has come up during several of my family's retellings of these stories. And we were told that a man by that name lives in Bath, who matches the description.'

The professor looked at Catherine sharply. 'I am not sure who has started the story of Stanley in the green house. It is a bit of a tall tale in these parts that a man or several people have appeared and disappeared in that house. There are accounts of murder and infamy, too. And none of these have ever proven true.'

'Is there an investigation into him?' asked Sebastian.

'That would be like investigating the disappearance of Cinderella's slipper.'

'Are you saying that Stanley does not exist at all?' said Catherine.

'A man by that name may or may not exist in the town of Bath. It is hardly so unexpected a thing in a town of that size. But there is no evidence of the other things they have accused the poor creature of.'

'Someone else has come before looking for him? Was it a man named Bently?' asked Sebastian.

'No, it was someone else connected to the treasure, much like you — James Talbot.'

Sebastian leaned forward. 'And what did you tell him?'

Whitmore looked put out, but he answered anyway. 'Not much. It was a brief visit.'

As Sebastian digested this bit of information, Catherine stepped in. 'Would you have any idea where the missing piece of this map might be?'

'No, I'm sorry. If there had been any evidence that it was still in existence, I am sure several bounty hunters would have located it by now. Because everything about this treasure has been torn apart to within an inch of its life.'

'Okay, you have been enormously helpful. And we thank you for taking the time to explain all of this to us,' said Catherine, standing up.

'You're most welcome. I wish I could have been more help with your family. But after prattling on for all this while, I feel you may not be after your kin after all? Good luck, and bon voyage.'

BACK IN THEIR HOTEL, Sebastian sat on the lounge chair in one corner, looking more brooding than usual.

'What's the matter?' asked Catherine.

He raised a brow. 'Isn't that the most laughable question?'

'You don't seem very amused. Why don't you just say what's on your mind?'

'My uncle was here,' he said.

'Why do you think he is looking for Stanley?'

'For the same reason we are — he is connected to the treasure.'

'So you don't believe Whitmore's claim that Stanley is a work of fiction?'

He shrugged, getting up and walking over to the window. 'Is any of this worth it to you?'

'Not this again,' said Catherine, hackles up.

'Yes, this again. Precisely this again and again,' he said, turning around. 'What is it you want, Catherine? You say it is treasure. But you are lying to yourself.'

'What do you think I am after? Clearly you have some ideas!'

'Answers about your past.'

She shook her head incredulously. 'So what if I'm looking for answers? Is that so wrong?'

'If I have learned anything in my life, it is that there is nothing to be gained from trying to hold on to what is lost.'

She stood before him angrily, hands fisted by her sides. 'I am not talking about a lover here. I am talking about my father. A very dear father who I had so very little time with and this is the explanation behind it all!'

'Well, at least we're getting somewhere. You're admitting you are looking for your father. Not the treasure.'

'Maybe it is both.'

'You think Stanley is your father?'

'Perhaps.'

Sebastian frowned. 'This can only lead to heartbreak. Or worse. You're trying to mess with time.'

Catherine remembered the warning in her father's letter, too. 'Not mess with it. I am not trying to bring back the dead. Just to get some answers.'

'There are no answers that will make it worth it, Catherine.'

'You can't know that! Look at everything he's done to bring me here! What happened, Sebastian, to make you so cynical about people? Was it Ophelia's rejection?'

Sebastian let out a bitter laugh. 'No, Catherine, I hate to disappoint you, but not all of us are romantics.'

'You told me to be honest about myself. Maybe it's time you did the same.'

He shot her a look that was icy cold. 'Tell me, Catherine, how is what Ophelia did to me so very different from what you did?'

'I beg your pardon?'

'Since I presume you know the entire story, you know she pretended to love me in order to get my dukedom for my uncle and herself. You pretended to want me in order to get the medallion.'

'It is not the same thing,' said Catherine, cut to the bone by his words. 'I flirted with a man, I kissed a man who seemed quite capable of taking care of himself. I didn't make anyone love me!'

'Don't worry, there is no risk of love here.'

She took a deep breath. 'I certainly didn't mean you to be here with me. You were not supposed to get hurt. And once again, if you wish to return, I will take you back this minute.'

'And come back here by yourself?'

'Yes. I will find a way to get the medallion back to you in time, I promise that.'

'I believe you.'

Catherine's heart sank. So this was it then. This was where they parted ways.

He put his jacket back on and made for the door.

'You want to return?' she asked.

'Yes,' he said, not looking at her. 'We must hasten back if you intend to keep your engagement in Bath.'

Sixteen

SEBASTIAN AND CATHERINE SPED through the miles back to Bath, reaching just in time to make themselves decent for the ball.

Sebastian had said nothing more about not attending. He had protested at first, but had to admit that getting to know a few locals better was a good idea. He just had a different way of going about it than she did. He had in fact acquired a jacket for himself for the occasion, though he would never have volunteered such information to Catherine, who was rushing through her toilet with the help of the innkeeper's young daughter.

When she emerged, Sebastian had to remind himself of what happened the last time he had allowed her to get close. But he couldn't look away. There was no way around it: Catherine was simply beautiful; her dark hair and pale skin against the yellow of the dress made from cloth so fine it was iridescent.

He wanted to do more than imagine touching her. So much more. He had been leaving their room early and returning late in part to avoid being close to her. To be attracted to her was one thing, but now she had him in an advanced state of confusion, too. How had she gotten it into her head that he wanted Ophelia still? By the time she had been done with Sebastian, he had been destroyed and it had been up to him to remake himself as a man all on his own. His family were content to let him languish in his misery and he'd barely spoken to his father in the years before his death.

And then, when Sebastian had finally become duke himself, their relationship, though long over, had been used to snatch his title away, with James claiming Sebastian was trying to steal his wife anew and had hatched a foiled assassination plot. With the help of James's connections, Sebastian had been stripped of his peerage and had narrowly escaped jail. Even now, if Ophelia's brother had his way, that was where he would languish.

It had been the most painful thing to set eyes on Ophelia again in Bath, just as she was as he had first seen her. But no part of that was a longing for what once had been. Anger had long since passed as well.

And perhaps even more confusing — why did he care what Catherine thought, anyway? She had pulled him into this mad world of time travel and alchemists. He shouldn't care, nor should he trust her, despite her obvious charms.

But there she stood, black lashes against the curve of her cheeks. She looked up almost shyly. 'Shall we proceed?'

'My lady.' He bowed down low, and as he straightened up once again, he was witness to the first genuine smile she had directed at him for some time. And he remembered why he had been avoiding her. She shone as bright as a star as he extended his elbow toward her. She looped her delicate hand around his arm and they proceeded down the stairs as was befitting a married couple on their way to a ball.

Sebastian had spent most of the past few days going from one town official to another in search of the mysterious Stanley or Captain Bently's identities. But it turned out no one could give him any usable information about either. He had heard of several Bentlys but none that matched the description of the man they met; Stanley's identity had remained stubbornly shrouded in mystery; but there was nothing on his being wanted by the law. Sebastian had even returned, far more discreetly this time, to keep a watch on the green house, where he had seen no activity at all.

Hopefully, this evening would settle the matter once and for all. If Catherine agreed to give up on the Stanley route, he had a few ideas about what they could try next.

Sebastian and Catherine entered just as some local dignitaries were addressing the assembly. Catherine began looking around for her friends and soon spotted them.

'You go ahead,' he said, 'I have a few people to speak with.'

He watched as Catherine joined Eliza and Judith, and the annoyingly attentive Thomas. Now that he knew Catherine was a married woman, he had reeled in his enthusiasm, but not as much as Sebastian would have liked.

He found a gentleman approaching — it was Mr. John Decker, a justice of the peace Sebastian had approached a few days prior. He had sent him away empty-handed, but now seemed more inclined to conversation. After the customary greetings and chit chat, he asked: 'Did any of your enquiries bear fruit?'

'Thank you, only a very little. I have been given to understand by an acquaintance that the tales regarding Stanley, whom we had discussed at our last encounter, have been exaggerated. Could this be true?'

'Your acquaintance is much mistaken,' said Mr. Decker. 'While I was rather indisposed when we last met, I made further enquiries. Stanley Parker is a known miscreant. We have had an eye on him for some months now and have linked him to several crimes in the area. There is no place for doubt, of course, so a thorough investigation into his origins has been conducted and we simply cannot find any trace of him prior to six months ago.'

'That is strange.'

'Quite. In addition, Stanley has broken into the house of a man I believe is known to you, perhaps even your relative, if my memory serves me.'

Sebastian went still. 'Is that so?'

'Yes. He was spotted near your family estate of Westlake after a break-in.'

'That is a remarkable a coincidence, if true.'

'Oh, I assure you, it is true. The family has been making inquiries as well — which is how I came to learn as much as I did after your visit to me. The question is, can it truly be a coincidence?' said Decker. 'What is your intention in searching for this man?'

'I have been forthright with you. I am wholly ignorant of the connection, having only just returned from New York with my wife after the better part of a decade. And I am not on good terms with my family and do not know of events that transpire at the Westlake estate.'

He frowned. 'That is a shame. I was rather hoping to learn something more about him from you. Perhaps she can aid us in our enquiries.'

'I am happy to make the introduction, sir, but I am afraid you will be disappointed. She is as in the dark as I am. In fact, more so. I have not told her many of the unsavory details I have gleaned about Stanley since our time in Bath has begun. I have spared her the pain of knowing that one of her last remaining relations may be such a rotten apple.'

'A regrettable business. Are you certain that she knows nothing?'

'Absolutely, sir. It was to find out more that I sought your help.'

'You'd do well to keep your distance from him. Anyhow, he is not currently in his house at Bath. It has been several days since the team watching the house has seen anything.'

'Is one Captain Bently a member of the surveillance team?'

'Not to my knowledge.'

'I thank you for your help,' said Sebastian with a bow.

As Sebastian went in search of Catherine, of one thing he was certain: there was no break-in at the Westlake Estate around the time of his uncle's wedding. He'd have remembered something like that. So it had been an invention to smoke out Stanley. The question was, what did James Talbot want with him?

Before he got much further, Catherine came to find him. 'There you are, I've been looking for you everywhere.'

'What is it, my dear,' he said. She pursed her lips at the endearment.

'Thomas is speaking with an admiral and wants to introduce us to him.'

They hurried back to where Catherine's friends were standing. Thomas was in conversation with the admiral and his deputy. As Catherine and Sebastian approached, he waved them into the fold.

'Would you allow me, sir, to introduce you to guests all the way from New York? This is Catherine and her husband, David Talbot.'

Sebastian needn't have feared discovery, for the admiral barely spent a moment on his face, focusing all his attention on Catherine instead. 'From New York, you say? Simply splendid. I was there last year and must confess to being completely charmed by your home.'

'I am delighted to hear it,' gushed Catherine. 'It is a wonderful city, and though I have only left a month ago, I miss it terribly.'

'Is your move permanent?'

'Our plans are unfixed,' said Catherine, looking up at Sebastian. 'For now, we are here. Perhaps we will return or perhaps some new adventure awaits us.'

'That's the spirit,' said the admiral with a laugh, clearly charmed not just by New York but by Catherine too. She really was a sight to behold in full flow.

She asked an array of questions that the admiral began to patiently address. And then she came to the point. 'Admiral, we had the pleasure of meeting one Captain Bently here in Bath. Do you know him? I fear you must have so many men under your command that you wouldn't know one lone captain.'

The admiral turned to his deputy with an enquiring look. 'Is there a man by that name in our squadron?'

'I confess it does not ring a bell.'

'Oh, I must be mistaken then.'

'Did Thomas say you are a Talbot?' asked the admiral, finally turning to Sebastian.

'Yes,' he said with a little bow.

'Talbot of the Westlake family?'

'The same.'

'I believe your relation James was here just now. He's an old acquaintance of mine.'

Sebastian looked at Catherine with alarm. That was their cue to exit.

'Right,' he said, 'he's a distant cousin.'

'Due to get married soon as well; I'm sure you'll both be there.'

Catherine changed the topic, reverting to her many questions for the admiral. As soon as he could, Sebastian put his hand on Catherine's arm. He had spotted James through the crowd; any moment someone would call out to him, making an introduction inevitable.

'Would you care to dance, my love?' he said. It was the only way to get out of view that Sebastian could think of.

She smiled her sweetest smile. 'Of course, my dear.'

The admiral and the party made some comment about young love as he led her away. Once in the ballroom, she immediately stiffened.

'I don't know this dance,' she whispered.

'The quadrille?' he asked, looking at the rows of dancers. It was still a dance in fashion in the 1851 England.

'We don't do this in America, I'll make a spectacle of myself.'

He cursed softly, leading Catherine away in search of another way out, careful to keep his back to where he had last seen the man who had done — or would do, rather — everything in his power to destroy him.

'There are two ways out of this place — one is on the far side of the hall, and our path to it is being blocked by the very man I wish to avoid. Several of his party may also identify me, and I see them circulating near the other exit. The dance floor will offer cover.'

'And I would love to, if they would only do a waltz.'

They moved around the room, in search of another way out. Catherine looked behind her.

'He's coming this way!'

They rushed past the crowd on the sidelines of the dancefloor, causing more than a few heads to turn. With just a few feet between them and the exit, Sebastian spotted a familiar face, an employee of the Westlake Estate, keeping guard at the door. He whipped around and saw a door on the opposite side of the entry vestibule. Grabbing Catherine by the hand, with the man's back to them, Sebastian crossed over to it and turned the knob.

It opened into a tiny closet.

He hesitated, shooting a glance at the exit once again just as his uncle joined his man at the doorway.

'We have no choice!' whispered Catherine, pushing him in and joining him herself, closing the door gently behind them. She almost tripped over him, the room was so small. 'Oof,' she exclaimed softly. He turned to face her, and they were inches apart.

'Of all the horrid turns of luck!' she cried.

'Yes, this act of impersonating others is rife with danger.'

She dismissed him with a wave. 'No, I meant that the stupid door led to a closet with no means to escape.'

'I must agree with you there,' he said, as his eyes grew accustomed to the dark environs.

She looked around. 'It is an odd place for a cupboard. Do you think there could be a secret passageway?'

'That is always possible in these old buildings. The Westlake Estate is full of them.' He pressed at the walls gently with his fingertips.

'Anything?' asked Catherine

'Not that I can find.'

And then there was a movement outside. He peered through the crack between wall and door. It was his uncle and his companions, standing very close.

He held a finger to his lip.

'There's no sign of this man,' said James.

'Who do you think he could be?' said his companion. 'Couldn't it be some distant relation who isn't so well known to the family?'

'The relationship he is claiming is one that simply doesn't exist. I have an uncle who went away to the New World, but then he went to Shanghai and inexplicably settled down there.'

Sebastian cringed. He knew this, of course, ruing the moment he stayed close to the truth. He could have chosen any other name, except Westlake or Talbot, and would have avoided all notice. Sebastian had thought the Talbot name would open doors for him, and it had, but at too heavy a price. But it was too late now. There was no choice but to escape this room and then flee Bath.

'His wife seems to have attracted some attention. Quite the beauty.'

'So it would seem.'

Sebastian looked out of the crack again. For the longest time, the group did not move.

Catherine stood on her toes to whisper in Sebastian's ear. 'What are they waiting for?'

Sebastian barely suppressed a shiver at the feel of her breath on his neck. He turned to face her, to tell her they would have to wait awhile, when he saw her eyes wide, her rosy lips parted. He searched her pale face, glowing in the sliver of light coming into the space.

There was a moment of recognition in her eyes, and a reflection of his own desire.

He felt the air between them change. She took a step back, coming up against the wood-paneled wall of the closet. He reached out and took both her hands in his, caressing her palms with his thumbs.

And then, his eyes never leaving hers, he lifted her hands to either side of her head, pinning her to the wall.

'Sebastian,' she whispered, looking up at him in the dim light of the room.

He swept down and claimed her mouth.

SEVENTEEN

CATHERINE SQUEEZED HER EYES shut.

This was nothing like their kiss on the bridge. This was a heart-stopping, knee-buckling moment of truth.

She kept her hands still, knowing she still didn't have his trust, knowing it was fair, knowing how much he was risking by letting his guard down again.

And then she couldn't think anymore as the kiss went from a tentative question to a full-blown answer. His mouth explored hers, and she arched her back, trying to get closer to him.

He let her hands go at last to cup her face, tipping her head backward as he traced a path of kisses down her neck. She wrapped her arms around his waist as she tried to draw him to her, but it still wasn't close enough. With so many layers of skirt between them, she needed more.

His mouth met the edge of her bodice, and her chest heaved with the unbearable delight of his breath grazing the tops of her breasts, pushed high by her corset.

'Sebastian,' she sighed.

'Shhh.' His hands caressed her, finding her taut nipples through the soft cloth and she let out a gasp which he silenced with his mouth.

She opened her eyes and saw his heavy with desire. 'Catherine,' he murmured, 'how I want you. How I wish it wasn't time to go.'

She sighed as he placed a kiss where her dress gave way to breast. 'Sebastian,' she said with a moan.

'Catherine, delicious Catherine.' He pulled away reluctantly. 'I think they have left.'

'They couldn't have. Not now, when they are finally coming to some use.'

Sebastian let her go and turned to peek outside again. 'Yes, they are gone,' he said with a sigh. 'And we must go too.'

She closed her eyes for a second and pushed him against the wall. He looked down at her darkly.

'Catherine, there are many ways I have imagined this happening, but this isn't one of them.'

She stepped back, feeling the warmth between her thighs as the pleasure of his words crashed into her.

He lowered his mouth to hers again, kissing her hard one last time.

Catherine took a deep breath as she straightened out her gown and hair. She'd look ravished despite her efforts, but there was nothing to be done for it. Catherine left the closet first to ensure that James was no longer about. Then she had to track down Eliza. If they were leaving Bath altogether, she didn't want to do it without saying goodbye at the very least.

'Leaving now? Whatever for?' she asked on hearing Catherine's rushed words of farewell.

Catherine shook her head. 'It is a long story, I wish I could share it with you. But we need to leave not just the ball but also Bath.'

Her blue eyes shone with concern as she took Catherine's hand. 'Good heavens! I hope everything is alright.'

Catherine nodded. 'Yes, but it's complicated.'

'Dear Catherine, a week from now, I am heading straight back to Salisbury. We would be delighted if David and you would join us there. Do you promise me you will come if you have any need at all?'

Catherine gave her hand a squeeze. 'It isn't often that you meet people with whom you have such a connection in so short a time. I thank you and will try to join you there. Please give my regards and make my apologies to Judith and the others.'

And with that, she returned to Sebastian and ushered him out through the back exit.

CATHERINE AND SEBASTIAN MADE their way around the building as quickly as possible. The carriage was parked across the road from the entrance, and Sebastian had found a local boy to watch the horses. They had one more corner to turn before it came into view, but just as they were about to make it, Sebastian pulled Catherine back and they pressed themselves against the cold stone of the hall.

'Where did he go?'

It was James's voice. 'If the justice of the peace is to be believed, this man has been making inquiries for about a week now.'

'It must be the man I saw at the green house.'

Catherine turned to Sebastian. It was Bently. She was sure of it. She'd never forget that menacing lilt.

'He gave me a story about being related to Stanley.'

'We have to get to Westlake now. We cannot wait here any longer.'

'Yes, a man cannot be late for his own wedding,' said a third man. And a laugh went up.

Catherine could hear the sounds of the men disbanding. It was several minutes till Catherine thought it safe enough to look around the corner. Bently was still standing in front of the building, but she almost did not recognize him out of uniform.

A few minutes later, they seemed at last to be gone.

'They may have only gone back inside,' said Sebastian, scanning the crowd in front of the building for familiar faces. 'But we have to take our chances.'

They hurried toward the carriage, Catherine's arm wrapped around Sebastian's waist, his head lolling to one side, as though he were a drink away from unconsciousness.

They crossed the narrow road to the carriage and Catherine climbed up into the driver's box as Sebastian abandoned the act under the cover of the coach, quickly paying the boy watching the horses and climbing in beside her.

'There!' yelled a voice. The captain!

Sebastian snatched the reins and they raced away. It was a long open road in front of the assembly hall, with nowhere to turn off. By the time they found the first lane, the captain and his cohort were in pursuit on horseback. Sebastian spurred their horses on as Catherine desperately kept a lookout for a place to hide.

'There,' she said at last, pointing at a little narrow lane off to the side.

Sebastian rode on. 'We will be sitting ducks if it's a dead end.'

The men and horses were behind them now by just a few hundred meters.

Then the road rose and dipped away again in front of them, and Catherine spotted an empty shed.

'If we go in now, they won't spot us from their position,' she said urgently.

Sebastian brought the horses to a grinding halt and coaxed them quickly and quietly beside the shed, obscured from the road by bushes.

They got off and stood by their horses. It was a few moments later that Bently and his men raced by, and from what Catherine could see and hear, they took the wrong turn further down the road.

'They might return,' said Sebastian, taking out a bag of oats from under the driver's bench and soothing the tired animals.

They waited another fifteen minutes. When there was still no sign of the men, they set out.

'Sit in the back this time,' he said as he took off his jacket and rolled up his sleeves. He traded his hat for a cap which he had taken off the boy who had watched the horses. Then he grabbed a handful of soil and rubbed it on his face. 'Will I pass as a coachman?'

'Not really, but you don't look like a Talbot either.'

'That'll do for now. Though they'll recognize the vehicle.'

Catherine took Sebastian's jacket and boarded the carriage, and he took his seat in front. They made their way back through the quiet side streets, avoiding all the major thoroughfares.

CATHERINE AND SEBASTIAN QUICKLY got their affairs in order once they arrived at the inn. It had taken twice the time it should have, given their circuitous route, but they had not seen their trackers again.

Sebastian rushed the innkeeper to settle their dues as Catherine piled all of their meager belongings into a trunk they had acquired earlier that week.

He came back to the room. 'We must leave at once.'

Catherine was ready and waiting. 'Yes, but not until you tell me what you have learned. You know more than you are letting on.'

He paced the room. 'Can't this wait?'

'No.'

He sighed, slumping on the bed. 'I heard only this evening that my uncle is claiming the man we know as Stanley broke into the Westlake home a few days ago. And it is not known what he took, and it is not known where he is at the moment.'

She turned to him. 'And?'

'And I know it isn't true. I would have remembered something like that.'

'Can you be sure?'

'Yes.'

'So they are trying to have him arrested,' said Catherine, standing up.

'Yes.'

Catherine paced, feeling a frisson of excitement running through her. 'This is it,' she said, pacing the room.

'I was afraid you'd come to that conclusion.'

He was up to something; he was working with them; they were so close now. 'We must stay and find him!'

'He isn't here anymore, Catherine. There's been no sign of him for days in Bath.'

'But someone must know where he has gone! We need to go back to the house. We can't leave like this!'

He grabbed her by the shoulders. 'Catherine, we cannot hunt for this man — it will get us killed!'

'It will be dangerous, but we can figure out a way. We'll disguise ourselves.'

'Catherine, if he wanted that, he'd have met you himself by now.'

'I don't know —'

'We must leave! It is only a matter of time before those people find us. And no matter what the truth is about Stanley, James and Bently will cause me harm if they get to me, of that you can be sure.'

Her shoulders slumped. 'Who is the captain?'

'I don't know, but he does not belong to the navy.'

Catherine had been fairly certain of this herself. Seeing him without his uniform, at what was a function for the military, made it abundantly clear that he was an imposter. 'Where do we you propose we go?'

Sebastian looked grim. 'We have two choices. Either we give up and return to our time, at least for long enough to regroup. Or we go to the one place that seems the most dangerous of all.'

'Where is that?'

'The Westlake Estate.'

Eighteen

IT WAS A HARROWING night. The journey, so close to the one they made to Bristol, had taken its toll on the wheel of their carriage, and they were forced to come to a grinding halt in the middle of nowhere. They had found a ramshackle inn, and though there were no fit horses to exchange, at least their present pair could rest, along with the driver.

The room was little more than a shed. They were both tired enough that they slept — or pretended to sleep. After the events of the closet, Catherine had wondered how their night would go. But they were too put out even for awkwardness. They each claimed a side, the bed a pile of unadorned hay, and all but clung to the rough wooden walls so as not to touch each other.

Catherine's mind refused to settle. Their explosive kiss had opened up all her concerns about lying to Sebastian, about where — or rather when — she was from. He knew well enough who she was. But if he were to learn the lie, he would trust her even less than he did now. Had she only come clean at the beginning, that first night after they fell through time, she would not have had to keep this secret.

But what if he learnt the truth now? What if he left her?

That was the feeling that scared her most of all. When had she come to want him? It was frightening, of course, being in this place, and it was reassuring to have Sebastian, who was a native of this time, to take the lead on some things. But it was more than that. Somehow he had come to mean something to her too.

Perhaps she'd wanted him with her all along.

And the closer they got to Westlake Estate, the more she feared for them both. First, there was Ophelia and the danger of her unsettling Sebastian again. But even though it twisted Catherine inside to think of him hurting, that was far from the greatest danger: the primary risk, of course, was the physical harm that might come from detection. It seemed insane that they would run away from Sebastian's uncle in Bath only to rush toward him the very next day on his own turf.

But Sebastian had made clear there was something he was after in the castle, though he had been insufferably vague about what that thing was.

WHEN THEY AWOKE THE next morning, they stumbled awkwardly around each other in the tiny room.

'I'm sorry,' said Sebastian, still looking exhausted. 'This was hardly an ideal situation.'

'You have no reason to apologize,' she said. 'The horses needed rest, and our wheel needed mending.'

'And to those ends, please excuse me. If you could prevail upon the mistress of this place to arrange for some food and water, we might be on our way by the time the carriage is ready.'

She could feel his distance already. And she knew that the closer they got to Westlake Manor, the farther he'd leave her behind.

Catherine wandered out of the stable, picking bits of hay out of her hair and off her clothing. What she'd give for a mirror and a decent bathroom.

The mistress of the changing station said she'd arrange bread and cheese for their journey. After freshening up, Catherine picked up the tidy little bundle and went in search of Sebastian.

She found him squatting by the wheel of the coach with some tools.

'How bad is it?'

'Not terribly. But there are no workers in this place at this hour. So I am trying to see what I can do.'

'Can I help?'

He looked up at her with an incredulous grin, a smudge of grime on his cheek.

Catherine put her hand on her hip. 'I can hardly be the first girl who has offered to help repair a carriage with you.'

'You seem to overestimate my experience with women.'

'You have quite the reputation.'

He gave her a spanner to hold, though she couldn't see what purpose it served. Then he got to work on mending the spoke as best he could, and then went off to wash his hands. When he returned, they sat on the driver's seat and ate their breakfast.

'I would kill for a cup of coffee,' said Catherine.

'Or tea,' said Sebastian.

'Where will we stay when we arrive at Westlake?'

'Not at the castle, that's for sure. My fifteen-year-old self might get a fright from which he would not recover.'

'I am sure you have always been made of sterner stuff than that.'

He looked at her with a vulnerability that took her by surprise.

'Anyhow, it's important that we aren't seen by anyone, but specifically by your younger self,' she said.

'Will the world bend and break in half, if that were to happen?'

'No, but think about it this way: when you were sixteen, do you remember seeing your future self?'

'No, indeed I do not. And it is the sort of thing I might remember.'

She nodded. 'If we are trying not to change the past, that seems rather important.'

She thought for a second. 'Do you think our actions here are predestined?' she asked.

'A weighty question for the morning after we spent the night in what I would describe as a stable.'

She nudged him with her shoulder, and he answered her with a smile.

'If I did not meet my future self as a teenager, it means we won't meet him today. Because it has already been that way for my past self in that castle — and with *me* sitting here with you now. Or something like that, I suppose?'

AND THEN IT WAS time to be on their way. There were no good choices facing Catherine and Sebastian. The problem with arriving at Westlake by night was that the guards around the castle, beefed up for the wedding, would be out in numbers. The problem with arriving during the day was that detection was so much more likely with the occupants of the castle out and about.

Sebastian pulled into a disused shed near the castle he had remembered from when he was a teen. He'd said it would be a good place to keep the carriage and horses as no one went there, and his expression had made Catherine wonder just what young Sebastian had got up to there.

'We'll do a reconnaissance before entering,' said Sebastian. 'If it seems too risky, we can reassess.'

'Are you sure no one will find the carriage here?'

Sebastian scanned the roof. 'I am more concerned about the building collapsing and killing the horses.'

Then it was on to the next problem on their hands: how to get into the castle without being spotted.

'If I remember correctly,' said Sebastian, 'the wedding is not for another day or two.'

'Why is it so crowded now in that case?'

'People arrived for this from all over England and even abroad. It was the social event of the season. And people who traveled here stayed for a while.'

Catherine could see the strain on Sebastian's face. 'We need not do this. We have options. We could go back.'

'No, if what I think is true, we must come back, anyway. The wedding, with all the crowds, provides us with a certain amount of cover.'

CATHERINE AND SEBASTIAN WALKED the remaining distance to the castle. Catherine had glimpsed the enormous estate from further away, but it was only now that she took in the full splendor of the place. What Sebastian called an estate was a fortified castle of sandstone, with too many turrets to count, and a vast entrance.

She saw at once what Sebastian meant: this was a good time to move around undetected. The grounds were full of people, and they had put tents up for the feasts and dancing to come.

Sebastian looked different here somehow. He held himself straighter and seemed a very great distance away from her. His hat was pulled down low over his head and he'd had no opportunity to shave, giving him a rakish air.

They went around the building, with Sebastian pointing out where the secret passageway would emerge from inside the castle walls. There was a wooden trapdoor in the ground, obscured by hedges. 'Can't we just enter through here?' asked Catherine.

'These doors only open from within. Believe me, I have tried several times to sneak in and out undetected. There is only one entrance to the passage, and it is in a small study on the ground floor.'

They passed through an inner gate with no trouble and proceeded along the broad driveway.

'So this is where you grew up?'

Sebastian nodded. 'You like it?'

'It is a truly a wonderful building, but I can't imagine it as a family home.'

He looked grim. 'Not to mention the squadron of servants and an extended family to guarantee intrigue enough to fill every room.'

'You weren't happy here.'

'No,' said Sebastian simply.

A young man came running to them, clapping Sebastian on the back. 'Look here, you slow top, we've been waiting on you this past hour to get a bit of a card game going. But it seems you have abandoned us for this girl you've charmed. Are you making her an offer of it then, planning to make it a double wedding?'

Sebastian was staring at the fellow — a boy, really, of about eighteen — with a befuddled expression on his face. 'I'm sorry, sir, but you appear to have mistaken me for someone else.'

'Oh, you hare-brained codpiece,' the boy said, slapping Sebastian on the back. 'What are you going on —'

And then he finally looked at Sebastian's face and immediately pulled away. 'Pardon me, sir, it is just that you have a remarkable resemblance to — excuse me,' he said, running off.

Catherine stifled her laugh as best she could to avoid further attention, but she could hardly stop her shoulders from shaking.

'What a mess,' Sebastian said under his breath. 'I hope you aren't offended by his crass words.'

'Don't be silly. There really is a Talbot look, isn't there?' said Catherine. 'Dark and imperious.' Though she wouldn't say it, what appeared in the others as arrogance was transformed in Sebastian by a humor and a readiness to laugh at himself. In other words, he was more handsome than the lot of them.

'We are a charming bunch, aren't we?'

'Who was that boy?' she asked.

'My favorite cousin Cornelius. One of the few members of the family I will stay in touch with.'

'He recognized you.'

But then, with a sharp inhalation, Sebastian grabbed her hand and pulled her through the nearest door and into an alcove. Their backs against the wall, Catherine was closer to the doors. Not at risk of being recognized, she turned to glimpse what had so alarmed Sebastian.

'Don't,' said Sebastian.

But she couldn't resist. Ophelia was striding across the courtyard, surrounded by a gaggle of brown-haired girls, golden head standing out in the crowd. Across the space stood Sebastian, Cornelius now by his side, so young it twisted something inside Catherine. He was watching Ophelia, clearly in love, and she looked up and smiled at the handsome boy.

Behind her entered James and his retinue. He was almost twice his bride's age.

Ophelia and Sebastian exchanged another furtive glance before they all headed off in different directions.

FINALLY, once they were certain the revelers had all cleared out of the courtyard, Sebastian and Catherine broke free of the crowds and headed toward the library. They strolled on in as leisurely a manner as possible. The library was up a flight of wooden stairs. And as they turned the corner, Catherine's heart was in her mouth.

But fortunately, this wing of the house was empty with everyone in the dining hall below. Sebastian went through the wooden doors of the room and shut them, shoving a chair under the knob to block it off to intruders.

'Do you know what we're looking for?' asked Catherine.

'One thing is staring you right in the face.'

She followed his gaze to a hanging on the wall. It was a beautiful hand-drawn map of the world.

'This is it?' asked Catherine.

'I think so.' He removed it from the wall and took it out of the frame. He rolled it up and handed it to her, and she put it into her reticule. He stowed the empty frame behind a bookcase.

'There are few other items that I thought might come in handy,' he said, leading her through the room to a cabinet filled with all sorts of objects.

Sebastian opened it and pulled out two of them — a silver box and an ivory letter opener.

'And that's it?' asked Catherine. 'We just waltz in and take these things?'

Sebastian gave her a confused look. 'Should it be more complicated? There is one more thing,' he said, browsing one of the massive bookshelves that lined the room. 'Here it is,' he added, grabbing a brown leather folio. 'Be careful with this one.'

The feeling of dread wouldn't leave her as Sebastian removed the chair from under the door, opening it just a crack at first.

'We seem to be alone,' he said.

Catherine put the other objects in her reticule, clutching it tightly to her chest as they left the room.

Back downstairs, they first checked if they could slip out the way they came in, but James and his friends were in the courtyard.

'They'll go in now for the feast,' said Sebastian.

'Shall we wait?'

But just then James threw a look in their direction, Sebastian tugged at his cap and took off down a corridor. Catherine held his arm and squeezed.

'Don't run,' she whispered, 'we'll seem suspicious for sure.'

He slowed down. She was confused as to their orientation, but Sebastian had assured her that there was only one way through the secret passages, and she couldn't get lost even if they were to get separated.

They passed by a group of playing children, and Sebastian ushered her through a pair of wooden double doors at the end of the hall and into a small study. They closed the doors behind them and crossed the room to a wall of bookshelves. Catherine kept watch as Sebastian felt along a shelf and, with the press of a button, the entire case swung forward just the tiniest bit.

Sebastian frowned. 'It's stuck.'

With a solid tug, Sebastian got it open just enough for her to slip through.

As Catherine passed into the passage behind it, she heard a voice.

'Who's there?'

NINETEEN

SEBASTIAN SPUN AROUND. HE leaned on the door to shut it the rest of the way as gently as possible.

It was Ophelia. Of course it was. Who else could smell trouble wherever it was and twist it to her own ends?

'Pardon me, madam,' he said, bowing low. 'I chanced upon this room and have been fascinated by the beautiful objects within. I apologize if I am trespassing.'

'No, it is I who should be sorry,' she said with a shy smile. 'The castle is overrun with guests at the moment and I am new here too in a manner of speaking.'

He nodded. 'New, but not a stranger. My name is Tobias Wentworth. And I have arrived from London just this morning. You are, I believe, none other than the bride to be?'

Ophelia blushed. He remembered that look well, remembering too just how empty of meaning it was. For to blush, truly, you needed to feel shame or embarrassment, two emotions she did not possess.

She gazed at him intently, and it was all he could do not to squirm. 'You look quite familiar.'

He smiled a brittle smile. She'd seen him in Bath; would she remember that?

'The family resemblance is remarkable, isn't it? Yes, you bear a strong resemblance to my husband-to-be.'

'How strange. It has been some time since I have met James. I'll be happy to see this resemblance for myself.'

She took a few steps toward Sebastian.

'I suppose it isn't a surprise, though. We *are* related after all.'

She stopped. 'Oh, is it? In what manner are you related?'

'A distant one, to be sure. We can explore it all at length during the stay here. I wouldn't like to keep you longer than I already have.'

'It is no bother. I must confess to being rather at a loss, not being much accustomed to such large gatherings or grand spaces.'

'Your family is smaller.' It was true. She was an orphan. A broken, rich orphan whose wedding had been arranged by an aunt who hadn't considered an age difference of almost twenty years between her ward and a duke's second son to be a deterrent.

'In my experience, one's wedding is not for the bride and groom to enjoy, but for everyone else.'

She cocked her head to one side. Sebastian knew that look too. She was measuring him up.

'So how did you say you were related? You must come with me and meet my husband.'

'I will confess to being rather weary myself after a long journey and would prefer to rest a little before venturing out into the party.'

'I see.'

'Yes, it was a pleasure meeting you,' said Sebastian, heading for the door.

'You are that man, aren't you?' she said suddenly. 'The one they're looking for? The man from Bath. I saw you there.'

She took a step back, blocking his way out.

'I don't know what you're talking about,' said Sebastian. 'I have been nowhere near Bath.'

'Lies. And it was you who gave away the signet ring to those scoundrels who appeared here and made such a nuisance of themselves. How did you get the family ring?'

She raised a hand as though to summon help, but there was no one to see her. In a flash Sebastian crossed the room and was by her side — if she made a move, he'd lunge for her, and she knew it.

'Why don't we just work this out between us,' he said. 'There is no reason for alarm. I mean you no harm.'

Her eyes widened a fraction. 'What are you doing in this house? How did you get in?'

'I simply walked in through the front door.'

'What is your intention in coming here?'

'My intentions are none of your concern. And if you let me go quietly, I needn't disrupt your wedding.'

'Let you go quietly? How perfectly ridiculous. Empty your pockets right now.'

He flashed a sardonic smile. 'Is it your fear that I have come here to steal?'

'Why else would you be here?'

'Money is not the only motivation for a man,' he said, barely containing his scorn. 'There are some things more valuable than coin.'

'Show me your pockets or I scream,' she said.

'You are hardly in a position to make threats, and these walls are rather too thick for that one to help you much. But I will show you anyway as a gesture of good faith.' He turned them out.

'Your jacket.'

He clenched his jaw as he took off his jacket and handed it to her. She went through the pockets, but still did not seem satisfied.

'You are looking at me as though I may have put some family heirlooms down my trousers.'

Ophelia did not pretend to be outraged. 'It would be a good way of stealing things now, wouldn't it?'

'It appears we are at an impasse for you can't possibly mean for me to strip.'

She looked him up and down clinically. 'No, there's no need for that. As long as you tell me who you really are.'

He lifted his chin. The Ophelia he remembered hated nothing more than diffidence. 'If that is what you insist upon, here you are. I am your husband's bastard brother, which might explain the similarity in our countenances. I am the son your future father-in-law didn't claim. I am not sure how well you know the man to whom you owe your entire future happiness, but I can tell you he has exacting standards. He has no time for weakness in anyone, including himself. And, as living proof that the great Duke of Westlake too can slip up, they never allowed me to step inside the gates of the manor. Once I had been thrown out, that is.'

'They threw you out?'

'Yes, I was born here as my mother was the maid.'

Ophelia flinched.

Sebastian was very young when it happened, but the story was the unfortunate truth. He had a vivid memory of that boy, Joseph, and could only hope that his father had taken care of him, wherever he was. Sebastian had tried to track him down during his brief tenure as Duke, but before he knew it, he had been fighting for his own life and had to abandon the search.

'You see why raising an alarm about my presence here might not be such a good idea?'

There was almost a moment where he could see her calculating coldly the risk of upheaval versus the awareness that this man might pose a threat to the family.

'What prevents me from calling the guards on you, or even my husband, and having you taken away?'

'Because if you do, I promise I will make a claim today that will embarrass your entire family to be and ruin your wedding, perhaps endanger it altogether.'

Ophelia walked up to him. 'Your bastard birth will not cause such a stir, surely?'

'My claim will not be about my identity. It will be about your conduct.'

Her face dripped with scorn. 'Whatever do you mean?'

'I did a bit of my own homework before coming here, you see. I know all about you and Sebastian.'

She was impassive, but he knew her every expression. And it was time to dig in.

'I know what you are doing with that boy, and what's more, I know why. So if you want your little scandalous secret to stay safe, I'd keep my pretty little mouth shut and go on my way.'

Her chest rose and fell, her face ashen. At last she gave an almost imperceptible nod. Sebastian opened the doors and calmly walked out of the room.

TWENTY

CATHERINE RAN THROUGH THE secret passageway as fast as her feet would carry her. It was just as Sebastian had described: there were a few cracks between the stones to let some shards of daylight in, barely illuminating the way before her. But the walls felt as though they were closing in on her with their rough surface. Twice she slipped, the floor slick and damp. She scrambled up and continued on, eager to put as much distance between herself and what she had just witnessed behind her.

Ophelia was beautiful, to be sure. But all else about her seemed wrong. In the way she was sizing up Sebastian; the way she measured everything he said.

It had almost been as though she could sense Sebastian's lies. It had made Catherine uncomfortable; seeing her naked desire up close.

For it was clear that Ophelia was drawn to Sebastian, and that Sebastian was drawn to her in return. The way she took him in, the way she came so close to touching him. A stranger in a strange house, on the eve of her wedding. It was positively chilling.

And then Sebastian had used her — and his own — past against Ophelia, and it had worked. Catherine had been right in suspecting young Sebastian's relationship with Ophelia had already begun, even before the wedding, in some form. She only hoped that Ophelia had been scared away from calling for help because she did not know what had become of Sebastian once he had left that room.

Catherine clutched her bag close as she finally approached what seemed to be the end of the passage. There were two shallow steps that led to the doors in the corridor's ceiling. She reached for the latch and pulled.

It wouldn't budge.

As she fought off the icy grip of panic, she worked it with fumbling fingers. Making no progress, her arms aching, she forced herself to sit down on the cold ground until she took a breath or two and then tried again.

In the tiniest of increments, she gained some traction. And then, at last, it sprang open.

As the relief rushed through her, she had to restrain the urge to throw the doors back. Because it was all too possible that there would be someone on the other side who might see her emerge.

She took three deep breaths and then swung the door out, climbing out of the passage, her lungs filling with fresh air.

She was mostly alone on the outside of the castle. There was a couple wandering in the woods, hoping perhaps for privacy themselves. They registered her sudden appearance, but then quickly averted their eyes.

Catherine followed the path back to the stable and, letting herself in, was relieved to find the horses were still there. She closed the door behind her and then began her wait for Sebastian.

He entered about ten minutes later, his face a dark, stormy cloud. 'Let's go.'

'And where do you propose we go exactly?' she said, her voice coming out angry and shrill.

Sebastian looked at her with a frown. 'Out of here, where do you think?'

But after what she saw, she was in no mood to comply. 'What was that back there?'

'We almost got caught. What did it look like?'

'Or was it you got precisely what you wanted? You came here to meet Ophelia, didn't you?'

He exhaled, closing his eyes. 'You are being ridiculous. Get into the carriage now.'

'No, you told me I must not seek my father, but you are happy running around in the playground of your past, trying to relive something that can be yours no more.'

'You think that's what happened back there?' he spat. 'Let's get out of here now, we'll talk about this later.' He grabbed her by the arm, opening the carriage door with his free hand.

'Let go of me,' she said, wrenching her arm away.

'Stop it, Catherine. You don't know what you are talking about.'

'I want to go. And I don't want you to come with me.'

'So you mean to leave me here, with no means of getting back to my world?'

'I'll take you back right now. Find me a bridge, anything tall. I'll take you, as I've told you, time and again.'

Just then Catherine heard the creak of the barn door opening. She swung around and felt the ground shift beneath her.

It was her would-be kidnapper from the beach in Portishead. He sized them up with a grin.

'Well, well, well. Fancy seeing you two here.'

Sebastian turned to her. 'Now,' he whispered, 'do it now. Let's go up the stairs there.'

She stole a glance at the loft above them and realized what he meant. It was utter insanity.

'I think we need water,' she hissed.

'What do you mean, you think? You don't know how this works?'

'No, I've made it pretty clear that I don't.'

The barn was a giant, cavernous space, and the intruder was still standing by the gate. They'd have time — just — to run up the ramshackle wooden steps and jump down over the haystack.

Catherine and Sebastian raced to the corner and up the stairs.

'Where do you think you two are going?' said the man quizzically, arms crossed before him.

'Aim for the hay,' Sebastian said. 'At the very least, we won't break our necks.'

'We'll just have this man think we're crazy.' She pulled the medallion out of her bosom. And he did the same with his.

'Ready?' he asked, looking her in the eye, wrapping his arms around her as she inserted the dagger into the body of the bird.

'Ready,' she said. She thrust the pieces together, and he propelled them away from the banister.

'What in God's name!' the brigand exclaimed.

As they fell, there was no slowing of time. They simply crashed headlong into a pile of hay that was far flatter and far less bountiful than it had appeared.

'Ouch,' said Sebastian. 'Are you okay?'

Catherine glared at him, but then, despite everything, they both began to laugh.

But then they saw the frowning face of the kidnapper looming over them, and they scrambled up.

'I hope my family showed you some famous Talbot hospitality?' said Sebastian, dusting off his jacket.

He grunted. 'You got us into a bit of hot water, you did.'

Sebastian pulled a shocked face. 'Don't tell me they didn't honor my promise and pay you for the ring?'

He held up his hand, ring still upon it. 'The only payment we got was a world of pain. Just as you had planned.'

Sebastian caught Catherine's eye and gestured to her that she should get into the carriage. But she was hardly prepared to cower in the carriage while he took on this man.

'And we met the Duke of Westlake's son, and he didn't look at all like you.'

'Oh, well. What is a little lie between friends? Let us part now, shall we?'

Just then the tall man, the muscle of the party, entered and took the scene in with delight.

'You would have figured by now,' said Sebastian with growing alarm, 'that you have more or less gotten what I'm worth out of that family. That ring was all I had, and they gave you nothing for it, which means you have nothing more to gain by hurting us.'

'That's a pretty carriage you've got there,' said the leader. 'We could do with a carriage, couldn't we, Smith?'

'You're asking for the one thing I can't give you,' said Sebastian.

'I thought that was your wife!'

Sebastian took a swing at him and missed, the taller man lunging at him from the side. Sebastian got out of his way, but there was only so long he'd be able to hold out against the two of them. Catherine desperately searched the barn for something she could use, her eyes landing on a pitchfork in the corner. She quietly ran to get it, hoping she wouldn't call attention to herself. Sebastian had seen her and was drawing them away from her.

Catherine grabbed the implement and flipped it around so the sharp tines were tucked safely away, holding it by the handle and swinging it over her head, hitting the bigger man on the back with a crack.

He slid to his knees, groaning in pain. The other one swung around to see what had happened and Sebastian wasted no time grabbing him from behind.

'Quick! Get something to tie them with!' he said as he wrestled the man to the ground.

She struggled to find anything except copious amounts of hay, till she spotted a rein attached to an old saddle hanging from the wall. She cut it on the pitchfork and rushed it over to Sebastian.

'Let's hope that none of their colleagues are waiting for us outside,' said Catherine as Sebastian bound the men.

'You won't be needing this then,' he said, grabbing his ring from the man's finger, who let out a howl of rage.

They then jumped into the driver's seat of the coach. With a crack of his whip, Sebastian raced the horses out of the barn.

Twenty-One

BY THE TIME THEY reached the nearest town, it was evening. They went to a small inn Sebastian was familiar with, where he secured the top floor with two bedrooms and a sitting area. The bed was comfortable, but sleep was fitful, her body aching and her mind on the man sleeping in the next room.

And then there was the worry about what was to come next. Instead of tossing and turning any further, she rose with the sun, stretching her sore muscles. Taking both maps out of her bag, she sat with them side by side.

Her map was an art student's copy of the image she had discovered back in New York. Now believed to have been created by none other than Tibeau himself. It was drawn in a confident hand in black ink, painted in fairly standard colors — brown for land, blue for water.

The map they had pulled from the Westlake wall was far more vibrant and whimsical, with bright greens and purples and rounder, less precise edges and no labels or markers on it at all.

She couldn't work out what Sebastian had found connecting these two.

She pulled out the leather folio next. It held together a loose sheaf of aging paper, covered in tiny writing and scribbles. She tried to read it but couldn't even figure out what language it was all written in, leave alone understand what it meant.

Unable to make any headway, she turned her attention to another problem her increasingly light reticule made clear: her dwindling funds. If they didn't find a cheaper way to live and travel soon, it would wring her dry before they even reached anywhere close to the treasure.

She heard Sebastian stir in the outside room and realized that she could not avoid him for much longer. She opened the door and saw him sitting there.

It was as though nothing had really happened, despite their kiss, despite Ophelia, despite their endless mess. His eyes raked over her. She was wearing the chemise she slept in, hair open. He'd seen her in all manner of dress by now, owing to their frequently cramped quarters, and she couldn't work up the energy to put up a show of false modesty that morning.

He noted the maps in her hands. 'I see you've been busy.'

'I can't make head or tail of them in conjunction with each other or apart. What makes you think these two even go together?'

'In part family lore. And in part hunch.'

'Start with the lore, please.'

'This was supposed to be part of the chest that came back from that ill-fated journey. After your ancestor had his way with mine, several of Tibeau's fellow journeymen were kind enough to send his belongings back to his family. This was amongst them.'

'And the medallion around your neck wasn't?'

'Not that I know of,' said Sebastian. 'I discovered it in a dusty corner of that same library that I took you to.'

This struck her as more than a little odd. 'It was just lying around for a child to discover — the key to turning back time?'

He grinned. 'If you put it that way. Not so different from our boy Ferdinand. Anyhow, the map was one of Tibeau's last possessions.'

'And it was framed and put on that library wall, despite generations of treasure hunters that came after him?'

'Yes, because it appeared to be meaningless. As you may have noticed, there is no writing on it, nothing to show its purpose.'

'And what about these other objects?' she asked, holding up a sheaf of brittle papers.

'His notes from the voyage.'

'I can't make head or tail of them, either.'

'Yes, I know.'

'You've tried to read them before?'

He nodded.

'Yet you claim to be the only one in the family with no interest in the treasure?'

'I never said I wasn't curious,' he said with a smile.

'And what about these?' said Catherine, pulling out the objects he had given her to put into her bag: a letter opener and a silver pillbox.

He looked at her, eyes gleaming. 'I haven't been exactly pulling my weight on this expedition.'

'This letter opener is going to save us from the poorhouse?'

'Yes, because it was once part of Anne Boleyn's trousseau.'

She raised her eyebrows, looking at it in an all-new light. 'Okay. But how are you going to prove such a thing?'

'Don't you worry about that. I know people.'

'You know people in 1831 who will buy priceless artifacts from you?'

'As a matter of fact, I do. Because these are the same people who will buy artifacts from me in 1845, and '51, and I am sure further into the future, if I ever get there.'

'You can't go to people who might recognize you; we've already been through this.'

He grinned. 'I know, which is why it is you who will be going.'

'Me? I know nothing about fencing ancient artifacts!'

'It is all quite straightforward.'

'This is crazy. How much could this even be worth?'

He took it from her, turning it over in his hand. 'To the right person, maybe fifty pounds. Maybe more? The letter opener is made from ivory from Botswana, with a handle inlaid with sapphires from China, and has passed through the hands of no fewer than three British monarchs.'

'All of them wife-killers?'

'Only one of them.'

'What a relief. But how will we figure out our next stop? The treasure should arrive any day now, and it will take us days to decipher this map, if at all it is possible.'

'With those papers, I hope to have better luck than that.'

'Where do we need to go to pawn this thing?'

'Salisbury. That's where my man is.'

'Your future man.'

'My future man can well be your current man.'

'If we're going to go to Salisbury, I have an idea to buy us some time. We should go stay with Eliza.'

He nodded. 'That's not a bad idea.'

'High praise, coming from you.'

There was a knock on the door. The maid had arrived with their breakfast and tea, and the two of them fell upon it hungrily. Bellies full, Sebastian's gaze fell on the pendant around her neck.

'Why do you think it didn't work when we fell from the loft?'

She sighed. 'I don't know. Perhaps it wasn't a long enough drop? Or perhaps it was the absence of water?'

'So when we are ready to go back, we have to be by a body of water?'

She stopped for a minute. 'Yes, it was always a part of Ferdinand's story.'

But not on her trampoline trip with her father.

'Catherine, is there something you aren't telling me?'

'No, nothing. Now tell me about this man of yours.'

'His name is David Cromwell,' Sebastian began. 'I met him just a handful of years after this when I began my career as an antiquarian. We were in Egypt, where an archeological dig was underway, and several highly anticipated artifacts were expected to be uncovered.'

In that moment, Catherine was utterly jealous of Sebastian. He had taken his disaster and had made the world do his bidding. She was in awe, not because she wanted him, but because she wanted to be him.

Or perhaps it was a bit of both.

'We got into a bidding war over them. And he seemed impressed by my knowledge of history and dealings with the archeological team. Soon after, Cromwell became too ill to venture much farther afield than the continent. So I would acquire them for him and sell them to him at a discounted rate over what I might get from other buyers, in return for his funding my expeditions.'

'I've been to your house, remember — you hardly seem like you needed his help.'

'In the early days after I left Westlake, I had nothing. That didn't last long, though, thanks to a few particularly lucrative trips.'

'Have you been to any of the places frequented by our ancestors — India, Burma, Mauritius?'

'No. But to Egypt and Shanghai and Brazil. There were approximately fifteen, or twenty such expeditions between the years of 1840 and 1851. When you met me, I had just come back from Greece.'

And in between, he had a short stint as duke, from which his uncle and Ophelia ousted him. Which he had no inclination to speak of. 'You have other buyers now?' she asked.

'Yes. Private collectors, big and small.'

'You are still in touch with Cromwell?'

'Oh yes, he still demands I show him everything I bring in. He's a genuine lover of antiquities.'

'An honest man?'

Sebastian flashed her a wicked smile. 'Honest is very much in the eye of the beholder. There is nothing a man like Cromwell wouldn't do if he found an object he truly wanted. But I would say he is the safest pair of hands for something like this.'

'And why is that?'

'Because he is not a schemer. He will see something of value, and give you a fair price for it, unless there is some competition driving it up. And there is one more thing.'

'What is that?'

'He has a penchant for a pretty face.'

Catherine rolled her eyes. 'Oh, thank you very much for sending me into the lair of some sort of ass!'

'Not an ass. He will simply be charmed by you.'

'Does this mean you find me charming, Sebastian?' she said, feeling herself flush.

He laughed. 'Despite your best efforts at the Crystal Palace, you are a horrible flirt, Catherine.'

'What! I did just fine, didn't I?'

'You did fine because you are a beautiful, intelligent woman; not because you batted your eyelashes at me like a hummingbird might flap its wings. I never know why women think that is attractive.'

'Neither do I. But it has ensnared a man or two.'

He gave her a dark look. 'Not men. Boys like William and Thomas.'

She threw a napkin at him.

He grabbed her wrist, sending a stab of desire through her. Their eyes locked, but then he abruptly let go, as if remembering himself, to her disappointment.

'What I mean is, Cromwell will be swayed by your many charms without holding your sex against you.'

'What is that supposed to mean?'

'Has it escaped your notice that 1831 is no place to be a woman?'

'It's not that different from 1851, if you ask me,' said Catherine.

'That unfortunately may be the case. But Cromwell is different.'

'I thank you for taking such good care of my modesty.'

Sebastian shot her another look that made her cross her legs.

'Okay, so that gets me through the door. Then how should I proceed?'

'It's quite simple. You show him the letter opener and tell him its provenance.'

'What is that precisely?'

'It came with the title of Westlake.'

'And if he asks me how I came upon it?'

'Men like Cromwell know better than to pry. Most people selling unique objects will not lay out their entire history to him.'

'But he'll need to know that it's authentic.'

'Yes, that he will. For that, you tell him you were referred to him by Stuart Johnson.'

'The inventor whose house we went to?'

'Yes, he too is a collector, which is how I met him.'

'How do you know he will go for it?'

'Because in the year 1847, I saw it in Johnson's possession.'

Her eyes widened. 'Can this really be how it got into his hands?'

Sebastian looked as awestruck as she felt. 'It can,' he said. 'This artifact was noticed missing a month after the wedding. There was quite an outcry later.'

He looked as though he was remembering something.

'What is it?' she asked.

He shook his head. 'Nothing.'

'Not nothing.'

He closed his eyes briefly. 'I remember a conversation at the breakfast table, just after my uncle and Ophelia had returned from their honeymoon.'

'You think she worked it out then that it was you who took it?'

'It's possible, isn't it?'

She clapped her hands to his surprise. 'Don't you see? That's a good thing! Everything we do that advances us toward our goal without changing the past is a step in the right direction. If it's happened before, it will happen again.'

CATHERINE WALKED DOWN THE cobblestoned road to the small, nondescript shop front that Sebastian had described. There was a wooden sign over the door that read 'Cromwell & Sons'. She had it on good authority that there were no sons involved. But the sign and name conferred an air of respectability Cromwell had sought.

'It sounds more and more like your friend Cromwell may actually be a thief,' Catherine had said on hearing these revelations.

'No more a thief than I am,' Sebastian had replied.

Catherine had bitten her tongue on this subject.

But now she realized she was wrong. She entered the room piled high with all manner of treasures, from carved wooden console tables to ornate oriental mirrors to stuffed monkeys to tiger-skin rugs.

Behind the desk at the far corner of the dark room was a tiny man. He already looked as antique as any of the surrounding objects. Catherine approached, making sure the awe on her face was quite clear. It was no effort really, it truly was a remarkable shop.

Cromwell rose to his feet with a little bow of greeting as Catherine approached. 'How may I help you?' There was a twinkle in his eye behind steel-rimmed spectacles, and she couldn't help but smile in response.

'I hoped that you'd look at something for me.'

'Please, take a seat,' said Cromwell, waving her into the chair across the desk from his. 'Before we begin, if I may, you don't sound like you are from here?'

'I am visiting from America,' she said. 'And that is part of the problem that brings me here.' She pulled the letter opener from her reticule. 'Stuart Johnson said you might be the man to help me.'

'Johnson sent you, did he?' His curiosity was piqued.

'I have an object of great value to my family and I have been told it is of great value in general.'

He indicated she should put it on the desk before him with a small tap. She placed the letter opener before him, and his eyes ran over it. 'How unusual,' he said.

'It is made of African ivory and on the handle are sapphires from China.'

'That I can see. It's the carvings which are so very intricate.'

'Made on special order for Ann Boleyn. My father had it from the Westlake family.'

'Oh, that is very interesting.' He couldn't contain himself any longer, picking it up and inspecting it with a magnifying glass. 'I must know a little more about how this object entered your family,' he said.

Catherine silently cursed Sebastian.

'My father was friends with the Duke of Westlake, and he gifted this to him as a token of his regard.'

'Are you quite certain there aren't more such artifacts that accompanied it? You could be sitting on quite the treasure chest.'

'It is the only one I know of. The Talbots may have more.'

He put the letter opener down and studied her face. 'It must be quite difficult to part with an object so irreplaceable.'

She nodded. 'But there is a time and place for treasuring a thing of beauty and a time for survival. And I'm afraid that the time has come to place survival first.'

'My dear lady, I wish there was something else I could do to help you apart from take this off your hands. But if it truly be the case that money is of the utmost importance, I will offer you twenty-five pounds for it.'

Catherine clenched at the paltry sum. 'Sir, surely there is something more that you could do? I was given to believe I could expect up to seventy pounds.'

His eyes widened with a surprise she hoped was contrived. 'Who has given you such an outrageous number?'

'I had it valued in America, and Mr. Johnson concurred.'

'I hold Johnson in high regard, but I feel that in this case, he was mistaken. However, I could go up to forty pounds.'

'Make it fifty and we have a deal,' said Catherine.

Cromwell smiled. 'Nature has bestowed you with both intelligence and beauty in equal measure. We have a deal.'

He stood up and walked over to a small cabinet on the other side of the room, unlocking a drawer and producing a bag of coins.

He handed it to her along with another object he pulled out of his pocket.

It was a little black box. As black as jet.

She looked from it to Cromwell. 'What's this?'

'Stanley said to expect you. And that I should give this to you once you arrived.'

Her heart dropped to her stomach. 'Stanley? There must be some mistake.'

'There is no mistake.'

'When was he here?' she asked, looking around, as though he might still be in that little shop, another wonder squirreled away by Cromwell.

'Six months ago. He had come in to sell me a trifle.'

'What was it?'

'A dinosaur bone from America. Quite remarkable. It has gone into my personal collection.'

'Can I see it?' she asked, heart pounding.

'He said you'd say that, and that I should tell you not to bother; that what you are seeking lies in this little box.'

She stretched out a trembling hand. 'Thank you.'

TWENTY-TWO

THE SERVANT LED THEM to a stately sitting room with windows that opened onto a sprawling garden. It was nothing compared with the Westlake estate, but Thomas and Eliza Franklin lived well.

'Sebastian,' said Catherine, 'be nice.'

He tried to look offended. 'Have you known me to be anything but nice?'

'Do you really want an answer to that?'

Footsteps pattered down the hall and Eliza burst upon the room.

'Catherine, you came!' she said, throwing her arms around her.

After a moment, Catherine pulled away, her hands on Eliza's shoulders. 'I'm so sorry to arrive unannounced like this. We didn't have time to write.'

'Think nothing of it. You are most welcome here, and most dearly anticipated. Judith, Thomas, and I have been talking of little else than our wonderful time together at Bath, short though it was. And we were trying to decide when you would come. We hope you will be with us for a while?'

She shot a look at Sebastian.

'We are uncertain how long we are to remain in the area,' said Sebastian.

Catherine clasped Eliza's hands. 'But we do so dearly want to spend some time with you before we leave.'

'No, you must not talk about leaving while you are only arriving! I will not hear of it. But you must be tired after your journey. Let me show you to your room. I will fetch Judith and Thomas for tea in an hour?'

CATHERINE AND SEBASTIAN HAD not discussed what happened at Cromwell's shop in any kind of detail. Now in the safety of their friend's charming guest room, Catherine placed her newest belonging on the bed. Sebastian stood over her shoulder as they both stared down at it.

'What do you think it is?' he asked.

'I wish I had a clue.'

'On the face of it,' said Sebastian, 'it's completely innocuous. It might be a decorative item.'

It was a simple disk of hardwood, with the engraving of a ship. On its rim were deep grooves.

Sebastian sighed. 'I think by now we both suspect Stanley is your father. You have an insight into his way of thinking that I don't have. What do you think he could be saying with this?'

'I really can't say. He predicted we would end up at Cromwell's shop. How I do not know. But it can't be unconnected with whatever else we have in our possession right now.'

'You think it connects to the maps?'

'I think it's the only explanation. He left this with Cromwell six months ago.'

'He must have known we'd go there after going to Westlake, with the second map in our possession.'

Sebastian picked the disk up and turned it over in his hand. 'I think it means we are on the right track. These elements must fit together somehow.'

NOT WISHING TO KEEP their hosts waiting, they freshened up and returned to the sitting room. Judith and Thomas echoed Eliza's joy at being reunited, and they quickly made plans for how to spend their time together.

'There's the most beautiful lake that we must visit. It would be the perfect place for a picnic,' said Judith.

'We're expecting another guest tomorrow evening,' said Thomas. 'He's an old friend of the family. And he, too, was traveling through the area. In fact, he's been to your relatives' home for their wedding.'

Catherine felt the weight of their eyes on them both, fists tightly clenched on her lap to conceal the anxiety that swept over her. Peace, it seemed, was not to be had.

'What is his name?' asked Sebastian somewhat sharply.

'John Banville.'

Catherine stole a glance at Sebastian to decipher whether the name meant anything to him. But it did not appear to concern him. So she could only hope he hadn't spotted them while they were at Westlake Estate. Either way, it was a complication they could do without.

After lunch, the women of the party called on friends in the area. Sebastian declined to join them, saying he had some correspondence to catch up on, and Thomas too opted for a siesta.

Catherine, Eliza and Judith rode to their friend Mary's house, a short distance away.

'We told Mary all about our time together in Bath,' said Eliza, 'and she was so disappointed to have missed it. This visit will cheer her considerably.'

'Mary's brother Stephen,' said Judith with a conspiratorial smile, 'has asked our Eliza for her hand not once, but twice.'

'Oh,' said Catherine, 'tell me more!'

'He's a nice man,' said Eliza, 'but very much like a brother to me.'

'It would be a suitable match,' said Judith, clearly not the first time they were having this conversation.

'Oh, Judith,' said Eliza with a little shake of her head. 'I can't be with a man for whom I feel no passion! That can't be what marriage is about!'

'No, perhaps not with your fortune. But he's a good man. And he understands you. What do you feel, Catherine?'

'I don't know him at all, I'm afraid.'

'You and Sebastian seem to have a deep connection,' said Eliza.

She started. 'Oh. I suppose it just happened for us. Despite all the odds, he came into my life and has taken over ever since.'

Eliza nodded knowingly. 'But that's just what I'm looking for! I want passion, not a person to spend the rest of my days with, who I would be happy to ignore in other circumstances.'

'I know that once upon a time, I felt the same.' She thought about her dates with Stuart. Had he been rich and eligible, would she have felt more warmly toward him? She didn't think so. A marriage of convenience would not be for her. She couldn't help but think of the match between Ophelia and James, and all the pain it had caused.

'How long have you been married?' asked Judith.

'It's only been a few months. We wed after a brief courtship.'

'How romantic,' sighed Eliza. 'Just as it should be! A man who understands me but is also passionate about me, a man with whom I can travel the world. Not one who wants to stay in Salisbury for the rest of his days, his only idea of adventure a trip to London in season.'

'Adventure might be a trifle overrated,' said Catherine. 'I think I've had my fill for a lifetime.'

They had reached their friends' house. Catherine was satisfied to stay in the background, listening to their companionable chatter. Mary's brother was perfectly charming and attentive, but Catherine was forced to agree that he seemed utterly boring.

THE NEXT DAY BROUGHT with it rain, and they spent the day indoors. After a night poring over Tibeau's papers and making no progress, Sebastian had stayed back in the room to try again while Catherine played the part of the good guest.

Catherine fought her nerves all day over the imminent guest from the Talbot wedding, but upon seeing him had immediate confirmation that she'd never laid eyes on him before. John Banville had once been an officer in the navy. He had met Sebastian's father and mother through some common acquaintances in town and had been invited to the wedding in such a capacity. He wasn't acquainted with the rest of the family intimately enough to detect Sebastian's lies.

'Do tell us all about the wedding,' Eliza said as Thomas passed around drinks in the parlor before dinner. 'They say it was the social event of the year.'

Banville gave Eliza the details she so craved. 'The wedding was quite the grand affair, almost like a fete besides a wedding. Much of the county was in attendance, and much of London too. And there was one grand dinner where thousands must have been served.'

She was suitably impressed. 'And what of the family?'

'They are a handsome lot, to be sure. But a mysterious lot as well.'

'What do you mean?'

'It appears to be a serious business being a Westlake, as there is a lot of unrest within the family.'

'How so?' asked Catherine.

He shot Sebastian a glance, who waved away his compunctions.

'The groom and his brother the duke do not appear to get on at all and make no secret of it. They have been living together since the death of their parents, and with the age difference being quite vast, James was almost brought up by the duke.'

'Then what could cause this falling out?' asked Judith.

'I can't pretend to guess. Perhaps David could shed some light on the matter.'

Sebastian gave a small shake of his head. 'I have been away for too long to be of help. But from what I understand, it is a rift caused by that thing which causes most family rifts.'

'Love?' said Eliza.

'No,' said Sebastian with a wry smile, 'the other thing.'

'Money,' offered Thomas.

'The groom is a second son. Our lot is not to be envied,' said Banville, with the air of one who knows.

'Who is the heir to the title?' asked Judith.

'The current duke has a son named Sebastian, an only child. Around sixteen, I would reckon. It is a good thing, too, that the line is secure. Because from what I understand, James Talbot is not the sort of man to be trusted with power.'

'Whatever do you mean, John, you must elaborate,' said Eliza, leaning forward.

'I don't think —'

'Don't hesitate on my account,' said Sebastian. 'Having aroused the curiosity of these young ladies, you mustn't disappoint them.'

'Very well then. I have heard that he traveled to India on board a naval ship, calling in a favor from a friend, which is how I learned of this. On his arrival, he traveled to Burma, hoping to trace a family heirloom of some sort.'

They looked at Sebastian, who gave them a brief nod. 'I always thought this tale of a lost heirloom a fiction, but there is such a story.'

'While he was there,' continued John, 'he had quite the reputation amongst the native women.'

'Scandalous to be sure, but hardly unique,' pointed out Thomas. 'By that definition, we should strip half the peers of the realm of their titles.'

Eliza and Judith hid their smiles discreetly.

'Yes, but that's not all. If what I heard is to be believed, he killed three natives and the ruling dispensation did not look kindly on the incident.'

'Killed them!' cried out Catherine.

'Oh dear! How can this not be widely known?' asked Eliza.

'They quickly dispatched him home, and the matter hushed up thanks to his family's influence.'

'That is shocking indeed,' said Sebastian, looking pale. 'Is there any evidence of it?'

'I believe there is amongst the men in the colonies.'

'Was the naval friend who secured his berth on the ship a man by the name of Bently?' asked Catherine.

'Bently, no.'

Catherine felt a wave of disappointment.

'But the privateer with whom James Talbot sailed back to England went by the name of Bently Phillips.'

SEBASTIAN WAS SILENT FOR the rest of the evening. Catherine too found it hard to concentrate on the game of whist being played, and when Judith took to the piano, she wandered over to the window where Sebastian was standing.

'This is massive,' she whispered.

He gave a brief nod of the head. 'Yes, knowing who this captain is gives us an advantage at last.'

'That's not what I meant,' she said. 'If this is the truth about your uncle, and you can prove it, you'll have your dukedom back soon.'

But from his face, Sebastian seemed less than thrilled by such a prospect.

TWENTY-THREE

SEBASTIAN DID NOT SEE Catherine much over the next few days. She had made plans with her friends, and Sebastian was quite happy to stay behind with his thoughts and Tibeau's scribbled notes. Every now and again, she would surface and he'd update her and they'd try to work through the material together. Not only were they having serious trouble decoding Tibeau's writing, but it made very little sense even once he had. Some of them were from his time in Burma, where he seemed to be in the grips of some sort of mania. Figures and drawings and sketches accompanied his scribbles.

One morning, about three days into their stay, Sebastian put the diary away. He was stiff from sitting all day and spending nights on the chaise in the room's corner. He pulled on his boots and headed out for a walk on the grounds.

He'd been walking for some time through the gardens when he found himself in an apple orchard. The dappled sunlight reached the grass, inviting him with its softness. He stretched out underneath a tree. As he did so, he glimpsed in its boughs a harvest juicier than fruit.

'Do you think?' said Catherine, legs dangling from the branch above him, 'that all of this is fated?'

He closed his eyes. 'Not this one again. For one moment can we forget this madness you have visited upon us?'

'I don't believe you answered my question last time.'

Sebastian wanted so badly to reach up and grab the leg dangling above him, to run his finger up it, to make her blush right there in the middle of the orchard. But he answered her question instead.

'I don't believe in fate. We always have a choice. Couldn't you have chosen to not come find me?'

'I rue the day I did not.'

'Those who blame their lives on the heavens are taking the easy way out. If our being here is fated, nothing we do will influence the future. Right?'

'I suppose,' she replied.

'If fate was so powerful a force, why would we have to bother with not messing with the past, as your father so wisely advised?'

'I don't know. I think that is what I am trying to find out. If it's not fate, Stanley is monitoring us closely. He is tracking our movements, figuring out our next steps, and then going back in time and planting the evidence or the signposts or whatever else we need to proceed.'

'That is plausible, given what's happened of late.'

'You said you don't remember a break-in at the Westlake house around the time of the wedding, yes?'

'No, I do not.'

'Do you remember when you found the medallion?'

He held his breath.

'Do you?'

'It was after the wedding,' he admitted reluctantly.

'Just after the wedding?'

He nodded.

'So isn't it entirely possible that it was Stanley who put that necklace in your library?'

'No,' he said with an adamant shake of his head. 'It can't be.'

'But it can, and I believe it is.'

'So you are saying that fate is whatever Stanley — your father — decided for us both, for the purpose he saw fit?'

Her face went through a range of emotions — from wonder to the same fear Jane had seen in their new friend back at the Crystal Palace. But then she seemed to come to some kind of decision, nodding decisively to herself.

'Stand up,' she said.

'Whatever for? The views from here are rather good.'

She glared down at him from her perch. 'Stand up,' she repeated with a laugh.

He did as she commanded, and before he could prepare himself, she had tumbled down from the branch and into his arms, almost taking them both down together.

The sun hit her face and lit her up. 'If you had only used the medallion just now, who knows where we'd be,' he said.

'I don't think this would have been high enough.'

'We really must figure out how that works, if we ever intend to get out of here.'

She shrugged. 'We know enough.'

And suddenly it all made sense. 'You don't have anyone to return to, do you?' said Sebastian.

'No,' she said simply. 'Here might just be as good a place as any, now is as good a time as any.'

These words hit him in a way he hadn't expected. For all of her chaos and dissembling, Catherine was all alone, much like himself, much like Ferdinand from her fairytale.

'Catherine,' he said.

She looked up, the green from the trees making her eyes glint like emeralds.

'I'm going to kiss you now.' The corners of her mouth turned up as he brought his head down.

She tasted of apples and herself, infinitely sweet. Sebastian felt a sense of contentment as she kissed him back.

But then, abruptly, she pulled away.

'That's it!' she exclaimed.

And before he knew it, she had leapt away from him and was racing back toward the house.

'IT'S NOT THE WATER. And it's not the height, though those seem to help,' said Catherine, back in their room, pacing like a caged animal. 'The key is the intent.'

'What are you talking about?' asked Sebastian, out of breath.

'The fairytale about the boy — Ferdinand didn't know where Stanley was, did he? Not really. He didn't even have all the details about how he would have to jump! He just chose the bridge because he meant to kill himself!'

'Okay. So?'

'So the only reason he ended up with Stanley is because he had focused all his intention on it. In the stable at Westlake, we hadn't decided on anything real, we weren't focusing on our destination.'

Sebastian tried to keep up. 'But that can't be true, because when we fell together the first time, I did not know where we were going either.'

'So what *were* you thinking?' Catherine asked, eyes aglow.

'Just that I needed to go with you. Since you had my medallion.'

She rolled her eyes. 'You didn't even know I was going anywhere! You thought you were saving me from a watery death in a puddle!'

He scowled at the memory. 'I suppose. Or perhaps more accurately, I didn't think it through, I just reacted.'

'Exactly, you felt it fully, whatever it was. Panic, fear, all put aside because you grabbed at me. Thinking that you would save me.'

'When you put it that way, you make me sound terribly silly.'

'No, it was actually terribly sweet,' she said with a smile.

He shook his head — who had he become? This woman had utterly bewitched him.

She was pacing again. 'But that's not the point: despite everything, it united us in purpose — I wanted to come here and you wanted to come with me. And that is how we need to get out as well.'

'So any height, no water needed?'

'Well, I think it's less scary to dive into a body of water, especially if it's deep, because there's a chance that you can swim in case it doesn't work. But no, I don't think it really matters.'

'If we only knew a bit more about this alchemist.'

'Did you find any answers in Tibeau's diary?'

'It is all a hopeless jumble. I've made some notes, some things that make sense with what I already know of what happened.'

She sat on the bed, poring over the papers, thinking aloud. 'We want to intercept the treasure from the hands of the officers of the Crown who took it as that will create the least potential impact on our families.'

'If that is what Stanley wanted, this clue,' he said, holding up Stanley's gift to them, 'must apply to it.'

She held up the disk for the millionth time.

'If he wanted me to know what to do, why didn't he just write it in the damn letter!'

She threw the disk onto the bed and stared at the map.

What would her father do? He hadn't written more in the letter to her because he wanted her to figure things out as she went.

But what if he had written to her after all? She held the map from Westlake up to the light.

'What is it?' asked Sebastian.

'How could I be so stupid!' she cried. 'I need a candle.'

There was a taper in the corner of the room, and Sebastian lit it and brought it to her. She held the paper over the flame.

'What the devil are you doing?'

'You'll see.' She moved it around so as not to burn the paper. And slowly, the writing appeared.

'Well, I'll be damned,' Sebastian whispered.

'Invisible ink was a favorite little trick of my father's. He'd leave scraps of paper for me to discover all around the house.'

'How do you do this?'

'It's very simple — you write with lemon juice and the words appear as if by magic when held to a flame.'

She ensured that not an inch of the paper was untouched by the soot from the candle. Finally she held it up. On it was only one word.

'Selsey,' said Sebastian. 'That's a tiny port town close to here.'

She jumped up. 'We must go there then, at once!'

'We shall. Once we have a plan in place.'

She threw her arms around Sebastian's neck, eyes wild.

'Catherine,' he said, 'if you don't take your hands off me, I won't be able to stop this time.'

She tipped her head toward him. 'I don't want you to stop.'

And with that, his mouth swept onto hers. She slumped against him with a sigh.

He wanted to possess her with that kiss, but forced himself to slow down, plundering her mouth at leisure, as though he hadn't been dreaming of this for weeks. He then ran his hands down her neck to her shoulders, his thumbs grazing the milky skin, impossibly soft. His hands meandered down till they cupped her breasts through the cloth and she let out a little gasp.

He turned her around, laying a path of kisses down her neck as his fingers worked the laces at the back of her dress. He got them loose, displaying the corset beneath.

'Insufferable clothes,' he said.

She spun around. 'It fastens in the front,' she whispered, a playful smile on her lips.

He dropped her dress to the floor, untied her skirts and pushed her gently down onto the bed. 'You work on those, then. I have other things in mind.'

He kneeled on the floor in front of her.

She propped herself up on her elbows. 'Sebastian, what are you doing?'

He ran a finger up one leg, slowly, steadily. 'You told me once that being in an open carriage shouldn't stop any mischief worth making. I have dreamed of doing this ever since.'

Twenty-Four

'SEBASTIAN, WHAT ARE YOU doing?' she said, her blood racing. She'd given up on her stays as she was taken over by the rush of feelings.

'You know this would be impossible to do in an open carriage, right?' she laughed, hardly able to recognize her own voice.

He stood up, smiling down at her, his hands still busy. 'What did *you* have in mind when you said that?'

But his hand had worked up to the junction of her legs, and she couldn't quite think anymore.

'I had nothing in mind. I just wanted you to — aah!'

He had pushed her chemise up and was staring down. 'What are these?' he asked huskily.

Catherine shot up as it hit her that Sebastian had just discovered her 1929 underwear. 'They are from home... they are knickers,' she said, face burning.

But he was too busy to notice. 'I like them.' He slid his thumb along the black fabric. 'Lie back down.'

She did as she was told, crying out as he played with her through the cloth, tracing his thumbs up and down, teasing her.

'Open your stays,' he commanded.

She finally got them open, and he slipped the chemise even further up, slowly, seductively, the soft material transformed in his hands. He pulled the cloth taut against her breasts, rubbing slowly from side to side. She arched her back with the exquisite pleasure of it all.

And just then, there was a knock on the door.

'Ignore it,' she said.

But there was another knock, and Sebastian closed his eyes for a moment.

'Stay right here,' he said.

The bed was tucked away in the corner, and Catherine could hear him fling the door open.

'Sorry to intrude, but you asked me, sir, to let you know if there was any trouble in the village. Two men from Westlake arrived earlier today looking for one of their relations.'

'And? Did they get any information?'

'No, but they will be on their way here next, I think.'

'Why do you say that?'

'I heard them, sir. They have orders to go to all the grand houses in the area.'

Sebastian thanked the man and sent him on his way. Then he returned to Catherine, collapsing on the bed beside her, running a hand down her cheek, an angry vein pulsing in his neck.

'My dear, you don't know how much it pains me to say this, but we had better be on our way.'

'What was that about?' asked Catherine.

'I had told the servant to keep an ear out in the village for people searching for us and it seems that they have arrived.'

'Do you think they know you were at the Estate?'

Sebastian shook his head. 'I don't know, but I know this: he won't let us get away so easy again after what happened in Bath. James Talbot hates losing more than anyone else I've met in my life.'

Catherine frowned, and Sebastian took her hands in his. She leaned into him, kissing him, sliding her tongue into his mouth. After a moment, he tore himself away, groaning as he held her at arm's length.

'Much more of this and we won't be getting out of here alive,' he said, his dark eyes boring into her. 'First, we must get to safety.'

CATHERINE WAS SAD TO leave her friends so abruptly. But with no time to lose, Catherine and Sebastian left Salisbury and headed for the port town of Selsey, certain now that it was the landing spot for Christie's ship.

Sebastian, concerned at being spotted thanks to the large number of family members who were now done with wedding festivities and might be in the area, abandoned his fine attire in favor of humble clothing quietly purchased from the footman before departure. There was less need for Catherine to disguise herself, as only Bently could identify her, on top of which she was safely and considerably more comfortably confined to the carriage.

They headed to Selsey at the same slow pace that had been driving Catherine crazy. 'Isn't there a faster way to get there?' she asked at one of their many rest stops.

Sebastian looked at her. 'There aren't trains yet. But we could travel on horseback.'

'Unfortunately, I only know how to ride a little.' She thought for a moment. 'This carriage of ours is rather grand, don't you think?'

'It was the best I could do under the circumstances,' said Sebastian rather stiffly.

'What if we trade it in for a smaller one? Would it make our travel any faster?'

'That depends on the carriage, but it might be more uncomfortable for you.'

'I don't mind, especially if it means we are less likely to be identified. Bently will recognize this carriage from Bath.'

And so, at their next stop, Sebastian conferred with the innkeeper on how he might exchange his carriage for a more lithe one. Half an hour later, he found Catherine again at the eating house. 'Your idea was a good one. I traded our carriage in for a more modern but smaller one and even got a little money in the bargain.'

'Really?' she said. 'I suppose I don't know a lot about carriages.'

He looked offended again. 'That was a coach fit for a queen.'

Catherine understood what Sebastian meant when she bounced around in this lighter, faster carriage. But it was worth it when they arrived at Selsey hours before they would have otherwise. Still, there was little time to find suitable lodgings and the best they could do was a little room above a public house. It was noisy; the door didn't close properly, and it quickly became apparent they would have no choice but to share a bed with no space to stand, let alone for a man to sleep on the floor.

They hadn't discussed the change in their circumstances, but one look at the dank surroundings and it was clear that nothing would happen in that room except sleep — and whether even that would be possible was doubtful, with the racket coming from below.

Exhausted to the bone after a full day's travel, they quickly undressed in the dark and took to their own sides of the bed. Catherine lay there for a minute, wondering what Sebastian would do if she were to reach out and touch him, but before she could decide, his breathing deepened, signaling that he was already asleep.

CATHERINE STIRRED FIRST THING in the morning, and it was with alarm that she noted a very large hand on her stomach. It was attached to a rather heavy arm that held her tight. At first, she lay there, enjoying the feeling of closeness and warmth that she had so craved and yet had so fought against since she had arrived in Sebastian's life.

But then Sebastian moved behind her, burying his face in her hair and taking a deep breath. He let out a soft groan as his hips made contact with hers, pulling her closer, running a hand from her hip to her breast.

And just then, a crash in the hallway, followed by the sound of a substantial mass colliding with their flimsy door and extremely colorful screaming, tore them apart. Catherine froze and Sebastian did some swearing of his own.

'If these bloody Talbots don't kill me, I will die of quite another sort of pain,' he growled.

Catherine turned to him, her body still on fire, smiling against his mouth. She kissed him and yet he pulled away.

'Catherine, dear Catherine. I'll have you, but not like this.'

She wished she could tell him exactly how little it mattered to her that this was against all of Sebastian's rules of propriety. She wanted to reassure him it was okay, but she didn't know how without betraying the very great difference that lay between them thanks to the eras to which they belonged. So all she could do was assure him of her desire.

'You aren't the only one in pain, you know.' She took his hand and put it on her breast. His eyes darkened as his fingers began to move.

And then there was another crash, and this time the body made it through their ruined bedroom door, collapsing on the ground in a heap. Catherine grabbed the blanket close as Sebastian shot up.

'Out!' he bellowed.

The large ruckus had been caused by a small and terribly drunk man, who stood up and stared at him with glazed eyes before continuing on his way.

Sebastian closed the door which would no longer even pretend to lock.

'Time to get out of here,' Catherine said, getting out of bed.

THEY HEADED STRAIGHT TO the docks. Catherine hadn't known what to expect. This town looked tiny; how big could its port be? But the dockyard turned out to be orderly and impressive, an array of vessels of all sizes soon coming into view. Catherine was enraptured by the largest of them, a naval ship that was undergoing repairs, its vast masts scraping the sky.

'Be careful, your pirate's blood is on show right now,' he whispered into her ear. She looked up at him and smiled.

'Can you say you aren't tempted?'

'I cannot.'

She blushed, because it was clear he wasn't talking about the ship.

There was a mad bustle all around them. Men shouting and jostling for space, loading and unloading cargo. There was plenty of trade activity from places as far as Australia and Hong Kong. But as predicted, there was no organized authority, no one to approach. How would they get any actual information? They were far from the days of radio communication, before even telegram, so how would they know when the ship would arrive?

'Sailors have ways of signaling to ships and sending word through faster boats or vessels,' explained Sebastian. 'But it is possible we will simply have to wait and see.'

They spent the next few minutes observing the surrounding activity and then were shooed away by a man carrying a large load on his back and another couple of men pulling a cart.

'Wait here,' said Sebastian.

Catherine tried to stay out of the way as Sebastian went in search of someone who might know something. Then there was a man who all but pushed her off the dock. He walked by without even turning back, shoving her hard with his shoulder. She stumbled and had to grab onto a ship's bow to straighten herself.

'Watch where you're going,' she called out.

The man didn't turn around. His hat was shielding his face, but suddenly she was struck by the sense that she'd seen him before. Before she could follow him, however, the voices coming from directly above her stole away her attention.

'Has the ship from Kallan arrived yet?' a man said.

Her ears immediately perked up. 'No,' replied another. 'I would have sworn they would have reached before us with their large sails.'

'After what that crew has been through, it's a miracle they will get on a ship again with that man at the helm.'

'He's a wild one, that's for sure,' said the first man.

And then they proceeded down the gangway.

TWENTY-FIVE

SEBASTIAN WAS WALKING BACK toward her. Catherine rushed to him instead, grabbing him by the arm and leading him away from the ships.

'Come with me,' she said. She jogged toward the sailors, quickly closing the distance. 'Excuse me, sir, may I please have a word with you?'

They turned around. There was an older man in his fifties, with a face worn by the elements telling of a lifetime spent on the water. His companion was younger and cockier, looking Catherine up and down. The leer didn't get past Sebastian, who put a protective hand on Catherine's back.

'I couldn't help overhearing you speak about a ship that will come in.'

The two men looked at one another. 'What's it to you?' asked the older one.

Catherine revived her most woebegone look. 'I believe my brother is a part of the crew you were speaking of, and we haven't seen or heard from him since he left home. I've come here with my husband all the way from America just to find him.'

Sebastian stepped forward. 'We'd be happy to take you both for a bit of breakfast if you could share with us what you know.'

The two men exchanged another glance and gave a reluctant nod.

'Thank you, gentlemen. My name's David and this is my wife Catherine,' he said, holding out a hand to the older man.

'Jonathan,' he replied, 'and this is young Frank.'

They proceeded down the path, Sebastian and Catherine in their wake. They walked back to the line of shops and businesses they had passed on their way to the dock, entering a pub.

The floor was sticky and Catherine tried not to think about what was on the table they sat at. Sebastian went about ordering food for them all and brought back several tankards of beer.

'Could I ask which part of the world you have arrived from just now?' asked Catherine.

'We've been sailing from the port of Cochin in India and stopped along the way in Mauritius.'

'Is that where the crew you were speaking of were?'

Jonathan shook his head. 'No, we met one sailor who had left and was looking for another passage back to England on Reunion Island. The rest of them were on Kallan Island and there being fewer ships that travel there, he'd had little luck finding another commission.'

'What was this man's name?' asked Sebastian.

Frank shrugged, but Jonathan narrowed his eyes. 'I believe it was Oliver.'

Catherine gave an exaggerated sigh of relief. 'I don't know why I am happy; I suppose it doesn't matter if my brother has defected or not.'

Jonathan nodded. 'I reckon there is little difference between one man stranded on an island and another man stranded on another island in that part of the world. They're all having a rough time of it. What is your brother's name?'

'William.'

The old man lifted his tankard of beer to his lips. 'I hope he reaches you safely.'

'There was trouble you said on his ship?'

'Yes,' he said, 'the very sort of trouble you hope to avoid as a sailor. There has been a near mutiny amongst the men.'

'What befell them?' said Sebastian.

The younger man, Frank, spoke this time. 'Rather ask what didn't befall them. There are actually two crews involved. Which is your brother on?'

Catherine looked at the men in confusion.

'The original crew had been told they were sailing for Mauritius. They left here last year under the command of one Captain Bently.'

She saw Sebastian's grip on his tankard tighten. 'I don't know,' she said with a shrug. 'He sailed from here some time last year.'

Frank nodded. 'Then he'd be with the first crew and you'd be lucky to get him back all in one piece.'

Catherine winced. There was a pause as the older man glared at his friend. Jonathan continued.

'There are very few honest men who'd be willing to set sail for Kallan. There have been talks of curses and witches and much mischief on that island for some years now. So when Bently steered the ship off course, he nearly had a mutiny on his hands. He finally landed ashore only because of the devilish storm that hit them, leaving the ship badly damaged and the men marooned.'

'What was their cargo?' asked Sebastian.

'Well, that was part of the problem, you see. There was no cargo. The men were to sail an empty vessel there, which they didn't mind as long as it hastened their trip, but in the storm they bobbed about like a twig in a typhoon. They landed hard and then were told that they had no right to ask questions about the mission. But it became clear fast that Captain Bently had arrived looking for treasure. Lost treasure. It's one that sailors around those parts are well aware of.'

'Tibeau's treasure?' asked Sebastian.

'How did *you* hear of it?' asked Frank, suspicion writ large across his face.

'We are acquainted with some of the original family. It has ruined them as well.'

Jonathan shrugged. 'It doesn't help to be greedy. Anyhow, the captain was just beginning to get his men back in line when another disaster struck: a fever spread through the men, picking them off like maggots on a wound. The locals forced them into quarantine and dumped the bodies of the dead. That's when the healthy amongst them mutinied in earnest. They were about to send the captain to a watery death when Davy arrived.'

'Who's Davy?' asked Catherine.

'A sailor who has no business at sea,' said Frank.

'He's been hired by someone to rescue the stranded men and complete the voyage,' said Jonathan.

'The men wanted to know who had sent Davy and who was paying for this expedition. They wouldn't accept his authority without promises of action against Bently, and a cut of the treasure when they found it. Finally, they began work repairing the ship, for Davy had arrived on a small boat to make up time, and they'd be stuck on Kallan till they could repair it.'

'Do you know who had commissioned Davy?' asked Catherine.

Jonathan shook his head. 'The men split into teams, one working on the ship and the other hunting for treasure. Davy had brought with him information that Bently had not had.'

'What was it?' Sebastian asked. Catherine could hear the urgency in his voice.

He shrugged. 'It was enough to get the job done. They found the treasure.'

Sebastian and Catherine exchanged a look.

The man's eyes twinkled now. 'Oh yes, they found it. After centuries of men trying and failing, this captain just stumbles across it lying there in the middle of a field, no one around as far as the eye can see.'

'How did they know it was Tibeau's treasure?' asked Sebastian.

'Sitting on top of it was a giant gold bell. As tall as a man, as heavy as a beast. The men grew even more alarmed when they saw it. For this bell is famed to have shipwrecked all who attempted to transport it. They refused to set sail with it.

'Captain Bently tried to take advantage of this fresh round of dissent and lead the men against Davy. It was then that Davy's first mate said that Bently should be tried for his crimes right there and then, and if he were found wanting, they should execute him. Bently's men knew that with their captain dead they couldn't be far behind. The fewer men to share the treasure, the better for the ones remaining. Bently challenged the first mate to a duel to settle matters. The first mate was losing when he jumped off the side of the ship and clean disappeared.'

Catherine could hardly contain herself. A man jumping off the ship and disappearing? It could only mean one thing.

'Where did he go?' asked Sebastian.

'No sign of him. It was as though he had vanished,' said Jonathan.

'Isn't it possible he drowned?' asked Catherine.

'Davy's men looked for him. Nothing. Not a scrap of clothing or the cap on his head,' said Jonathan, thrusting out his chin. 'And that's when talk of Bently practising witchcraft began. Not being altogether stupid, he stole Davy's smaller vessel and made his way back here with what was left of his crew. And that was the last our friend Oliver had heard of him.'

Catherine's eyes were wide. 'That is quite the story. What was the first mate's name?'

'Stanley, I believe it was.'

Her nostrils flared, and she gripped her knees under the table to stay calm.

'And where are they now?' asked Sebastian.

'Before we set sail, we heard they had only a few days' work left. With the size of their sails, I was sure they would arrive before us. The entire way was just the right amount of calm.'

'In that case, they'll be here in a day or two, I would imagine,' said Sebastian. 'Catherine, there is hope you will find your brother soon.'

The two men exchanged a skeptical look, but they held their tongues this time. Clearly they harbored little hope on her behalf that he would still be alive amongst all the bloodshed.

'And I wonder what became of all that treasure,' said Sebastian.

Jonathan shook his head and drained his beer. 'I'd rather be a poor man till my dying day than get a piece of that cursed pile.'

SEBASTIAN PAID THE MEN a small token for their time. Pleased with their lot, they went on their way, leaving Sebastian and Catherine behind at the pub.

'What's on your mind?' asked Sebastian.

Catherine shook her head. It was as clear as day now: Stanley was her father. He was there on the ship, trying to get his hands on the treasure. Or to set it up for them. It was impossible to know how many times he had been here, or on the island. He had moved through time repeatedly in search of the one thing he wanted — but that one thing had not been Catherine.

'We need a plan now,' said Sebastian. 'Any moment now that treasure will arrive, and we have to think about how we will get it away from a dock full of people and a ship full of crew. We can't steal the treasure on the water. It is lunacy to even try.'

Catherine nodded. 'My father has led us here for a reason. He has brought us here for a task and has given us what we need to accomplish it.'

'I think you're right,' said Sebastian, 'which means we need to be ready to intercept the men on the ground. We have one advantage.'

'And what is that?'

'We know who will take the treasure away: James Talbot.'

Catherine frowned. 'That is a bit of a leap, is it not?'

Sebastian looked grim. 'My uncle will double-cross Davy and hand the treasure over to the Crown. He'll use this to one day win himself a dukedom.'

Catherine gasped. 'Sebastian, are you sure?'

'It fits,' shrugged Sebastian. 'Do you know how hard it is to disinherit a peer from his rightful title? It took an act of Parliament for him to get rid of me, with only the flimsiest of evidence that I had tried to kill him.'

'Had you?' she asked softly.

Sebastian looked surprised at the question and then smirked. 'No, I did not.'

She shook her head. 'I don't understand. If he had the treasure, why not just keep it and spare himself the trouble of stealing a peerage from you twenty years from now?'

'Because money was never his object. It started out as a plan for revenge against his brother, and me. This treasure is all the leverage he'd need.'

TWENTY-SIX

SEBASTIAN WENT OUT FOR a walk to clear his head after everything he had just heard. He had for some time now suspected there was more to his involvement in this quest than simply providing the missing piece of Catherine's amulet. There was a definite method to the madness that was Stanley.

He and Catherine were connected of course through generations of rivalry between the Talbots and the Christies, and at first he had thought this was some sort of poetic extension of that, someone's idea of a joke. But could it be that Stanley was providing him with a means of changing his fate? He had no reason to do so, as far as Sebastian knew.

When he returned to the pub, Catherine was waiting outside. 'Where have you been? I couldn't sit in that hole any longer.'

'Hole?' he said with a wry smile. 'That place was undoubtedly Selsey's finest.'

Catherine gave him a funny look. 'Are you sure you're okay?'

Sebastian nodded. 'It's strange how our families have been so caught up in this drama, and I never thought I'd be the one to go down this rabbit hole. The world is so full of treasure that this one held no interest for me. But despite my best efforts, here I am and here you are, and no doubt I will see my uncle again soon enough.'

Sebastian and Catherine headed back to the docks. What Catherine had learned from her research was limited: the ship was to come into harbor, and the customs officials would seize the treasure. Somewhere between Kallan and the Crown's coffers, they would lose the Bell of Dhammazedi again because though the sailors had told them it had been found, no record of this remained. It was possibly already gone, and they could only hope the rest of the treasure was worth the trouble.

There was information to gather about how a large ship might be unloaded. Sebastian found the harbormaster at last, and asked him more questions than he seemed inclined to answer, but they finally learned that the dockyard could accommodate only one large ship at a time, and currently that spot was being taken by the naval ship Catherine had been awed by that morning. He did not know about any ships coming in from Kallan.

Catherine and Sebastian thanked the man and walked to the shade of the five-masted ship. The scale of the vessel brought home the size of their problem. 'If it is only in one spot that they might anchor, this is where we need to be, ready to intercept,' said Sebastian.

'And how will we do that?'

Sebastian grabbed Catherine by the elbow and spun her around so she faced the ships.

'Do you propose we simply load up and get out of here?' she asked.

'No, look at what they are doing with their cargo.'

There were lines of barges in the vessel's shadow.

'You can't mean —'

'Do you have a better idea?'

THEY BEGAN THE JOURNEY back to the hotel, when Sebastian glimpsed a familiar form with a start. He grabbed Catherine again and turned into the first door he could find, which was a tailor's shop. The man behind the counter looked up. 'May I help you?'

'Just looking,' said Sebastian quickly.

'What happened?' she whispered.

'He's here — Bently — I just saw him on the road.'

Catherine swore under her breath.

Sebastian peered around the rack of clothes — all that stood between them and the glass front of the store through which they could easily be seen. He could have sworn Bently had seen them too. As Sebastian waited to see if he would walk by, he heard the tinkle of the shop door opening.

Sebastian's grip on Catherine's arm tightened, and he saw a pair of leather boots on the other side of the clothing rack.

The tailor stepped forward. 'Mr. Burr! What a pleasure! What can I help you with today?'

'I would like to order a gown for my wife,' came the voice that was decidedly not Bently's.

Sebastian and Catherine let out a sigh of relief and saw themselves out of the store cautiously, unsure of what they would find outside.

'We need to get out of the street.' He led her back toward the public house, pushing the door open a crack to check whether it was safe before ushering her in. 'This is moving fast now, and we need a plan.'

They were seated once again in a corner at the back of the room, Sebastian's back to the door, and Catherine keeping watch.

'We know where we need to be now,' she said. 'We know this is the right time — Bently being here is proof of that.'

'And they've chosen this small port over one of the larger ones presumably to avoid attention of the authorities.'

'The question is, how do they go from trying to dodge the authorities to landing straight into their hands?'

Sebastian shrugged. 'That's not a mystery. That is down to the future Duke of Westlake.'

She bit her lip. 'Can we really be sure of that? If you are right, why wait so long? Why not use the leverage while it's fresh to unseat your father?'

'I don't know, maybe he tried. But it doesn't really matter to what is happening at the docks. We don't know exactly when the ship will come in, but neither do they. And Bently is the only one here who has seen us. We can use both these things to our advantage.'

'What do you suggest?'

Sebastian smiled. 'The captain is looking for a man and a woman, right? So what happens if we pose as two men instead?'

Catherine's eyes widened. 'Where would we get such a disguise?'

'It doesn't have to be complicated: I am a man and you can be my page, passing you off as a young boy will be no impressive feat. You are a tiny little thing.'

Catherine rolled her eyes. 'Why thank you.' She sighed. 'I'll need a set of clothes and a pair of scissors. And you will need a giant powdered wig.'

They gathered their supplies and found a new inn, slightly more suitable than the last one. Sebastian had a moment's pause as he set down the scissors. There seemed nothing Catherine wouldn't do to get to the treasure. He had to wonder if he wasn't expecting too much of her, and she wasn't expecting too much of herself.

It was late, and they had no appetite. And then Catherine took to pacing their tiny space.

'Catherine, what's the matter?'

'What if there is another way? What if we were to go to the island before all these crews arrive and look for the treasure there? What happens if we get it ourselves instead of stealing it from these people?'

'How many reasons do you want me to list?' said Sebastian. 'For one, we do not have any idea where it really is apart from a secondhand account of two sailors.'

Catherine shook her head. 'Stanley was with Davy, and the men said they arrived on Kallan with some evidence that Bently hadn't had, which helped them find the treasure with ease. What if that evidence is with us right now? We have the maps, and the disk, if only we could read them properly!'

'Catherine, this was your plan all along — to come to the only place we *know* the treasure arrived for sure and intercept it — and it is a good one. It was you who have been so insistent that we in no way interfere with known historic events. We know this ship is meant to dock here because they have documented it in 1851, we know the Crown will seize it and the only reason we are taking it is because —'

'Because we don't like your uncle or Bently,' she said with a glare. 'It's as simple as that!'

'Well, they *are* both scoundrels and murderers!'

'We aren't stopping any of that, remember?'

'How would we even do that? The bloodshed this treasure has caused is legion!'

'But if we only go there, maybe —'

'Maybe what?'

Catherine stood up again, as restless as a caged animal.

'What are you looking for, Catherine? If you can't be honest with me, at least be honest with yourself.'

She rubbed her eyes before hanging her head in her hands, as though all the fight left her all at once. 'I saw my father today,' she whispered. 'My father is here, and he walked straight by me. I think he pushed me in the way of those sailors, so I'd hear them.'

'Oh Catherine,' he said gently, 'you knew he was watching.'

'Yes,' she said, throwing her hands up. 'He's watching, to be sure that we get the treasure. He left my mother and me for this, he died for this! He has made me — us — into puppets in his hands. The only thing that matters is that we discover the treasure that is so precious to him! And all I want to do is look him in the face and ask him if it was worth it!'

Sebastian crossed the room and put his arms around her, holding her to his chest as her body was wracked with sobs. He held her till they stopped, till she pulled away from him, rubbing at her face again.

'I'm sorry, Sebastian. I thought I knew what I was doing, but now I find myself completely in over my head.'

'It feels like he is just out of your grasp, doesn't it? Like we're chasing a shadow of a man. And perhaps we are.' He smoothed her hair back, stroking its length almost absentmindedly. 'You know, when we were back at Westlake, I so wanted to see my father. When he died, things were difficult between us.'

He looked down at Catherine's tear-streaked face and saw the surprise in her eyes.

'You thought I was there for Ophelia, but she is the last woman on earth I would choose to see.'

'What happened?'

'He was so scandalized by what had transpired between Ophelia and I, we hadn't spoken in years when he died. And then that day, I had the chance to see him. I heard his voice while we were in that alcove; he was just around the corner in the dining hall. But I realized that to look into his eyes wouldn't have helped. And also, what could I say that wouldn't change the trajectory of our lives? What would that mean for me and you, standing there from the future? I am not a religious man, Catherine, but I am a humble one. But if you need to meet your father, that's what we'll do.'

Catherine smiled wanly as Sebastian pushed the hair back from her face and cupped her cheek.

'Time to cut my hair,' she said, voice laden with emotion.

He looked at her with horror. 'I don't think I can do it.'

She grinned. 'Don't worry, I wouldn't trust you near my head with a sharp weapon. Who knows what you might do?'

In about twenty minutes, Catherine's dark curls carpeted the floor of their room. He swept up the evidence and threw it away. If it upset him, she was unperturbed. 'It will do?' she asked, running a hand over the still beautiful mane that ended at her shoulders.

'You don't mind?'

She winked. 'It's hair, it will grow back.'

'You really are one of a kind,' he said. 'And yes, it will do, though a haircut isn't enough to hide your beauty.'

She flushed with pleasure; her gaze warming him inside out. But then she looked down, and there was something in her expression that gave him pause.

'Sebastian,' she said, picking at a button on his coat, 'there is something else I must tell you.'

TWENTY-SEVEN

THERE WAS A KNOCK on the door and they both jumped. Catherine reached for Sebastian.

'Don't open it please,' said Catherine. 'I have a bad feeling about this.'

The knock came again. It was more persistent this time.

'Open up,' came the innkeeper's voice.

Sebastian gave her shoulder a squeeze. 'Whether or not we open it, whoever is on the other side is coming through.'

Sebastian opened the door just a crack, bearing down on it even as he did so. He peered around it, but Catherine could see the innkeeper trying to push his way in. Before they knew it, the door was forced open with a sudden jerk, throwing Sebastian off balance. Catherine leapt out of the way as Sebastian righted himself. It was the man from outside Stanley's house in Bath, Bently's muscle, and he had come with orders to fight.

Sebastian took guard against him, having pulled a knife out of his boot, a knife that Catherine had been for the past weeks completely ignorant of. She looked on with horror as the intruder did the same.

'Who are you?' demanded the innkeeper. 'This man here says you are murderers.'

'Well then, you better hope he's wrong,' growled Sebastian.

The man lunged, swinging the knife at Sebastian's face. But Sebastian was quick too, dodging the blade and taking a stab at the man himself. By now Catherine had been backed into the very corner of their tiny room, with no place to escape.

Sebastian knew it too. With a blow to the man's upper arm, he knocked the dagger out of his hand, sending it scuttling to safety under the bed, from where Catherine grabbed it. The innkeeper fled the room as Sebastian charged at the intruder, knocking his legs out from under him. He fell flat on his back with a loud crack. Catherine looked on in horror, afraid that the man's skull had cracked rendering his accusations against them prophetic, but he seemed only to be briefly incapacitated, already trying to get to his feet as Sebastian jumped on his huge chest and held the blade against his neck.

'Catherine, quick, get some rope!'

She flailed for a moment, no rope in sight, before scrambling to one of her dresses, using the scissors to cut off a sizable stretch of it. She tossed it to Sebastian, who bound the man's hands behind his back. Then she tore off another piece, and he got to work on his legs.

Sebastian wordlessly indicated to her that she should quickly gather their things. She knew he meant only what was most needed: the maps, the disk, and their rapidly depleting money. Once she was done, she went to him, still crouched on the man's back, sweat running down his face.

'Go to the stables,' he mouthed.

She ran down the stairs, past an angry innkeeper who looked poised to go out in search of help. Their time was limited. She was in the stables, where several startled hands watched her burst through the doors. Luckily, Sebastian couldn't be far behind.

But while Catherine was waiting by their own carriage, Sebastian rushed in and went straight to the largest horse in the stable, a tall, already saddled black mare. He grabbed Catherine by the waist and hoisted her up onto the creature, then swung in behind her, to the shouts of the men.

'Tell your bastard of a boss that he can have my carriage and horses as payment,' he yelled as they charged out.

ONCE AGAIN, SEBASTIAN AND Catherine were racing down the road, and all she could do this time was hold on for dear life. The town fell away from them. It was dark and lifeless all around and by the time the horse had slowed they were very much alone, and very much in the middle of nowhere.

'We need a place to stop for the night,' said Sebastian.

'Perhaps a barn, or a pasture.'

There was a small bend in the road, and on the other side of it stood two men. Catherine started as one of them stumbled toward them, before realizing they were merely drunk and unable to stand straight. Sebastian rode past without comment and he didn't speak of stopping again till they had traveled at least another mile.

'It looks like we've hit farmland,' said Catherine. 'Maybe we can seek shelter in one of their homes.'

Sebastian sighed behind her. 'I am afraid our friends may have sent out word for people of our description. It would be too great a risk.'

They passed a house and then another one, all in darkness. Something about the second cottage by the road caught Catherine's attention. She craned her neck to get a better look. 'Sebastian, stop.'

At first she thought she was seeing things, but a second glimpse confirmed it: on the side of the building was the curious shape at the center of Stanley's disk. 'Look at that. It can't be a coincidence, can it?'

They got off the horse, and Sebastian tied it to a post in front of the house. There was no one in sight. He came to stand behind her as she knocked. There was silence within.

He turned to her. 'I'm going in.'

He shoved the door, and there was enough give for hope. She stood aside as he pushed again and again till it flew open. They stood at the threshold, unclear of what to expect, but certain that they were meant to be there. It was yet another breadcrumb from Stanley. Her father, the puppet-master.

Sebastian entered the small cottage and groped around till he found a candle. Catherine reached into her reticule for the box of matches she'd been carrying around for emergencies and handed it to him.

'It isn't much,' said Sebastian, surveying the tiny room. 'But there is a cot and a fireplace, and for tonight it will have to do.'

TWENTY-EIGHT

'SEBASTIAN, THERE'S SOMETHING I need to tell you.'

She began again with the words that scared her most, scanning his face, knowing that what she was about to say could be the end of everything. But there was no way she could keep it secret any longer, with all that lay ahead of them. He had a right to know and more pressingly, they needed to figure out how they'd escape with the treasure.

'I've never known you to shy away from speaking your mind,' said Sebastian.

She paced the room, but it wasn't large enough for the size of her dilemma. She opened her mouth once, twice, and then finally blurted it out.

'I am not from 1851.'

She stood before him, completely naked, watching for any sign of anger, but all she saw was a shadow creeping back into his eyes, the shuttered look she had grown used to during their first days together in Bath. It pained her that no sooner had he let her in, she was about to ruin whatever it is they shared. She couldn't name what she felt for him; she dared not when she would spend the rest of her days without him. There was too much separating them now; eighty years of time was just one of them.

He was perfectly still, sitting on that dusty cot, as she looked down at him, pleading almost. 'Sebastian, say something, anything!'

The fire crackled away, its light dancing across his face.

'Tell me more,' he said, voice cracking.

Catherine breathed a sigh of relief. It wasn't much, but it wasn't outright rejection. The words tumbled out. 'I came to you from 1929. Almost everything else I've told you is the truth. Except that I hadn't seen your picture in the photograph in the newspaper as I had said, instead I found you thanks to a series of clues my father left me. I knew nothing about time travel or the true nature of the medallion till my twenty-fifth birthday, when I got a package from my father's lawyer. That's how I began on this path.'

Sebastian finally raised a hand up. Catherine waited, she could see him processing her words.

'The amulet...'

Catherine nodded. 'Yes. It works without the pair. I am not sure how, but it does. I have been afraid to test it again, not knowing where I would end up, and whether I could get back. But I believe that when used alone, the two pieces of the medallion seek each other out.'

She waited, but he fell silent once more, staring instead at the fireplace, leaving her to continue on her own.

'I fell from my time and into yours with only a vague idea of what would happen. I knew you were the one I needed to find, though I still did not know why. And then I landed in your yard.'

This finally broke through his reverie. 'In my yard?'

She nodded. 'I landed, quite gently, in the garden in front of your house in Twickenham. I believe it was the night before you left for

London. You came to the window, as though you heard something, and naturally I hid.'

Sebastian laughed suddenly, making Catherine jump. 'Naturally, you say? Of all the words to use, I certainly wouldn't have chosen that one.'

Catherine would have agreed with him had she not been so nervous. 'The next morning when I returned to your house, you had already left. Your housekeeper was kind enough to show me your collections, and that's when I realized you were a treasure hunter yourself. I didn't know if you had Tibeau's treasure already, if that was why I was being led to you, but I knew I had to find you to get the other piece of the medallion.'

'So what you are saying is that with both parts of the medallion, you can choose where you want to go in time, but with only one part you will go to the time and place where the other half of the medallion exists?'

Catherine nodded. 'At least my bit worked that way. I don't know about yours.'

He was fidgeting, raising a jerky hand to run it through his hair, bouncing his knee, eyes darting around the room as the possibilities cascaded over him. 'Makes you wonder how they got separated in the first place.'

'Yes,' she said. She'd thought of this endlessly as well. How had her father gotten around with only one piece of the medallion?

'I believe there is only one explanation — he must have left you the dagger and then traveled back to my time with some other object.'

'He died at home?'

'Yes. But I don't know how it all works. Perhaps we *are* each at liberty to return to our timeline just as we please, and that would be wonderful, but I couldn't risk being stranded again and not being able to come back to you.'

Sebastian's eyes narrowed. 'You mean to the treasure.'

She flinched. She deserved that, perhaps. 'To begin with, yes. Of course, I won't deny it. But even then, I had no desire to leave you stranded here.' She thought Sebastian was about to laugh again. 'I know you have no reason to believe me but trust me when I say I never meant for you to be a part of this and I have no desire to see you suffer as a result.'

Sebastian leaned back against the wall, his face an impenetrable mask. 'Why didn't you tell me any of this before?'

She clenched her hands. 'I wanted to, and not just since we grew closer, I've wanted to for some time now. But at the beginning, I had no real idea what kind of person you were. In 1851, you might have taken me for a witch, especially if you had no foreknowledge of the medallion. And if you knew about it, what was to stop you from trying to steal it from me? And then when we got here, you didn't trust me as far as you could throw me. It just didn't seem right, or even necessary.'

'And it is necessary now?'

Catherine looked at him, tears in her eyes. 'Yes,' she said, her voice a strangled whisper.

'Why?' he asked. He wasn't about to make this easy for her.

She straightened her back, refusing to let him see how much she was hurting. 'Because if we are right about the treasure coming in tomorrow, there will be no time to figure out what to do with it after that, and where to go. We need to make a plan for how to safely get the treasure back to our time, and right now, I don't know when that time is.'

Sebastian nodded.

'Say we've got it already, and we've split it, we need to get you back to 1851 and me back to 1929, with no knowledge of how much we can do with just one medallion.'

'Well, that bit's easy,' said Sebastian. 'We go back together to 1851. You leave me there and take the medallions and return to 1929.'

Catherine couldn't meet his eyes, staring into the dancing fire instead. 'You'd do that? You just give this away?'

Sebastian shrugged. 'I have no intention of doing this ever again. I had no intention of doing this at all, yet here I find myself, with the most exasperating woman I have ever met in my life.'

Her head snapped up. He smiled at last. 'So you aren't angry at me?'

He stood up and came to her, cupping her cheek like he had before they had been so rudely interrupted back at the inn. 'No. If anything, it explains quite a lot. I had chalked up much of your difference to being from America, but now I know it is beyond that.'

'Are you saying that I am strange?'

'You are most unlike any woman I have ever met.'

Under other circumstances Catherine might have said that he would probably have felt the same in 1929. She'd fit into her own time pretty much as well as she did now. And Dolly aside, Sebastian might be the closest she had ever got to a genuine friend. But she held her tongue, because he was looking at her with eyes dark with desire, and she had no intention of making that look go away.

'Sebastian,' she said, when she couldn't take the intensity of his gaze anymore.

'Catherine,' he said, resting his forehead against hers, 'it occurs to me that this is the last night we will spend together. And we have unfinished business.'

With that, he kissed her. She responded with a passion that took her by surprise, pouring everything into that kiss, everything that she was too afraid to say out loud.

There was a new urgency between them, and she didn't wait for him to work his way around the tiny buttons on her bodice this time, opening them with fumbling fingers herself.

His lips teased her skin as she slipped her gown off. He spun her around, unlacing her corset and dropping it to the floor. He pulled her hips against his, and she gasped as he rocked into her, kissing her neck, cupping her breasts, teasing her nipples through the cloth.

She turned to face him, picking at his buttons, but he held her at arm's length. She stood there, as she had so many times before, in just her cotton chemise, pulling it off over her head in one fluid motion.

He drew in a ragged breath. 'Catherine, you are so beautiful.'

'Too many clothes in 1831,' she said, smiling as she helped him out of his jacket and cravat, the linen of his shirt soft against her bare skin. He cradled her face in his hands, looking deep into her eyes and teasing her mouth once again. He traced his tongue from his lips to her sensitive jaw and down her neck.

Desire raced through her as his mouth dipped to her breast, her hands weaving through his hair. He was rubbing his thumbs over her nipples, squeezing just so till she was gasping.

'Every night sleeping an arm's length away from you, when all I wanted to do was this. It's been torture, Catherine.'

'I've wanted you too.' But for all the times she had imagined this moment, she had not known it could feel like this. So wondrous, so treasured, so full.

Her back arched as she gave in to the sensation filling her and spilling over. He lifted her up and placed her ever so gently upon the narrow cot. The fire licked both their bodies, and she reached out to him.

Sitting on the edge of the bed, he bent down to take a nipple in his mouth, playing with the other.

'Sebastian,' she said, impatient with desire, 'I need you.'

He barely looked up. 'I'm going to bloody well take my own time over this.' He ran one hand down her stomach and then the other, cupping her hips in his hands, the delicious friction between her legs making her shudder.

'Catherine,' he whispered, 'I need to know if you have done this before.'

She shook her head. He kissed her again, infinitely tender. 'Then we'll be taking it extra slow.'

He traced one finger down her pelvis, running it gently down her slit. She held onto his shoulders, crying out as he found her most sensitive nub with his finger, probing her gently with another, massaging her in slow, luxurious circles until her back arched off the bed.

He took her breast in his mouth again, as his fingers continued their relentless pursuit. It was almost too much, beyond anything Catherine had ever experienced, but she needed him closer still. 'Sebastian, I want you.'

'And you'll have me, my love,' he said without pause.

She grabbed his hair as the pleasure racked her body, not being able to hold back the tide, collapsing in a limp heap.

She opened her eyes and took in Sebastian's face. He lay down beside her as she closed her eyes again, the awe washing over her.

'What have you done to me?' she gasped.

'You liked that?' he said with a smile, leaning over her.

'We should have done that weeks ago,' she said.

He laughed, the sound of it warming her once again.

She turned to her side and traced a hand down his bare chest, to the bulge that was straining in his pants. She rubbed up and down his length as she looked up at him shyly.

He grabbed her hand. 'Are you sure you want this, Catherine?'

'More sure than I have ever been of anything in my life.' She sat up and straddled him, delighting in the feeling of him through the layers of cloth between them.

He grabbed her. 'Easy now,' he said, placing her back on the bed.

He kissed her mouth and began his slow exploration down her body once again. Then, when he was sure she was ready for him, he undressed at last, and Catherine memorized every line of his body as he stood there, beautiful in the firelight.

He slowly slid one finger into her, sending a shiver of pleasure in places she'd never felt before. And then he eased in another, and another.

'Are you okay?' he asked.

She nodded. He bent over so their mouths were inches apart.

'This might hurt,' he warned, as he slowly thrust into her. She let out a gasp of pain this time, and he stopped, waiting for her to open her eyes. She gave him a nod as he went deeper. It hurt, quite a lot to begin with, but less and less as he moved, slowly, gently. And then, alongside the pain, there was pleasure. He rocked into her with growing intensity. As she gripped his shoulders, his finger found her once again. She felt full to the brim and spilled over, her climax ripping through her as he cried out his own pleasure.

Twenty-Nine

SEBASTIAN WALKED INTO THE room, opening the ramshackle door as quietly as he could. Catherine was still asleep, not a surprise after the night they had shared. She took his breath away, lying there wrapped in his shirt. The morning sun was streaming in through the crooked window and he placed the cloth parcel he was holding on the small, battered sideboard. Much as he wanted to join Catherine in sleep, he would have to wake her instead. At least he could think of a pleasurable way to do so. He sat on the edge of the cot, leaned over and kissed her.

She stirred, raising her arms above her head in a stretch. Finally, her eyes fluttered open, a smile filling them at once.

'You're up early.'

Sebastian nodded. 'I brought food, too.'

That got Catherine's attention, and she sat up.

Sebastian first passed her a jug he had filled with water from a nearby well. Catherine drank greedily. Next, he brought the bundle over to the bed. He opened it, revealing a veritable feast of bread, cheese, and a bit of cold ham he had purchased from a neighboring farmer.

They both took a minute to enjoy their first food since the pub with the sailors the previous day.

'You've been busy this morning.'

'The horse needed water and food, so I rode over to the nearest inhabited farmhouse. It is two miles away at least, and they had no idea there was anyone in this cottage.'

'Which is a good thing,' she said.

He nodded. Particularly if they were right about Stanley leading them to this place. Perhaps it was more than a safe spot to spend the night. But they had searched everywhere and found nothing that revealed a hidden purpose.

'Sebastian, do you think we might be wrong about this entire thing?'

'What thing?'

'Our approach to this?'

Sebastian shook his head. 'No. Everything that has happened once will happen again, except one thing — who walks away with the treasure. Which means we have plenty of work to do this morning.'

She nodded, pushing her curls behind her ear. Still getting used to its length, she seemed annoyed when it sprang back out.

Sebastian reached over and smoothed it back, and she gave him a smile. It was enough to arouse him again, the tiniest touch, the merest hint of her enjoyment. And something constricted in his chest, knowing the very next morning she would no longer be by his side.

He pushed her back onto the bed, gathering up his shirt and pulling it over her head. 'So these tiny little knickers... they are from the future,' he said, running a hand over them, feeling her heat.

'Yes,' she said, eyes darkening with desire again. 'I figured no one would see them so I could take a chance.'

'I am overjoyed you were wrong,' said Sebastian, sucking one nipple and then the other, taking his time as she squirmed beneath him. He reached down, and she was wet for him again.

'You know how many mornings I've wanted to wake you like this?' he said, rubbing his thumb along her through the material.

'Why didn't you, Sebastian?' she said, moaning against his mouth.

If only he had. If he had showed her before what they could be, maybe it would have made a difference. But now, it was too late. He and she would never be in the same year again, let alone the same place.

Sebastian got off the bed and pulled Catherine to her feet, slipping her drawers off. He stripped down and sat at the edge of the cot. He inserted two fingers deep inside her, making her gasp, a thumb at her apex. He opened his mouth for one luscious rosy nipple, and then the other, plunging in and out of her warmth with his fingers.

Breaking away, Sebastian looked up at her face: lips parted, eyes half closed as she moaned his name. She grabbed his wrist, making him stop, as she held out a tentative hand toward him.

She was still shy about touching him. It was almost too much as he watched her hand clamped around him, running along his length, and it was his turn to gasp as she brushed against his tip.

He hoisted her on to his lap, guiding her over him and they sat there, locked in an embrace, closer than they'd ever been. She began to move, riding him with eyes aglow, hair wild, the most beautiful creature he had ever beheld. She arched her back as he matched her thrust for thrust, and they both came apart together.

He cradled her in his arms as they caught their breath.

'That was... unexpected,' she said with a smile.

'Was it, really?' He searched her face. She looked happy and content, but he couldn't find any sign it was anything more for her. He kissed her hard once more before placing her beside him on the bed. 'Nothing about you surprises me anymore. But now we really must go.'

SEBASTIAN AND CATHERINE GOT ready with care. Catherine had gathered all they needed before running out of the hotel. They left their other clothes, all they had left, in neat piles. They didn't know if they would make it back here.

Sebastian's 'disguise' was from his own wardrobe. The fine jacket he had purchased in Bath, pantaloons and boots as usual. The crux of it lay in a bushy white wig, quite unfashionable for the time, but would serve their purpose rather well.

'How do I look?' he asked.

Catherine, who was getting ready behind an opened door to a wooden cupboard in a sudden bout of coyness he found enchanting, took in his appearance with a smile. 'The wig does wonders, really. I think it should do. Particularly with your newest accessory.'

Sebastian arched his brow. 'And what might that be?'

'Your nubile young valet, of course.'

Catherine stepped out from behind the door, and even Sebastian, who had spent the better part of the night in her arms, could hardly recognize her. A simple white shirt tucked into a pair of faded brown pantaloons and worn black boots. An oversized lumpy jacket hid her curves, and her natural leanness insured no one would question she was who she said she was: a young boy in Sebastian's employ. She pulled a dirty brown cap down over her forehead, the last article they had purchased from a tradesman the previous evening. Catherine's newly short hair was just long enough to be restrained by a ribbon.

'Will I do?'

Sebastian was at a momentary loss for words. 'Always.'

She looked away, and for a moment, he wondered if she might be feeling the same as he did about their impending separation. But then she smiled, spinning around. 'This is the first time in weeks I haven't been in a corset.'

'Aren't there corsets in 1929?'

'Goodness no. And women can wear pants too, or short dresses.'

'Perhaps 1929 isn't so bad after all,' he said with a grin. 'You look quite fetching in those trousers, and I very much prefer the underwear.'

Catherine froze for a second and then searched his face. 'Would you come with me?'

Sebastian's heart soared. He had been wondering much the same thing for the past twelve hours. What if she were to stay with him, what if he were to go with her?

She beamed at him. 'There is so much more we can do together, maybe we can even find my father?'

And there it was — it seemed the reason Catherine wanted to be with him was not at all the reason he had in mind. So instead of answering, he smiled. 'We'd better be going now.'

Catherine closed the door of the cupboard, but then she halted, eyes fixed on a spot on the wall next to it.

'What is it?' he asked, rushing to her side.

'Do you see that stone?'

Sebastian immediately knew what she was talking about. One stone in the wall definitely looked out of place, the crumbling mortar around it making it appear as though it might have been recently moved. He squatted on the ground and gave it a tug, expecting to see something stuffed behind it.

It didn't budge. Instead, there was a loud metallic click that seemed to have come from within the armoire. Catherine and Sebastian exchanged a shocked glance. Catherine opened the doors again, moving a thick coil of rope, the only item in the cabinet, to the side and reached a tentative hand into the cavity. She pulled open the back as though it were a door. Behind it was a panel made of iron.

Catherine shook her head slowly. 'Of all the places he could have put a secret compartment, he chose the easiest to miss.'

'This cottage has been lying here abandoned for who knows how long. He had to ensure that this was for your eyes only.'

'A heads-up would have been nice.' Catherine felt around the panel, looking for a way to open it. 'I can't find anything. It feels solid.' She gave it a knock, and there was a decidedly hollow echo. 'No, not solid.' She reached around again, splayed her hand across the middle section of the door. And then Sebastian caught her spark of excitement.

'What is it?' he asked.

'There is a round, raised ridge in the center here.'

Sebastian looked over her shoulder, trying not to block whatever light was reaching it.

'I see it,' he said.

Catherine's head and chest were deep inside the cupboard. 'There doesn't seem to be any way to open it.' She moved to the side so he could see, and he was equally confounded.

'Wait!' Catherine cried, crossing the room and rummaging in her little bag. She pulled out the disk.

'You think it fits in the indentation?' he asked, moving away to give her room.

Catherine carefully positioned the disk into the void. Sebastian noticed there was an engraving on that ring of metal, and it lined up with the design on the edge of the disk. There was another click. Catherine gasped as the panel swung open.

She leaned in till she was hanging over the cupboard shelf and into the cavity revealed by the door. Sebastian held onto her hips, just in case.

'It's empty,' said Catherine, straightening up.

She stepped aside to let Sebastian have a look. The cavity was enormous. It must extend into the ground beneath the house. From what he could tell by reaching around, it was lined with some sort of metal too.

Catherine threw her hands up. 'A note, a sign, a word. Any of those things may have helped us figure out what this all means. This is simply useless.'

Sebastian shook his head. 'Oh no, it's not useless. It's how we're going to get the treasure out of here.'

Thirty

IT WAS AN AUDACIOUS scheme, one in which so much could go wrong. It was also so elegant that Catherine knew it was the only way as soon as Sebastian suggested it the night before.

The night before. And the morning, too. They had slept little, between the magic of finally being together and the endless discussion on what needed to be done.

Even in the midst of the madness they were living, Catherine couldn't imagine it ending. But one way or the other, end it would. With the discovery of the vault, all the major pieces were in place.

In her young man's garb, she entered the tailor shop she and Sebastian had stumbled into before.

'Yes?' said the elderly man behind the counter.

'I would like to pick up an order my master, Mr. Barr, placed yesterday.'

He seemed convinced enough that she was a footman, going into an immediate tizzy.

'Now? How could he send you when I told him the dress would be ready only later today!'

'I don't know about that, sir. He sent me, so here I am.'

He threw his hands up in despair and then retreated to the backroom to see if the garment was in fact ready.

With the shop empty, in slipped Victor, a young man of about Sebastian's height. Catherine gave him a curt nod and monitored the window, every moment expecting Sebastian to arrive, knowing that at that very moment he could be in grave danger.

After much discussion, considering the options available to them, they had decided upon a caper of distraction. Sebastian would walk by the dock where the Westlake gang had assembled in numbers. She and Sebastian had kept watch on them from a safe distance earlier that morning, to ensure that none of the immediate Talbot family that could identify him were around, though having seen the gangly sixteen-year-old Sebastian, Catherine could vouch that the man she spent the previous night with bore very little resemblance to his earlier self.

Sebastian was in a coat of a startling shade of parrot green, with a brown wig, parading by the dock to draw attention to himself. Having achieved this, he'd swiftly proceed to the tailor shop. By his side would be a young woman, Susan, hired that very morning thanks to her head full of brown curls, not unlike Catherine's.

They would enter the tailor's shop unseen, and in their place, out would go Victor, who was the brother of the girl by Sebastian's side, wearing Sebastian's obnoxious green coat, with Susan on his arm.

The trick would hopefully lure Bently away from the dock on a wild goose chase. As the only man who had seen the real Catherine and Sebastian back in Bath, they counted on him being the one deputed to apprehend them. And as the man who had failed the mutinous sailors on board the ship that was soon to arrive, he might even be a liability at the dockyard. With the captain out of the way, Sebastian and Catherine, dressed as man and servant, would move in.

Catherine was flooded with relief when she saw Sebastian striding toward them through the glass frontage. She was in position by the time he entered, stripping the jacket off him and slipping it over the shoulders of the younger man. Sebastian took off his brown wig and pulled it over Victor's head. Susan was dressed in a simple but pretty red dress guaranteed to catch attention. The pretenders walked out just as the captain rounded the corner in front of the shop, by which time Sebastian had put on the white wig, blue coat and had turned his back to the window.

As their decoys boarded a carriage and started off down the road, the captain and his henchman who had burst in on them the night before came charging down the street.

It seemed to have worked.

Catherine and Sebastian promptly left the shop, turning in the opposite direction toward the dock. She finally allowed herself to look at Sebastian, heart in her throat. 'That was almost too easy,' said Catherine.

He looked stern. 'If it makes you feel any better, I had to cavort quite enthusiastically by the docks before I gained Bently's attention. I was standing far enough away that I was assured of maintaining safe distance between the two of us, but that meant he couldn't see my face.'

'And your uncle?'

'Not on the scene yet.'

'This is too good to be true.'

'He is a newlywed after all, recovering from a week of festivities. But have no fear: there are plenty of other hurdles. We don't know how long the captain will be gone. If he gives up and turns back, we will have a fight on our hands as he might recognize us, even in disguise. And there is still the matter of making off with the treasure.'

Catherine looked past the bustle of the dockyard. 'Is that it?'

A ship — three proud sails billowing against the wind — had just come into harbor. She was battered and careworn, but still a towering presence.

'I'd think so,' said Sebastian.

From chatter around them they learned the ship was going to dock by afternoon, with the naval vessel scheduled to move out at any moment. They had several pieces to put in place, and preferably before Bently resurfaced.

The biggest logistical challenge was that they needed a canal boat which they would be in no position to return, with no money left with which to purchase one. It was a plan that made Catherine deeply uncomfortable for its slowness. At no point had she missed the twentieth century more, where a car would make swift work of their getaway. The idea of loading a priceless treasure onto a barge and floating gently down a canal powered by a horse was unsettling. The only consolation was that those who'd be in pursuit would be equally disadvantaged.

It was, however, their only option. Sebastian emerged from the shop sometime later and gave Catherine a nod.

'It's done?' she asked.

'I have instructed him to collect the barge from the house and the horse from Hangman's Cliff as payment.'

'Did he accept the deposit?'

Sebastian smiled. 'The useless silver box you so berated me for lifting from my dear family's home finally came to some use.'

She raised her brow. 'The promise of getting a free horse for one afternoon's hire would be his primary incentive, I would imagine.'

Sebastian hitched the horse up to the boat, to ensure everything was in proper working order. 'Have you ever used one of these?' asked Catherine.

'Not on my own, but I've seen it done several times coming home after an expedition.'

Despite Catherine's reservations, the barge also gave them a place from which to watch the comings and goings at the dockyard without fear of detection. Sebastian brought them water to drink and hand pies to eat. They spoke little, aware of every moment that passed as one of their last together.

Sebastian finished his meal and dusted off his hands. 'What will you do when you go back home?'

His dark eyes on her in their cramped quarters made her squirm. 'I don't know, really. If there is enough money, I might open a boarding school. For orphans like me.'

Sebastian smiled. 'I can't accuse you of being mercenary, in that case.'

'What will you do?' Her mouth was suddenly dry; it couldn't be ending so soon, so suddenly. But while Sebastian hadn't rejected the idea of them continuing together, he hadn't responded either. She couldn't bring herself to suggest it again. 'If you are still duke, will you be happy?' she asked instead.

Sebastian shot her a look of such intensity it made her stomach flip.

'I don't know about happy. I think I was as happy as I ever will be digging up antiquities in foreign lands.'

'Perhaps you could continue with that,' she said, looking out at the water.

'Perhaps.'

And then Sebastian's head snapped up.

'What is it?'

He rose and went out onto deck, ducking back in. 'She is moving now, it can't be long.'

AS THE NAVAL SHIP sailed out and the pirate ship sailed in, Catherine and Sebastian got into position on the wooden pier. The ship's decks were teeming with men tired after months at sea and shipwreck, but there was an eerie silence aboard, as though they sensed further trouble.

'Where's your captain?' called out Sebastian to a man putting the gangway in place. He didn't even look up.

He called out again. 'Davy!'

The captain spun around, trying to locate the voice that called out his name so audaciously. He finally spotted him, glaring down.

Sebastian craned his neck up. 'Davy, there is no time, James sent me to tell you that the customs officials will be here any moment and we need to take away the cargo immediately.'

Captain Davy looked around. 'James Talbot? Where is he, anyway?'

'He will be here any moment, but close on his heels are the customs officials. They sent me ahead to take charge.'

'Who are you?'

'His nephew.' He held up the hand which bore the signet ring.

Davy squinted suspiciously, then sized up the barge.

'Any moment now they will be here. Quickly, have your men lower the material on to the barge. It will await you in safety.'

The man examined Sebastian one more time. The family resemblance was so strong that no one could doubt he and James were kin. Even the wig was very much like the one the duke had worn in Bath.

'Come on, man!' urged Sebastian. 'Will you lose us our bounty after all we have done to get it back? If that be the case, you explain yourself to my uncle, as the Crown walks away with years of his effort because *you* ignored his orders! Did you think you could just sail into port and unload that chest without detection? The talk of your crew's misfortunes made it all the way to London weeks ago!'

This argument seemed to sway Davy at last. Their bounty was too notorious and their expedition too beset by calamity for the news not to have carried.

Davy disappeared abruptly from Catherine's view, and Sebastian looked down at her. Her heart was racing. There was no doubt in her mind that he was coming back with a pistol, a sword, anything to get rid of them.

Just then came the sound of horses racing down the path. It was Bently. She squeezed Sebastian's arm.

'Hurry down to the boat now,' Sebastian whispered.

Catherine clambered down the rope ladder and made the perilous jump into their small vessel.

Never in a million years would she have imagined that Bently's arrival might be a boon.

'The customs men are coming!' Bently yelled. 'They are only ten minutes away!'

Pandemonium erupted on the ship's deck. In a second, the news had spread, and if Davy had been in two minds before, he knew now he had to act fast. Catherine kept her attention firmly on the bow where Davy's face had earlier appeared.

The men aboard the ship still reviled Bently. Even with the frantic activity, several of them stopped and spat at him. Davy would not confer with him, getting ready instead to unload the treasure.

There were tense moments as they waited, and then Bently turned his attention to the two of them, Sebastian on the horse and Catherine, whose face was carefully averted on the canal boat below.

'Who are you?' he asked.

Sebastian pretended not to hear.

'I say, who sent you here?'

Catherine stole a furtive glance as Sebastian gave him a withering look. 'I am here on the instructions and authority of my uncle James Talbot.'

Bently glared at him. 'I just left him — he said nothing about sending a man.'

Catherine's heart was racing. But just as he took a step closer, a chorus of shouts went up behind them. Her first thought was that they were too late; that either the customs officers had arrived already or it was Sebastian's uncle, both of which would leave them with no choice but to make a hasty and empty-handed getaway. But when Sebastian looked down at her with wide eyes, she knew she was wrong.

Amidst the chaos, all she heard was one name: Stanley.

She ran the length of the barge, but couldn't see a thing, her view blocked by the giant vessel in front.

And then she heard shouts: 'He's stealing the horse!'

'That man is supposed to be dead!'

'What does a dead man need with the horse!'

Catherine ran to the rope ladder and clambered up, despite Sebastian's protestations. She finally glimpsed him in the distance, unmistakably the man who'd shoved her toward the sailors the day before. He jumped on the horse's back and spurred it forward with his heels, racing right past them. Catherine knew then with no doubt that it was her father, though his face was obscured as he touched the brim of his hat, speeding by with not so much as a throwaway glance in her direction.

Catherine was about to run after him, forgetting where she was and who she was meant to be, but Sebastian grabbed her around the waist from behind.

'Let me go!' she cried, with only sense enough not to scream. The tears were running down her face, and her voice was strangled.

'Stop, please stop,' whispered Sebastian in her ear. 'They are about to lower it down. We need to go back to the boat.'

Catherine looked in the direction in which her father disappeared one last time.

'Please, Catherine,' said Sebastian.

She reluctantly turned back to the ship where, besides several men who seemed petrified enough to throw themselves overboard, was Davy, roundly telling them off. And before Catherine knew it, there it was — a giant wooden chest being hoisted off the deck.

'My Lord,' mumbled Sebastian. He tied the horse to a post, and clambered down the ladder, Catherine in his wake.

Secured by thick ropes, lugged by ten men, the trunk was bigger than they had imagined, and would have to be positioned onto their tiny vessel. And they would have to do it fast.

The men aboard the ship thankfully knew what they were doing. As it descended the final feet, Sebastian and she centered it as best they could before cutting the main ropes, leaving the bindings intact.

'And that's it.' Sebastian gave her a look as if to check that she was alright. But it was all they had time for. Leaving Catherine on deck, Sebastian climbed back up to the dock, untied his horse, and they were off. Though excruciatingly slow, all the men on land or aboard the ship — Davy and Bently included — turned their attention away from the centuries-old pirate treasure they had just lost and toward the ghost of a dead man that had appeared before them, stolen a horse and ridden away.

THIRTY-ONE

AS THE BARGE TURNED the bend in the canal, Catherine knew why her father had chosen the house he had. What was a twenty-minute ride by road to the dock was only five minutes upstream on the canal.

How long had it taken him to plan this? How many visits had he made to this time; how many versions of their future together had he witnessed? Was this the outcome he had worked so hard to achieve?

They pulled up to the house and Catherine, so distracted by all she had seen, so distraught about all she had not seen, had not bothered to consider how they'd get the chest into the house. But then she realized her father had thought of it all: there were two pulleys hanging from the embankment by the house over the canal. As Sebastian ground to a halt, Catherine threw down the anchor. There was no ladder here, so Sebastian jumped off his horse and tied it to the old oak tree before reaching down to hoist Catherine up.

'The rope we saw in the cupboard, we need that,' she said.

Sebastian dashed inside and returned with it, and Catherine took it from his hands and strung it through the ropes that bound the casket, both the pulleys and then threw it over the branch above them. Catherine and Sebastian grabbed the rope and pulled with all their might. With each pass Catherine felt her hands scream in protest. Finally, when they were almost there, Sebastian jumped back down onto the barge to give it a final boost onto the bank.

'Now to get it into the house.' Sebastian took position behind the trunk and Catherine joined him as they pushed it in excruciating increments to the entrance of the little cottage.

'They could see our barge any moment now. We'd be sitting ducks,' said Catherine.

'We just need to get this inside and leave — unless they come up the canal there is no way to spot us.'

They made it just past the threshold and then somehow maneuvered the trunk to the cupboard.

'How do we get it in?' said a panting Catherine.

'Wait,' said Sebastian, getting into position and heaving the cabinet out of the way. 'Now we can just slide it in.'

Catherine inserted Stanley's wooden disk and the metal door swung open.

With a last effort, they pushed the trunk with a shout. It slipped into the cavity with a bang that echoed through the house. Then they watched in awe as the metal door closed on its own, and Sebastian moved the cupboard back in place.

'And now we must get as far away from here as possible.' Sebastian grabbed her by the hand and they raced out to the horse. He hoisted her onto it one last time before mounting it himself. As they galloped away from that house, Catherine felt a crushing sense of defeat, despite knowing what they had just achieved should be considered a resounding victory.

To put distance between the house and them was the intention in choosing Hangman's Cliff as their getaway. It was a brief ride away, and as it came into view, Sebastian slowed. He secured the horse as promised for the boatman to find, and they raced up the hill.

Catherine already had her hand on her medallion as the edge came into view. She looked down at the sheer drop: there was water, but there were rocks too. After their ignominious fall back at the Westlake Estate stable, she was nervous. What if it didn't work?

She turned to Sebastian. 'First, your time. Remember, we have to focus all our desires on that.'

He nodded, reaching for his medallion.

But it was not to be.

'Not so fast.'

A voice behind them chilled Catherine to the core. It was James, and he was breathing down their necks, too close by to risk a jump. With no time to prepare, they could easily hurtle to their deaths. So instead, Sebastian and Catherine stuffed their medallions back under their clothes hastily.

Sebastian spun around, pushing her behind him. That's when she saw that by James's side was Bently. And a step behind him, Ophelia.

'We finally catch up with you,' said James, knife out and poised for use. He circled them like a shark. But Catherine's eyes were on Ophelia.

'Is this the man you saw at the house?' asked James.

'Yes,' said Bently. 'It's them.'

But Ophelia was silent.

What Catherine didn't know was whether she or James had figured out exactly who it was they were dealing with — that the man they were looking at was Sebastian returned from twenty years into the future. If so, it would mean they knew about the medallion, and what it did. Keeping it away from them would be the most important thing.

'You think you have gotten away with something, but I can assure you this is just the beginning,' said James.

Catherine saw Sebastian's chin shoot up. He was not one to take threats lightly, particularly not from the man before him. 'And what precisely do you think I'm getting away with?'

'Don't play dumb with me, that is my treasure you stole, and I am going to have it back.'

Sebastian put his arm around Catherine's waist. She snuck a nervous look at him.

'Get away from her,' snarled James.

Sebastian dropped his arm as James gestured to Bently, who stood menacingly before them.

'David Talbot and his beautiful bride.'

Despite it all, Catherine felt a rush of relief. As long as James didn't know their true identity, they had the upper hand. Sebastian stole a glance at her that told her he was thinking the same thing. His eyes then went to the cliff — their means of escape.

'How long have you been searching for this treasure?' asked Sebastian.

'Oh, for years. My father made my brother and I swear we wouldn't make any attempt to retrieve it. The treasure was cursed, he said, enough Talbots had lost everything in their blind pursuit of it. My brother, assured of a dukedom, had no use for it. But what was I supposed to do? Be happy with my lot as an officer in the military? I had no such desire.'

James walked up to Catherine. He ran a finger down her cheek and she jerked her face away.

'Get your hand off her,' hissed Sebastian.

James looked from her to him with a smile. 'If you don't tell me where that treasure is, your wife will die.'

'You would kill for this treasure?'

'I won't need to. Launching an expedition of this sort is not a minor task. I didn't do it without help. All I need is to hand you two over to my associates, and they will do whatever it takes to get it back. If you know what is good for you, you'll hand it over today.'

James tossed his head at Bently, who grabbed hold of Catherine, an arm around her middle. She cried out as she felt the tip of his dagger at her throat. Sebastian lunged, but James grabbed him by the arm, restraining him.

'Watch what you do there,' said James. 'As long as you answer my questions, she'll be fine. What were you doing in the castle?'

Catherine did her best to stay calm as Sebastian threw him a scathing look. 'I am surprised your wife mentioned that.'

James frowned. 'My wife?'

Ophelia shook her head and laughed nervously. 'I don't know what he is talking about.'

Catherine's mind raced. If she had kept Sebastian's secret, then why was she here? For a moment, Ophelia looked frightened, and it dawned on Catherine that she had her own suspicions about the identity of the man she'd met in the study. And she'd wanted to get another look at him.

That's when Catherine knew that whatever else happened later, in this moment, Ophelia loved Sebastian. Not the man before her, but the young boy back at Westlake Estate.

James looked from Sebastian to Ophelia, who had pulled on her mask again. 'Did you see this man at the castle?' asked James.

'No, darling,' she said, hand on his arm. 'I mean, there were so many people, I can't even tell the difference between one Talbot and another.'

James looked at Sebastian sharply. 'A Talbot, you say? You think he is telling the truth?'

She winced. 'I don't know, I just —'

'Who are you?' James asked.

'You seem to have your own ideas,' said Sebastian.

Bently's grip on Catherine tightened, and she cried out as the tip of the dagger broke skin.

Sebastian's hands balled into fists. 'Let her go!'

'You left behind quite a mess in that old shed,' James said to Sebastian. 'We discovered those thugs you bound and left there, who had quite the story to tell. Show me your ring.'

Sebastian raised his hand defiantly, and James examined it. 'A fake ring? Claiming to be a Talbot? What game are you playing?'

He stood toe to toe with him, examining his face. 'You know what, Ophelia, I think you are right. It *is* more than a passing resemblance.'

Ophelia stared at the ground before her.

'Who are you?' asked James.

'You have caught me out,' said Sebastian. 'There should be a resemblance. I am your father's son, after all.'

Bently tightened his grip, and Catherine held her breath. He was sticking to the story he gave Ophelia then.

James's eyes narrowed. 'How dare you,' he said, voice icy cold.

'Imagine that!' spat Sebastian. 'Outrage, from you? Do you forget so quickly the bastard son your father had by the maid who disappeared when the resemblance grew too strong for the great duke's liking?'

James looked away for a moment. Such a boy did exist, after all. 'It hardly matters who you are,' he said at last. 'Stop wasting my time. Where is the treasure?'

'Take that knife away from my wife's throat or I tell you nothing.'

James glared at Sebastian, who did not flinch.

'Darling,' said Ophelia, stepping forward, 'is this really necessary?'

He stared at his bride for a moment before waving a hand at Bently. He removed the knife away from Catherine's throat, returning it to the sheath in his belt, but his grip around her didn't loosen.

'The treasure. Tell me where it is now!' James demanded again.

Sebastian's face was a mask.

James pulled back and struck Sebastian in the stomach. He doubled over with a groan. As he straightened back up, Catherine watched Ophelia's grimace turn to shock.

She followed her gaze and saw with dismay that Sebastian's medallion had swung free of his shirt.

'Tell him, please!' shouted Catherine.

But Ophelia was not to be so easily distracted. She rushed forward and grabbed the pendant. 'The necklace!'

Sebastian's face went stony. The young Sebastian would have just found the medallion back at the castle. Perhaps he would have shown Ophelia. Perhaps she had seen it in a moment of early intimacy.

'What of it?' James demanded.

Ophelia searched Sebastian's face. Then, struggling to compose herself, she shook her head and turned around. 'I'm sorry, I must be mistaken. I thought it was something else.'

James looked at his wife quizzically and in that moment of distraction Sebastian swooped down and grabbed his knife from the inside of his boot. At the same moment, Catherine struggled against Bently enough to put some space between them, swinging her hand back with all her might and driving it into his groin. He let out a howl of pain, and as he buckled over, Catherine twisted out of his grip and ran to Sebastian's side.

As James hurled insults at Bently, Ophelia looked gray.

James and Sebastian faced each other, knives out.

'Now then, let's all just calm down,' said Sebastian. 'I am going to tell you where the treasure is, and then you will let us go.'

'The treasure never left the dockyard. It is still there, with one of my men watching over it, waiting for you all to leave. Or kill each other. Whichever comes first.'

'That's ludicrous. We would have seen it!' Bently cried.

'It is covered in a simple tarp. Sometimes the best place to hide something is in plain sight.'

James's eyes narrowed. 'How do I know you are telling the truth?'

'You will have to find out for yourself.'

'I can't let you go till we have recovered it.'

'We can tie them up, sir, and go check,' suggested Bently.

'Oh no, you won't,' said Sebastian, dagger at the ready.

'You can hardly expect us to take your word for it,' said James.

'It is all you are going to get.'

Bently lunged at him, and Sebastian punched him in the nose, sending him reeling with a cry of agony. As James moved in, Catherine jumped onto his back, disorienting him thoroughly as she clawed at his face with her nails, jumping off before Sebastian struck him in the pelvis.

As he doubled over in pain, Sebastian grabbed Ophelia by the middle.

'If either of you make a move, she gets it,' he said. They moved back toward the cliff, one step at a time, Catherine by Sebastian's side, Ophelia in his arms.

Ophelia was remarkably calm. 'It's you, isn't it?' she whispered.

Sebastian paused for a second, but then continued on.

They were up against the very edge of the cliff.

Sebastian looked at Catherine. Her hand went to her medallion.

Pushing Ophelia away from him and onto the ground, Sebastian whipped off his necklace and tossed it to Catherine, grabbing her round the waist as his eyes locked with hers. Before they knew it, Sebastian had tipped off the cliff, taking her down with him. A shout went up as they hurtled toward the rocks below, and she saw the horror-struck faces of James and Ophelia watching at the top of the cliff. She pressed the dagger into the body of the bird.

Thirty-Two

AND SO IT WAS in time's gentle embrace that Catherine and Sebastian descended on Serpentine Lake, falling with nary a bump. They stood up, gasping, clutching one another in the darkness. Sebastian looked up at the bridge, and it was empty. There was no sign that Catherine and he had been standing there, surrounded by guards about to arrest him what was hopefully only seconds prior.

He turned to see whether the lovers he had noticed before their own dramatic departure from Hyde Park were still cavorting by the tree. It was as though not even a second had lapsed, his arms wrapped around her midriff, his lips on her neck.

He gazed at Catherine, seeing his shock mirrored in her face.

'I can't believe that worked,' she said. 'If all has gone to plan, your carriage will be upon us at any moment.'

'Can we know that for sure? There is no reason for it to come if I was never chased by those guards.'

'There is only one way to find out,' said Catherine.

Sebastian nodded and turned to the shore. 'Shall we?'

The sound of them wading through the water at last interrupted the ardor of the lovers by the tree, who registered them with shock and hurried away. Sebastian could feel the weeds underwater tugging at his boots. Catherine lifted her blue skirts, and he realized that not only had they returned to exactly the same moment in which they had departed, they had returned to the same state, the same clothes.

Reaching the bank, Sebastian helped Catherine up, the water weighing her down terribly.

Right on schedule, Sebastian saw his carriage approaching. The coachman saw Sebastian, his eyes flitting over Catherine, before averting them. Peter's training had been thorough and simple, his only remit was to drive and to never ask questions. Sebastian was satisfied that even given such scenes, he did not violate the terms of his employment.

Catherine stood in the grass, trying to wring as much water out of her skirts as she could, but it was a losing battle. Sebastian, even in his much more fitting garments, could feel the weight of it. And he wondered if it wasn't a bit of something else: having fallen twenty years into the future, perhaps the laws of nature didn't know quite what to do with them?

Sebastian pulled the door open for Catherine and she looked up.

'It's best we leave, Catherine. I will arrange clean garments for you at the earliest.'

Catherine nodded and stepped into the waiting coach.

'Peter?'

'Your Grace?'

'I am the Duke of Westlake, is it not?'

Even the unflappable Peter started at this question. 'For some time now, Your Grace.'

'Well, then.'

Sebastian was about to close the door to the carriage when Catherine held out a hand.

'What do you think you're doing?'

Sebastian could barely look her in the eye. 'Traveling in a closed coach with me in your present state, as I had occasion to explain once before, will mean certain ruin for you.'

Catherine's face cracked into a wide grin which became the beginnings of laughter which just wouldn't stop. When she finally got control of herself, Sebastian looking on with some alarm, she shook her head. 'You've got to be kidding me, right?'

Sebastian climbed in beside her.

THE DUKE OF WESTLAKE had a house in town, of course, and it was there that he'd been staying. 'You may be the duke,' said Catherine, 'but you still have business of some sort at the Great Exhibition, which means perhaps you are the treasure hunter that you've always been.'

Sebastian nodded, but could not share her enthusiasm for the present that he found himself in. So much of the last years would be different, and he couldn't even begin to understand how he would navigate conversations with people who had known him, whom he seemed to have no memory of except from his own life. How would he explain any of it? Not for the first time was he filled with regret. The dukedom may be his, but what he lost was perhaps of even greater value. And then he looked at Catherine's face, tired but smiling still. Excited about discovering the treasure anew, and what her future would hold. What was certain was that her future would not hold Sebastian. And for all he could see, this was not a state of affairs she was in a hurry to remedy.

They arrived at the grand house at which he had spent so much of his youth, not knowing what to expect. But it was effortless: the housekeeper quickly ushering Catherine into a spare room, declaring that she would arrange clothes and he was not to worry. She too knew better than to ask questions.

Sebastian retired to his own room, where a closet of dry clothes awaited him. His entire body was filled with an intense languor, and as he stripped out of his clothes, he knew that both Catherine and he needed rest. He also knew that he needed time to think. He sent instructions for dinner trays to be sent up for both of them. Everything else would have to wait for the morning. Sebastian crashed into bed and drifted off into a dreamless sleep.

THE NEXT MORNING SEBASTIAN woke early. For a long while, he lay there, wondering if Catherine was up too, aching for her worse than ever before, knowing that in a few short hours, she would leave him.

She came down to the dining room for breakfast an hour later.

'Good morning,' she said, beaming. If she was hurting, she didn't show it, eyes twinkling and in a pristine white dress.

'Lovely as you look,' he said, 'that gown won't do.'

Her brow furrowed as he poured her a cup of tea. 'Why not?'

'You'll be landing in the Thames, if I remember correctly. You'll want something darker. And a jacket too.'

'Thank you for always being such a gentleman,' she said.

'I don't know if you could rightfully call me that.'

He sent a man off to get the clothes, and as soon as they arrived and Catherine had changed, they set out for the house by the canal.

It was nightfall, after a day of hard riding, when they reached the stone cottage. They had spent the hours chatting about everything except what mattered most. It was pleasant and companionable, without the fear of imminent death or injury, which was a nice change of pace for them, but neither of them broached the subject of the future.

The house appeared unchanged, as though they had been here just moments ago. Which they had been, but at the same time, that moment was two decades ago. Were these two timelines layered on top of each other, or had one completely erased the other? Sebastian hadn't had time to reflect on what any of it meant, and he only hoped that when they entered the cottage, some answers would await them.

Catherine and he disembarked and approached that blue door, still slightly crooked, with paint flaking off and its metal rusted. Once again no one opened, and once again he entered through brute force, battering it with his bruised shoulder. It gave way, crashing open, revealing a room unchanged by time.

She grabbed his arm, but Sebastian found it difficult to look at her face, to register her excitement, when all he felt was loss.

Catherine already had the disk in her hand, crossing the room to the cupboard. She threw open the doors and clicked it into place. Sebastian heard the metal moving, and the lock opening. He at last came to stand behind Catherine and saw the top of the chest, still bound by ropes. Now, with time and leisure, they moved the cupboard away for easier access.

'Open it,' said Sebastian.

Catherine looked up at him, her eyes ablaze. The dagger twisted in his side, but he smiled down at her, anyway.

Catherine reached down, her torso and head disappearing into the cavity once again. She first tried to unravel the ropes that still bound the wooden trunk. 'I can't get it to budge,' she said. Sebastian handed her his knife, and she attempted to cut through them. After a minute hunched over, she sat up straight and shrugged. 'You have a go.'

He worked his way through the knots, reluctant to cut more than necessary, for these ties were still their best way of removing the wooden chest from the hole.

'It's done,' he said at last, standing up and dusting off his hands.

'Let's open it together.'

Sebastian shook his head. 'No, you should.'

She gave him a curious look, but then leaned in, grabbed the metal clasp and pulled. The heavy wooden lid took a good heave to lift, and Sebastian could smell the sea. It was a time capsule of the folly of men, his ancestors and hers. And now it was theirs.

'Sebastian,' said Catherine in a hushed voice. 'You have to see this.'

Sebastian leaned forward again, and even in the darkness of that vault, he could see the piles of gold and gems, and sitting at its very top, like a body in a grave, the Bell of Dhammazedi.

Despite himself, Sebastian felt something stir. This treasure had claimed so many lives. But none of that was why Sebastian had gone along with Catherine's plan, and now, with his dukedom returned to him, there was even less reason for him to want what had cost so much.

'You did it.'

'We did it!' He could see her confusion. 'What is the matter, Sebastian?'

He shook his head. 'What's next, Catherine?'

'I don't know. I've never been rich before. I want to open that school, but first there is something I need to do.'

Sebastian clenched his fists by his sides. And here it was.

'I need to know why my father did this. Why did he lead me down this path? Who is he even? Why didn't he do this himself, because he must know that he could have. Why me, why you?' She looked at him imploringly, but it wasn't him who could provide her the answers she was so in need of.

He nodded. 'Those are good questions.'

She grabbed his arm once again. 'Sebastian, come with me! We are such a wonderful team. We could do this together, and who knows what else?'

Sebastian cupped her sweet face in his hands. 'No, Catherine, I am not coming with you. I find my appetite for messing with history is very small. I can't take this journey with you.'

He took the medallion from around his neck and held it out to her. 'This is for you. You have unfinished business, but my place is here. You can go where you need to go as long as you have both parts of the medallion. I won't be needing it anymore, I'm not sure I ever did, except...'

'Except what?' said Catherine, tears falling from those exceptional eyes.

He shook his head. 'It was you who made me Duke of Westlake once more. And this is what I can do for you. I can set you free to be who you want, when you want, where you want.'

She took a step back, a hand on her chest, her eyes on the dagger-shaped piece of the amulet. And then she shook her head. 'I don't want to do it without you.'

'But you won't be at peace till you've tried. And I understand that. The treasure is yours. I have all that I need already, thanks to you. I'll keep this house safe for you to discover when you return to your time. And you can open it and find what you need within.'

THE CARRIAGE TOOK THEM back to Hangman's Cliff once more, and as they climbed to the peak, Sebastian could feel Catherine move farther and farther away from him.

They stood in the same spot as they had in their last confrontation with James. With no danger in sight, Sebastian took in the vista before him. Catherine would fall from here and go to the exact place and time she had exited her world, and they would never even exist on the same plane again.

Catherine wiped away a tear and then threw her arms around him. Despite himself, Sebastian wrapped himself around her too, and as she tilted her head back, he pressed his mouth to hers one last time, wanting to remember everything about her taste, the velvet of skin, the strength of her spirit.

He broke away and took a step back, forcing his hands to stay at his sides.

As Catherine prepared herself for the next leap, she gave him one last look. 'I'll miss you.'

And with those words, she hurled herself backwards off that cliff, and he watched her fall. He may have imagined it, but he thought she had reached a hand out to him. Then she disappeared, as though enveloped by a sudden mist.

THIRTY-THREE

'I DON'T WANT TO do it without you.'

'But you won't be at peace till you've tried.'

Catherine searched his face, for what she wasn't sure. She had known that it was a long shot. He had made no secret of the fact that her obsession with her father was something he couldn't abide.

In truth, she didn't know what she really wanted. In that moment, what she wanted was Sebastian. But standing there in the house that her father had somehow arranged for her to find hundred years before the last time she had seen him, she knew she couldn't give up so easily. Maybe she'd take a while to figure out what to do next, but she wasn't ready to let go of that man who had ridden away on horseback from her at the dock, creating the distraction that allowed them to slip away with the treasure.

What she hadn't expected was how hard it would be to let go of Sebastian. The last few days had been so frantic, and she hadn't been able to process it. All she knew was that standing next to that dusty cot in the corner of that cottage, the memory of Sebastian's hands on her body, his mouth on hers, felt as real as his rejection.

But how could she blame him for wanting no further part of her madness? Particularly when in this world, who knows what awaited him? He was duke once more, which meant that Ophelia — who had witnessed the man she finally had recognized as Sebastian hurtling himself off a cliff and into oblivion — hadn't betrayed him. What about James? Did Sebastian and Ophelia perhaps have a chance in this world?

So she decided she would walk away, and though that parting kiss on Hangman's Cliff was almost her undoing, he had already felt so far away that she couldn't be sure how he'd react if she offered to stay.

Raw and vulnerable, tumbling off toward her future was almost the simple thing to do.

HAVING LEFT 1929 IN London, it was to London she returned to much excitement. It wasn't every day that people landed in the Thames, having jumped from Tower Bridge.

After being fished out by the irate captain of a tourist ferry, she gratefully made it to land without injury. Upon confirming that it was indeed 1929, Catherine thought she would want to rush to the cottage. But she found herself lingering in town. She was behaving like a sentimental old fool, she told herself, strolling down the quiet pathways of Hyde Park, with no sign of the Great Exhibition of eighty years prior. And Sebastian, whom she had seen, touched, kissed just a few days before, was most definitely dead.

The last place she wanted to be was London. Had she known how the medallion worked before setting out, she would have spared herself the trouble of an Atlantic crossing and the pain of reliving these memories. As she ran her hand along the railing of Serpentine Bridge, where she had first embraced Sebastian, had tricked him, she wondered at how willingly he had stayed by her side, had taken such a crazy journey with her, and had wanted nothing in return except her happiness.

And it was only then that she realized what a fool she had been.

FROM THAT MOMENT, THERE was no time to waste. Catherine booked her berth on the liner back to New York and then hastened to the cottage in Selsey. Thanking her stars for the advent of the automobile, she was there in two hours.

The house was just as she remembered, but Catherine had a moment's pause when she recognized signs of life within: the chimney was smoking, the grass had been recently cut, and there was the smell of baking bread.

She opened the gate and approached the door, no longer crooked or blue. It was now red and quite sturdy. Catherine lifted the brass knocker and announced her presence.

An old lady opened the door and inspected Catherine genially. 'Yes?'

Catherine almost lost her nerve, not knowing quite where to start. 'My name is Catherine Christie.'

The woman nodded, as though she had been expecting her. She opened the door wide and ushered her in.

Then she stood at the threshold. 'I'll leave you now,' she said, closing the door behind her.

Catherine took in every detail of the small cottage. The inside had a few changes. The fireplace was where it had been, but the cot where Catherine and Sebastian had spent their one and only night together had been replaced by an overstuffed chair. There was a modern kitchen where the wooden table had once stood. It appeared as though a room had been added on to the back of the cottage, too.

She imagined Sebastian coming here, setting all of this up. Visiting as an old man. Talking to the old lady and leaving her instructions for what to do when someone named Catherine Christie came knocking in 1929. It had been only days since she'd seen him, but in reality, she'd missed his entire life when she could have grown old by his side.

What was still very much in its place was the ancient wooden cupboard. Catherine approached it gingerly, aware that the answer to the rest of her life lay behind it. She swung that creaking door open again, and with a shaking hand inserted the disk into the depression in the metal.

She heard the gears turning within as, with a loud clank, it swung open.

Catherine reviewed the contents of that vast hole with a smile, reaching in greedily.

THERE WERE MATTERS OF business to wrap up in New York. She had some days ahead of her, adrift on the Atlantic, to consider each of her next steps with care. So once on land, it took her only a handful of days to put her plan into action.

She returned to her own home, to gather her belongings. She called Dolly and told her she had decided to go to London to search for her family. Her friend was distraught, particularly at her insistence that they would not likely meet again.

'I don't know why you can't come back. It's only a steamer-ride away,' she said.

'I'll try,' said Catherine, 'but I really don't know where life will take me. I don't want you to worry.'

'I have news of my own to share, Catherine, and I'm not sure how you are going to feel about it. Stuart has asked me to marry him!'

'Oh Dolly, that is wonderful! Congratulations! I always said you were perfect for each other!'

And with that, Catherine could be perfectly at peace on the road ahead. She had little to pack. Where she was going, there wasn't much she'd need. She bought the sturdiest knapsack she could find, and into it put the remaining gold from her safe, an opal pendant her mother always had around her neck, her most treasured photographs and a few clothes. Before packing the box from her father, she placed a new letter in on top of the old one.

It was one of the handful of items she had taken out of the vault in the cottage. She knew its contents now by heart.

My dearest Catherine,

Forgive me. Forgive me for keeping so much from you, forgive me for not reaching out to you, forgive me for not holding you tighter when I had the chance.

By now you know everything. Or almost everything. You don't know how much pain it gave me to pass you by so many times and not be able to look into your beautiful eyes and tell you how exceptional you truly are. But know that I did so for fear of changing what was not mine to change.

I still am not sure where in time and space you will read this, so instead of trying to explain what I cannot explain, I will finally tell you all that I should have when you were a little girl.

I came to your time from the future. And as crazy as it may sound, it is you who led me to time travel.

The easiest place to start is at the beginning. I went to a museum as a young man in 1999 (does this make you older than me?). Our family's history of piracy fascinated me. At the museum, there was a special exhibition dedicated to the treasure looted from the East Indies by Tibeau and Christie, donated by the Duke of Westlake. In it I saw a medallion rumored to have been created by a man known as the Alchemist of Yangon, a man who it was believed could play with time.

There is no easy way to say this next part: I stole that medallion. It had been talked about in our family for generations, dismissed as a myth. I wanted to see for myself, and to tell you the truth, I was already a bit of a miscreant. Which may not surprise you now.

Having got the medallion, I spent some time trying to figure out how it worked. And then I went into the history books in our family's collection and found a sliver of a tome, a fairytale which you know well. I treated it as a sort of instruction manual, and I found myself most inexplicably in seventeenth-century England, next to pirate treasure on a boat captained by none other than Tibeau himself. I was completely unprepared, and I quickly used the medallion once again to move back into the future.

As you might have gathered by now, the medallion works in one of two ways: either through the intention of the wearer, or through the magnetic property of the metal, which seeks itself out through space and time.

I landed on Tibeau's ship because the medallion was there. This we know. I landed next in 1900, while I was still experimenting with it, and then I met your mother. I didn't expect to fall in love, but I did so swiftly and completely. There was only one problem: she couldn't time travel with me.

There is just so much about the medallion I don't understand still, despite all my travels. It doesn't work on some people at all; it works best when your whole heart is in it; it sometimes blocks you (which is why water — or a trampoline, as you may remember — are good choices when jumping).

I wanted to stop, but Maggie wanted me to continue. I had worked as a kind of amateur detective, and she was convinced it was important work that I must continue. And so, on my travels one day, I chanced upon a young lady named Catherine, just like my baby at home, who was the spitting image of my wife, as I tried ineffectually to soothe a lost child outside the Bath Abbey. And by her side was a man by the name of Talbot, of the same Westlake family that had donated the relics of their Portuguese pirate treasures to the museum, from which I had stolen it.

You might imagine how my mind spun in circles. How could it be possible? Could it be a coincidence? Could these other time travelers have used another medallion from Tibeau's treasure chest? Time travel has a way of playing tricks with your thoughts, cause and effect are forever warped once you know that things in the past can affect the future, that you can change things too.

So I will never know what came first: my giving the two of you the medallion, or you somehow being in the past. In my mind it had to be me who gave you the medallion, and so I went about effecting that with what I believe to be the minimum possible potential for damage.

I knew that if I left both parts of the medallion to you, the bird's body and wings, you might spin through history and the future much like I did. Call me selfish, but I didn't want that life for you. I wanted you to know home and love and stability in a way that I wasn't able to till I met your mother. I also needed you to find Sebastian, because I knew you already had.

So I put in place the pieces of the puzzle for you to solve: I created the vault in the cottage, I left the disk with Sebastian's associate, and I led you to the myth of Stanley. Stanley is not real, of course, except if you consider that sometimes I pretended to be him and I rented that house for a few months and made a grand old nuisance of myself.

And then I had to do a very ridiculous thing: I had to return to the island when the treasure was being discovered, in order to get another piece of the Burmese alchemist's work. And then I went to the Westlake library and left one part of my first medallion for Sebastian to find and used the new one to get back home.

It was my worst nightmare to die at the hands of those brigands on Kallan Island and not be able to return to you and Maggie at all. When I made it out alive, I decided I would put an end to the madness. It was my last mission — I came back, and I put away the medallion, and I said nothing about it again. You were only a child then, and I wanted very much to see you grow into a lady.

But you know that isn't the last time I used the medallion, because how else would this letter be in your hands now? When I realized I was dying, I wanted you to have the answers I saw in your eyes that day at the dock. I didn't have to be a time traveler to understand that they were the eyes of a girl who was looking at her dead father, wondering why he was being such an ass. So I came back to this vault, and though I don't know exactly what you have done with the treasure, I know that leaving you this letter, and this second medallion, is the right thing to do.

It was the honor of my life to be loved by your mother, and an absolute miracle to be your father. The only way to truly stop time is to have children in whose eyes you see your future.

Even if your father is technically from your future, and you are from his past.

You now have not one but two medallions, and I can trust that you will use them well. There are others, in different forms, scattered around the world. I believe those of us who have them are their guardians.

I hope this gives you the peace that you need, Catherine. The last thing I want for you is a lifetime chasing my ghost.

All my love to you (and Sebastian, who seems like he might even deserve you).

Your adoring father,

Philip

CATHERINE HAD LOST COUNT of how many times she had read that letter, each time discovering something new to wonder at. Her father had thought of everything. She'd only been too stupid to see it.

For in the end lies the beginning.

THIRTY-FOUR

THE IMPOSING CASTLE LOOMED before her. She'd been there just a few months before, uninvited guest at the wedding of James and Ophelia.

She shuddered at the very thought.

As she dismounted the carriage and walked toward the entrance, she took comfort from the evidence of Sebastian everywhere. In this world, he had been duke uninterrupted since his father's death almost two years before. The grounds were home to sculptures and architectural artifacts from around the world.

She took her time, stretching out these moments of uncertainty, unsure of what lay before her. She stopped to examine a phantom marble doorway that looked like it belonged in Greece, and a fountain that looked very much like the one that held pride of place at the Crystal Palace.

Just then a big brown dog ran up to her, sniffing at her cloak. If Catherine felt a moment's alarm, it dissipated as soon as the giant beast prostrated itself to demand affection.

She smiled, bending over to do its bidding. 'The Duke of Westlake should be happy he has human guards who aren't as easily won over as you.'

It had hardly been a few weeks since she had seen Sebastian last. When she came back, she did her best to ensure that she kept true to time: both she and Sebastian had returned to their lives together, and though one leg of her journey had involved jumping eighty years into the future, and eighty years back, she hadn't seen Sebastian for as long as he hadn't seen her. She was beginning to understand what her father meant about time travel messing with your mind.

Whether Sebastian wanted to see her again at all, however, was the big question.

Before she could knock on the massive castle door, it swung open. The man before her was familiar, and she realized it was the butler from Sebastian's house in Twickenham. But in this world, Sebastian had never had a house there, and the butler had never seen her before.

She introduced herself, and was informed that the duke was in residence, however he had stepped out for some errands.

She said she would be happy to wait and was shown into a small parlor and brought a tray of tea and scones. But Catherine was far too nervous to eat, and though she had brought a book to keep herself company, she did not read a single word. She stared anxiously out the window instead.

Catherine did not know how long she had been waiting there when the door opened. She jumped up in surprise. Sebastian stood there, his eyes burning embers in his face, just as beautiful as she remembered him.

'Sebastian,' she said, twisting her hands.

'Catherine!' he said, stepping into the room almost tentatively. 'I hope you are well?'

She managed a smile as she sat back down, arms aching to hold him. 'I am well, thank you.'

He looked relieved at first, till his concern gave way to hauteur once again. 'What brings you here, Catherine?'

She stood up again, wishing she weren't quite so short so she could look him in the eye and not at the immovable chest before her. 'I came to see you.'

He gave a brisk nod. 'How are the travels going?'

Catherine knew what he meant. He wasn't talking about visiting relatives in distant places, or beachside holidays for leisure. The only travel that was on his mind was through time.

'They're going well.'

'You have found the answers you needed?'

'Yes.'

'Good,' he said, 'I'm glad.' But the smile on his face was tempered by sadness, and in that sadness lay hope.

'Yes, but not in the way you think. How long has it been since you've seen me last?'

He frowned. 'Two months, I believe.'

'It has been two months since I have seen you too.'

She waited for realization to dawn, but all she saw was confusion. 'After I left you here, I traveled back to New York, to my time, to settle some business, but then I came back directly.'

He turned away and crossed to the window, but not before she heard his sharp inhalation of breath. 'And why is that? The medallion —'

'Is working just fine. And in fact...' she said, holding out her outstretched palms, in each of which was a complete, identical pendant.

His eyes widened. 'Where did you get that?'

'When I got to London, in 1929, I went to the cottage. You had kept your end of the bargain, and the home was well taken care of. Inside the vault were four objects.'

Sebastian looked at her, aghast. 'What about the treasure?'

She put the medallions away in her purse. 'I'm coming to that. One object was a letter from my father. The second was this medallion. The third was the deed to the cottage in Selsey, in your name, dated 1831. The fourth was another note in my own hand.'

His brow furrowed. 'In *your* hand?'

'Yes, it is all rather confusing. But I essentially had confirmation for what I had already decided: that I only had one use for my medallion, and that was to come back to you.'

Sebastian's face was a mix of incredulity and restraint.

'You see,' she continued, 'it didn't take me long to decide you were right. That chasing the past was foolish and dangerous. And I had no desire to be anywhere except by your side.'

She looked up at him slowly. For all the passion they had shared, for all that they had been through together, they had never once talked about how they felt, and laying her heart at his feet was the most frightening thing she'd ever done in her life.

Sebastian turned to her, arms crossed. 'Do you understand what you are saying? That to be with me means giving up the dream of racing through time to find your father? I couldn't bear what it would do to you time and again. I couldn't bear what it would do to me.'

Catherine nodded. 'It took me maybe five minutes of life without you to realize this. And you need not worry about me regretting my choice, because I have all the answers I need. Except one.'

'And what's that?'

'What happened to Ophelia and young Sebastian?'

Sebastian looked confused for a moment.

'Ophelia recognized you on that cliff. What happened when she went back to the castle?'

He shrugged. 'Those memories belong to another being, the one who was erased when we returned to Hyde Park. But I know that James never attempted to unseat me.'

'So there has been no conflict at all?'

'I don't know about that. From what I gather, we've butted heads plenty of times. But they've gone to America to make their fortune, and to the best of my knowledge, have found success. Why does any of this matter?'

'I thought, perhaps, that the two of you might have another future together.'

Sebastian shook his head impatiently. 'You never did understand that it was over between Ophelia and I years before I ever met you.'

She looked down. 'Yes, I have been quite silly, haven't I?'

He shot her a look, eyes still filled with doubt. 'You said you had the other answers you wanted?'

She showed Sebastian the letter from her father. He read through it haltingly, turning to her for explanations when he couldn't follow. Once he had reached the end, he was filled with awe. 'It was he who brought me the dagger — *after* he saw us together?'

She nodded. 'You found it right before the wedding, didn't you?'

He nodded.

'And you'd shown it to Ophelia.'

His face darkened at the memory. 'Yes.'

Catherine held up the second medallion. 'And this is how he did it. Are there more like this in the chest?'

Sebastian looked up in surprise. 'What do you mean? You really don't know?'

Catherine gave him a wry smile. 'When I went back to 1929, I visited the cottage to ensure everything was in place. I had already decided to come straight back. But my past self had already emptied the vault and left a note clarifying that it was upon my own wishes.'

She watched a range of emotions flit across his face, registering with horror that he was wondering if she had come back for the treasure. And she knew there was no way she could fight it: he had to believe that she wanted him, treasure or no treasure. But she wouldn't beg.

'Sebastian, you once told me we would get the treasure because it had already happened. This is the same thing. I had arrived to ensure the treasure would be yours and mine, here and now, and because I had done so once, it had already been so in my future. This is what's meant to be.'

Sebastian closed his eyes, letting the words sink in. 'You have always been with me. You always chose me.'

She put her hands on either side of his face, and when he opened them, they were filled with tears.

'And I would time and time again, in every time, in every life.'

He crushed her to him, holding her in his powerful embrace. At last, he tilted her face up toward him, brushing her tears away with his thumbs, and lowering his mouth for a kiss.

'You are here. You do not know how I have longed for you, my dear maddening Catherine.'

She kissed him again, and then wrapped her arms around him, feeling his steady heart beating in his chest against her cheek.

'I've been like a ghost in my own home. For all the world I am the duke, the lord of the manor with not a care in the world. And yet, I have come from another place in time altogether, having lived an altogether different life. One where I had you.'

'And now you have me here too.'

He grabbed her face. 'You'll be my bride?'

Her eyes filled with tears again. 'Yes, yes, yes.'

Sebastian touched his forehead to hers. 'Well then, that's all I need.'

And with that, he scooped her up, carrying her up the vast wooden staircase, every servant in sight watching with mouths agape.

EPILOGUE

IT WAS A WEEK before Catherine and Sebastian finally went to the cottage in Selsey. A week spent enjoying each other without holding back, wondering what their future would hold, and planning how they could transport the treasure to the Westlake Estate with some measure of discretion. Their only interaction with the outside world was with Sebastian's friend Jane and her brother William. In this universe, William kept his admiration for Catherine to himself, and Jane's husband had no reason to hate Sebastian. But luckily Jane still took Catherine shopping.

Now, with their wedding date set for a month away, Catherine had convinced Sebastian to dispose with convention altogether, and when they set off, he joined her in the carriage without putting up a fight.

'I still don't think I can fully understand this highly convoluted situation,' said Sebastian. 'The cottage in Selsey is already mine, and now we have to fix it up and install a family to live in it, just so you can go there in 1929 and discover you came back to me in the past?'

Catherine thought it through for a moment before giving him a nod of approval. 'Yes, that sounds right.'

.

Sebastian shrugged. 'Okay, but it seems like a waste of money to me.'

She laughed. 'My father bought this house for you — for us. Not to mention that without it, we'd never have got the treasure out of 1831.'

'You make a compelling argument.'

Catherine was using her powers of persuasion in other areas, too. Such as Sebastian's insistence about not wanting to time travel ever again.

'In the future, there will be many ways to get around quickly,' she said, and he had devoured her descriptions of ocean liners and airplanes. 'Just imagine, Sebastian, how many more places you can travel for all your digs if you use this medallion? No more mucking around on ships that take months to arrive, and so often visit death or disease upon voyagers!'

Thus far, Sebastian had assented to the use of the medallion only for their honeymoon. Though they were divided about where to go — Venice, which Catherine had always dearly wanted to visit; or New York, where Sebastian wished to see how Catherine had lived.

She couldn't say the idea wasn't attractive. 'I don't see why it makes such a difference which year we visit. It is not like we are going to seek my pre-1929 self out to spill the beans,' she said as they rolled out of London.

'I can see that if I agree to any of your wild schemes, you will soon ignore my compunctions regarding further time travel altogether.'

'I wouldn't dream of ignoring them,' said Catherine quickly, 'but there is certainly no guarantee that I won't try to talk you out of them.'

Sebastian silenced her with a firm kiss.

'And now,' she said, putting her hand on his thigh, 'I am very interested to see what scandalous feats you can *actually* accomplish in the confines of a covered carriage.

THEY ARRIVED IN SELSEY by nightfall and stayed at an inn. Fortunately, there were several more pleasant options than the two they had sampled in 1831. Once again, rising at daybreak, they had several pieces to set in motion.

Sebastian had sent a man ahead to get repairs done on the house and begin the search for a potential tenant. His next task was to organize a crew on the day of Catherine and Sebastian's arrival there, having decided that the easiest way to get the chest out of its subterranean pit was to dig it out from the outside.

Standing in front of the house, hand in hand, Catherine remembered vividly the darkness that had overcome her the last time she was here, faced with the realization that Sebastian no longer lived. 'We must ensure there is someone to manage once we both die,' said Catherine, squeezing his hand.

'Perhaps we might have children who will do it for us one day?' said Sebastian, looking shy for one who had committed unmentionable acts in the back of a carriage only a few hours before.

Catherine pressed her hand to his cheek, still overwhelmed at the feeling of constantly being by his side — being *his*.

When the crew arrived on site, there was no more time for intimacies. They immediately got to work digging up the earth outside the cottage wall, revealing a huge metal box as tall as a person. Stanley had evidently heard the lore about the bell being as tall as a giant as well. It had turned out to be significantly smaller in girth, though no less wondrous than promised.

Just as they were about to despair of a way of cutting through the thick metal walls to retrieve the chest, Catherine, conducting a thorough examination of her own, brushed away the earth from one of the side panels to reveal another round depression, just like the one within the house. She called out to Sebastian triumphantly.

'Stanley really thought of everything,' said Sebastian.

'It's Philip,' Catherine corrected him, 'and he really did.'

This door too opened with the disk, and then three handsomely compensated men lifted it up and onto the floor of Sebastian's carriage, where it took up an inordinate amount of space. Quite uncomfortable this time, thanks to their cramped quarters and priceless cargo, they set out immediately for London.

Once back in the castle's safety, they finally opened it. There sat the Bell of Dhammazedi, nestled amidst the gold, gems and artifacts that filled the bulk of the trunk. They stood and stared at it and then looked at one another.

'It is utterly magnificent,' said Catherine.

'And utterly useless,' said Sebastian.

Catherine started. 'Why do you say that?'

'What will you do with it? You can't melt it down, that would be a tragedy and I won't allow it.'

'I wouldn't dream of it,' said Catherine, slightly offended he would even suggest she'd do such a thing.

'You could sell it, I suppose, to the right buyer. It would go a long way in financing the school, but would you do that?'

She shook her head. 'There is enough gold here to get us started without the bell.'

They had already put the plan in place — an abandoned wing of the castle and some of the grounds would be dedicated to the project, and they would live in the rest of it. They'd start small and grow as they needed to take more children in. Sebastian was happy the enormous castle would finally be put to use, he had said.

Catherine looked at Sebastian, watching for a reaction. 'I did one additional piece of research when I went back home. The princely family that are the rightful owners of this piece have offered a very generous reward for the return of the Bell of Dhammazedi.'

Sebastian's face lit up. 'Is that right?'

She nodded. 'What we have here would be enough to pay for the repairs for the building. And then if we claimed the bounty, we'd have enough to run it for several years.'

'The only question is how we get it to them.'

Catherine beamed. 'In the year 1851, such a thing has never been easier.'

SEBASTIAN AND CATHERINE DROVE into Hyde Park on a crisp Saturday morning, the autumn air swirling with excitement. The Great Exhibition was in its last month, and activity had picked up once again with visitors pouring in from all over the country.

Standing in front of the Crystal Palace, Catherine spun around like a child, giddy at returning to the spot where she and Sebastian had started their mad journey. She spotted many a familiar face, including that of Mrs Riley. But none of them had any idea who she was, as though she had never even met them before.

The crowd thronging the Koh-I-Noor was still in place, and the lines outside England's first public flushing toilets too. Catherine smiled to see it, but then a very serious thought struck her, and she grabbed Sebastian's arm. 'We need one of those in Westlake,' she said.

'This might be a very expensive trip to the exhibition,' said Sebastian with a smirk.

'Given what we are about to do, that is a given.'

And then they arrived at their destination: the Italian zone where the Prince of Dhammazedi was in attendance to marvel at the Great Exhibition's myriad attractions. Thanks to Sebastian's good standing, getting an audience with him had not been a problem.

The prince was a handsome man of about thirty, square shouldered, chiseled, and projecting a calm confidence.

After the introductions, Sebastian and Catherine accompanied his party around the hall. Sebastian and he quietly chatted. It wasn't till they stood in front of the remarkable facsimile machine that they had the chance to pull away from the crowd enough to speak without being overheard. Catherine braced herself.

'We'd like a word with you in private, if we may,' said Sebastian.

The prince looked surprised. 'Now?'

'If possible, yes, on a matter of some urgency. We have something we believe belongs to you.'

Catherine could hear her blood pounding through her body as the prince followed them out to Sebastian's carriage, which had been waiting in front of the Crystal Palace's rear entrance.

'Here?' said the prince with alarm.

'Just a minute, Your Highness, and all will become clear,' said Catherine, boarding the carriage and flipping the lid to the trunk, before jumping back down beside Sebastian.

The prince's eyes glistened as he saw what was inside, but he was otherwise impassive.

'You don't seem surprised,' said Catherine.

His eyes flitted over her and Sebastian. 'There have been rumors ever since Tibeau's treasure was discovered that the bell was on English soil. We suspected the Crown had hidden it away, though why it should be more squeamish about revealing this when the wealth of several other nations is happily on display was never clear to me.'

'It was on English soil,' said Sebastian, 'but it never reached the state coffers. And now we would like to return this masterpiece to you.'

'Why?' he asked archly.

Catherine flushed. 'We believe it belongs to you.'

He gave a brisk nod. 'That it does. But I expect you are also seeking the promised bounty in return. Which is fair enough, though if left up to me, I would not pay for what belongs to my people. But it was my father's promise, and I am bound to honor it.'

Catherine suppressed her excitement. After Sebastian and the prince discussed where and how the item would be transferred, he gave them another inscrutable look. 'I see you make no mention of the alchemist's medallion?'

His words were like a battering ram to her stomach. Their guilty expressions told the prince what he wanted to know. 'I thought as much,' he said. 'When tales of the bell's mysterious recovery and disappearance traveled back to my land, it became clear that the power of the medallion had been unleashed.'

Catherine looked from Sebastian to the prince. 'What do you mean, unleashed? Could you tell us more about how it works?'

'I wish I could. But the alchemist of Yangon was not one to reveal his secrets.'

'How many more are there?'

'He made only a handful of objects before he lost the power. Precisely how many, no one knows. But have no fear — I will not be asking you to return what is in your possession. If it is in your hands, it has been called to you.'

Catherine felt the weight of this, so much like what Philip had said in his letter to her. 'Is there a purpose behind it all?'

The prince gazed into the distance. 'Only you can answer that question. Let me ask you this — how do you intend to use the bounty and your medallion?'

'We are opening a school for orphans. About the medallion, we weren't sure what we should do, really.'

He nodded. 'Be open to the ways of the universe, and all will be revealed. You will be called upon if needed. Be prepared for when that happens.'

As the prince strode away, Catherine and Sebastian watched after him in silence, his parting words reverberating like a prophecy.

Finally, Catherine slipped her hand into Sebastian's and smiled. Heavier things could wait for the moment. With the bell off her conscience, she was free to turn her attention to their forthcoming nuptials. 'Now that we have the prince's sanction, will it be New York or Venice, Your Grace?'

He looked down at her, wrapping his arm around her waist. 'Keep calling me that and we'll only make it as far as my bedroom.'

Her eyes went to the chain around his neck, his dagger medallion disappearing beneath his shirt, feeling the metal of the other half against her own skin. Their promise to one another that wherever they were going, it would be together.

Catherine smiled up at him. 'What are we waiting for?'

Thank you for reading
The Time-Traveler's Daughter!

<u>Check out these other titles in the</u>
<u>All Who Wander series</u>

Time & Again
The Promise Of Time
The Shadow Of Time

The Time-Traveler's Secret

You can also read the prequel novella
Time & Again for free by joining my newsletter. You'll hear first
about all her new releases and bonus content. Head to
www.emmastrike.com now!

If you enjoyed this book and have a moment to spare, please
consider leaving a review on Amazon or Goodreads. Thank you!

Made in the USA
Monee, IL
16 April 2023

31963768R00176